THE SOURCE

THE
SOURCE

Origins

A.J. Witt (signature)

A.J. WITT

SPRING CEDARS LLC

Printed in the United States of America.
First edition, 2019

Book cover, design, editing, and maps by Spring Cedars LLC

ISBN 978-1-950484-00-3 (paperback)
ISBN 978-1-950484-01-0 (ebook)

Published by Spring Cedars LLC
Centennial, Colorado
info@springcedars.com

CONTENTS

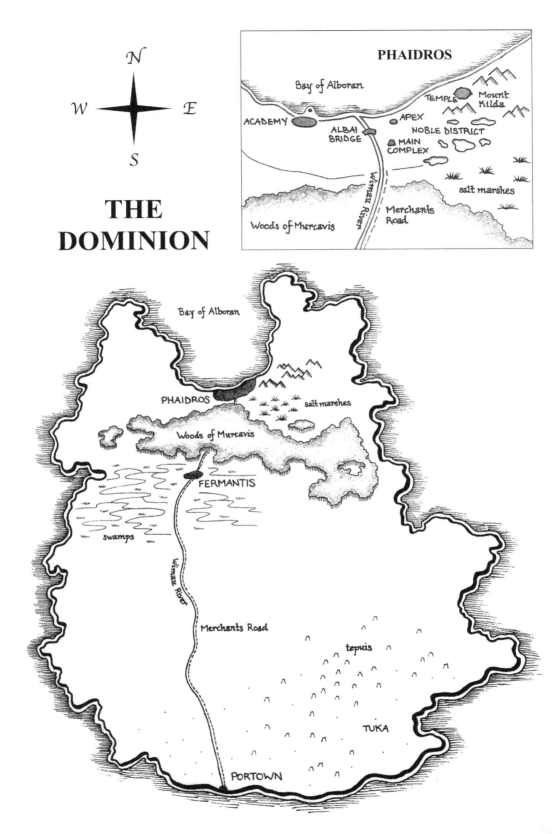

THE DOMINION

PHAIDROS

Bay of Alboran

TEMPLE

Mount Kilda

ACADEMY

APEX

NOBLE DISTRICT

ALBAI BRIDGE

MAIN COMPLEX

salt marshes

Woods of Murcavis

Wirnau River

Merchants Road

Bay of Alboran

PHAIDROS

salt marshes

Woods of Murcavis

FERMANTIS

swamps

Wirnau River

Merchants Road

tepuis

TUKA

PORTOWN

PROLOGUE

Conception 1:2

1 *They used something greater, and they exclaimed, "Let us control the stars!"*
And they became so great that they created life itself.

2 *And when they witnessed all that had been created, they rejoiced.*
For they had become Gods, destined to reign from their cities of Red.

[…]

Hubris 5:8

[…]

5 *But when they saw It, they wept.*
Colossal tears, filling entire oceans, sweeping through the lands.

6 *Because only then did the Gods comprehend the strife that had accompanied It.*
And only then did they realize the outcome that was bound to occur.

7 *"Did we not reveal to you the secrets of life?*
Did we not reveal to you the provisions of space itself?"

[8] *And in our pride, we ignored them.*
Using It to fulfill our greatest desires, to quench our selfish thirsts.

[…]

Castigation 14

[…]

[14] *And despite our protests, we were cast to start anew.*
Forever bound to the earth.

PART I

CHAPTER ONE

Kyran would often gaze at faraway stars, reveling in the thought of sailing among them, just as the Dominion's forefathers did before being cast down by the Gods. It was an impossible dream. And besides, the aura of dawn was already succeeding the dark night sky, glimmering specks of light fading until they could no longer be seen.

The young man was sitting at his usual place near the rear of the hall, close to the high-arched windows that offered a spectacular view of Phaidros. A perfect distraction from Zarkat's dreary lessons, especially in the morning, when Kyran would survey the great city as it came to life. Now, something else drew his attention.

A new Overseer had been assigned to monitor Zarkat's class, replacing a crusty old woman who had despised every Adept at the Academy and considered them filthy blasphemers daring to partake in sin forbidden by the Gods. She had met an unceremonious end, much to the pleasure of the students.

Mutual hate between Adept and Overseer was deeply rooted, stemming from the frightful Dread Days. A time many centuries prior when the Dread Shepherds, a group of renegade Adepts shunning the pacifist teachings of the Academy, used the Source to spread war and terror. In Dominion lore, they leveled entire villages. *No way that actually happened.* Though only Adepts could access energy from the Source, Kyran had trouble imagining such a display of power.

The Academy cracked down on the Dread Shepherds but

lost what little goodwill existed between the factions. The Dominion's two most prominent institutions seemed destined to clash, until a compromise was reached. They established the Council of Five, composed of an Adept from the Academy and an Overseer from the Temple, as well as three impartial lords from Phaidros's ruling Noble Assembly. It maintained a fragile peace, enacting laws designed to placate the Temple, while providing the Adepts with enough autonomy to remain in the arrangement. One such provision allowed a number of Overseers within the Academy's walls to observe lectures and ensure none of its students or teachers were planning a rebellion. *Or to prowl through the hallways with stern faces.*

Only in recent past had Adepts started venturing into the western neighborhoods of Phaidros, and little was known about their capabilities. This subjected the small minority to Dominioners' wild imagination which was often boosted by the Temple's public relations efforts. Incredible Source-powered technologies developed at the Academy yet shared with everyone failed to remedy the perception that Adepts were withdrawn and dangerous. Moreover, current events yielded a surge of support for the Overseers. Mystifying attacks left towns on the Dominion outskirts ravaged, with accusatory fingers pointing at the Academy. And then, an unthinkable assault on the Council itself, so savage it had shocked Phaidrosians to their core.

The Overseers smelled blood, Kyran saw it in their leering eyes and pathetic grins. *Gods, I hate them all. Wait … maybe not all.* The new monitor in Zarkat's course that morning was not the archetypical Overseer, and Kyran had trouble keeping his eyes off her. During his years of studies, though few, he had never come across a Temple official quite like this one. They tended to act rigid and sour. *She seems much more carnal.*

Barely older than the students, she introduced herself as

Gwen. Standing near the front of the classroom, the Overseer had her back to the high-arched window closest to the instructor's dais, and as the sunlight engulfed her figure from behind, Kyran could make out the sensuous shape of her legs beneath the long white dress. *Lucky I came to class today. I'd be missing a revealing sunrise.* She shifted her weight slightly to the left and brought her thighs close together. Kyran's heart leapt. Her voluptuous hips appeared ready to burst through the clothing. When Gwen turned in his direction, her dark hair shimmered in the sunlight. The young man looked away. *Did she see me staring?*

A glance back and, much to his relief, Kyran found Gwen's amber eyes focusing elsewhere. The Adept moved his gaze down her body and wondered how he would ever pass the class. *Not that I learn anything in the first place.* He shook his head to clear his mind, but any effort to concentrate was short-lived. Gwen walked toward the window. The Overseer's entire body moved with a seamless flow, each step more pleasing than the previous. Kyran conjured up suggestive images in which they were alone. She was kneeling, a lustful smile on her lips, playfully sliding the dress up and off her body.

"Kyran!" barked Zarkat. "Would you please focus on the task at hand, rather than on our Overseer's backside?"

Horrified, the student found Gwen staring at him, a look of indignation contorting her otherwise enchanting features. *How embarrassing.* Kyran heard concealed snickering from his peers.

"Good, now that I have your attention," Zarkat said, "perhaps you can answer the question I have just posed to the class."

The young man realized that since the start of the lecture, he had not captured a single word from the teacher's mouth. "Can you please repeat the question? Uh … sir." Kyran ran his fingers through his long hair, trying his best to appear annoyed.

"Well, if you paid attention," responded Zarkat, "you would know what to say. Instead, you were too busy contemplating other matters." Following the overt barb, the class found little need to mask its laughter, much to the teacher's delight.

A lonely student by his own volition, Kyran had few friends at the Academy. *Anything to avoid living in his shadow.* The young man's predicament kindled a nascent fury, and everything started to anger him. Zarkat's obnoxious smile, the laughing students, Gwen's disapproval. A flush of heat ran through Kyran's face, and he knew his eyes were shining brightly, just as they would for any Adept drawing energy from the Source.

"Stop right now!" Zarkat shouted.

Kyran ignored his teacher. That he was in grave violation of Academy rules, specifically those prohibiting Source usage outside of supervised classroom activities, bothered him little. Then again, his lack of obedience on the matter was not a newfound issue. Kyran relished the surge of energy in his body. It percolated through his core and pulsated in his veins. The Source made him feel stronger, more powerful. Zarkat's muted shouts were coming from a distant place, and Kyran pictured himself in a bubble, one that could roll over anything. Had he seen Gwen's expression change from disapproval to one of concern, maybe he would have stopped. *But I can almost touch the Source. Taste it on my lips.*

A powerful shock wave reverberated through the lecture hall. Papers flew in all directions, jugs of water were knocked over, and the chalk splintered into pieces. Kyran opened his eyes to survey the damage and was met with looks of stupefaction and condemnation.

"Get out of my classroom!"

CHAPTER TWO

Peering out of a window high in the South Tower, Edvon cringed as the restive crowd thickened. He could sense the hate emanating from the group gathered down below. *Dread them! Don't they have anything better to do?* Students joined him to see for themselves what was taking place outside. The rioters were now shouting in unison to draw the attention of anyone who cared to listen.

"Rapers, murderers, pillagers, stay away from our villagers! Rapers, murderers, pillagers, stay away from our villagers!"

Edvon rolled his eyes. As a beacon to Source users throughout the ages, the Academy had repeatedly been the target of such aggressions. These were increasing as a result of the unexplainable attacks on Dominion villages. *How could they think we're responsible for such atrocities? Just because we make for an easy scapegoat.*

That the Academy allowed for such demonstrations to occur within its walls was puzzling, yet the Court of Grievances did permit those with objections to Adept practices to voice them peacefully. *Those shouts don't sound very peaceful.* Edvon shook his head and noticed the worried expressions around him. "They can protest all they want," he said to provide reassurance, "but it won't ever diminish our abilities."

They were skeptical. "I hope you're right," one of them replied. "Though you have less to fear than the rest of us."

Edvon shrugged off the compliment, one he had grown accustomed to hearing during his time at the Academy. While the young man self-acknowledged his superior talents, he avoided flaunting them. The Adept's humility stemmed from the fact that although he had been gifted with Source drawing capacities, he spent countless hours practicing and refining them. A diligent work ethic combined with an unpresuming attitude earned him high regard among his peers. Edvon was well-liked, and he knew it. Dubbed a prodigy by his teachers, the star student carried himself with pride. Some even pegged him as a future major source manipulator.

"You know, maybe the preceptor should just close the Court of Grievances," someone suggested.

Not a bad idea. Marrek should ... Marrek! The thought of the preceptor snapped Edvon back to reality. *I'm supposed to meet him in five minutes.* He spun around. "Sorry, got to go." Politely pushing his way through the small group of students gathered by the window, the Adept dashed toward the wooden door near the back of the room. He swung it open, revealing a steep staircase serving as the South Tower's sole entryway. Often congested with people, Edvon was pleased to find the path unhindered. He made his way, making sure not to slip on the uneven stone steps. *Got to be careful.* Too many times students would race down the stairs, only to crash at the bottom.

The Academy, a splendid architectural landmark in Phaidros, was a circular building. An outer ring, through which Edvon ran, contained modest living quarters for the students. The raised inner ring was more luxurious and housed the teachers. Each had his or her own suite with a personal washroom, in stark contrast to the communal showers Edvon used every morning. In the middle of the Academy rose the Ivory Tower, home to the preceptor. Visiting Marrek required traversing several buildings and climbing many staircases, a veritable expedition, yet one that Edvon found worthwhile.

The young Adept crossed the narrow courtyard sandwiched between the rings, picking up sweet honey scents from the jakarhandas bordering the walls. They were blooming in the wake of a long and harsh winter, exhibiting a stunning array of purples. Students occupied benches under the trees, socializing or reading from thick leather-bound tomes. Edvon sighed, realizing he too had much studying left. *One thing at a time.*

He followed a long flight of steps to the Crimson Garden, named after the red brick covering its ground. Teachers or the occasional Overseer frequented the outdoor space separating the inner ring from the Ivory Tower, providing the young man with an excellent reason to hustle along.

"Edvon!"

Exactly what I wanted to avoid. The Adept grimaced and turned around, expecting the worst. A bulky man was walking in his direction, wearing the Temple's distinct white robes. "Broque," replied Edvon with a half-hearted wave. "How are you?" Though most Adepts despised Overseers, the young man found himself rather indifferent to their presence at the Academy. *Fake courtesy when required and otherwise ignore.*

"By Auralus, I'm doing well!" exclaimed Broque. "And I'd be doing better if you'd accepted my offer." The large Overseer grinned, teeth visible underneath his bushy beard. Soft hazel eyes and a lethargic demeanor made Broque look approachable, unlike his more reserved and unsociable brethren.

Edvon assessed the sincerity of the smile. "I appreciate your offer, but I'm sorry to say … I'm not interested."

"You'd be happier at the Temple."

"And why is that?" asked Edvon.

"Leave this place and you'll find out."

"Not a risk I'm willing to take."

"Ah," Broque replied in a subdued tone. "Well, the offer

will always be on the table. Remember one thing, Edvon. Whatever magical powers you Adepts possess isn't everything in life. Strong men like you, with character and integrity, are always welcome at the Temple."

Edvon nodded, repressing an urge to laugh as Broque walked away. *Character and integrity? What a joke.* Overseers had been trying to persuade him to defect to the Temple for years, and it was always the same pitch. Given their rejection of the Source, most relied on brute strength to achieve success, making Edvon a natural target of their overtures. From an early age the young Adept had been blessed with incredible physical prowess. Standing a foot taller than most, he spent considerable time exercising and toning his impressive physique. With perfect abdominals and well-defined muscle lines running from his traps to his calves, Edvon had even been recruited by the professional baqua associations of Phaidros. He preferred to remain at the Academy where both his skills and looks—curly brown locks with green eyes and a strong clean-shaven jawline—earned him the attention of his colleagues.

"See you around," called out Broque.

Gods, I hope not. Edvon sprang up the Ivory Spire's steps, recognizing he would be several minutes late to his meeting. *I'll just say I had to fend off Overseers on the way.* The Adept walked through the spire's entranceway, taking in a sight that never ceased to amaze him. From the foyer, one could see all the way up to the preceptor's office, accessible via a Source-powered elevator. The hollow spire was made of white marble, and its architects had incorporated natural light intending to give the space a feeling of tranquility. Edvon hurried toward the only means of access to what lay above.

Despite having been in Marrek's office multiple times, he was thoroughly frisked by guards at the bottom of the elevator shaft. They ushered him into the lift which started a slow and steady ascent. As he stood waiting, Edvon realized the purpose of his upcoming meeting was unknown to him. The previous night in the Great Hall, Marrek had asked the young man to come to the office without the slightest indication of his reasons. The elevator lurched upward. *I guess I'm about to find out.* Predicting the preceptor's intentions was difficult, and Edvon had no desire to establish a habit of trying.

He was directed to Marrek's waiting room, located just outside the luxurious and spacious sanctum he had seen more often than any other student. As he turned the corner, Edvon laid his eyes upon another Adept sitting with his head bowed. *Well, almost any other student.*

The visitor had long brown hair down to his collarbone, and he was tall, perhaps one of the few Adepts who rivaled Edvon in that respect.

"It's always one step too far with you, Kyran. Just one step too far."

He was being scolded by the Academy's second-in-command, an officer by the name of Elias.

"How many times do we have to deal with you and your uncontrolled actions?"

Edvon entered the room, and the student raised his pointed chin to look at the star Adept. His gray eyes flickered as he broke into a mischievous grin. *By all the Gods! What now?* Edvon marched toward his little brother.

CHAPTER THREE

Aiden sighed. "Okay, let's start over. The shopkeeper said he noticed the man before or after the Source Powered Carrier came around the bend?"

"The shopkeeper said, and I quote, 'Right as the SPC drove around the corner,'" answered a junior agent as he looked down at his notes.

"And we've established our bomber came down the alley?" Aiden was pointing at a sketch on the wall. He left no time for his subordinates to answer and skipped straight to a more practical question. "Have we interviewed the residents of the alley?"

"Yes, we have."

"And no one saw this guy?" wondered the chief. "It's not like he was easy to miss, with the vest he was wearing."

The room remained silent.

"We've got to retrace his steps, figure out where he came from." Aiden sighed again. "The longer we wait, the less accurate our potential witnesses. Does the other end of the alley lead to the flower market?"

Another junior agent replied. "Yes sir."

"Then we take it to the next level, and we interview each stall keeper." The group was not prepared for an order of such magnitude, and Aiden sensed the skepticism in the room. "Need I remind you this is the murdering of Council members we're talking about?" The chief closed his eyes. He loathed bringing a victim's social status to the table. *All cases are the same, whether a Council member or an indigent.* Aiden also knew idealism rarely mattered. He looked over to Criss. She was sitting off to the side, staring at him emotionless. *By Gods, she hates me. Not that I blame her for it.* "I want our entire team to canvass the flower market today. Someone must have seen him walk through. Anything that can help us establish his identity." The agents filed out. "And reconvene this afternoon!"

Only Criss remained behind. She scribbled another line into her notebook before shutting it and following the chief out.

"We should review the motives involved. I think we're missing something here."

"Understood," answered Criss.

"I'm still convinced someone paid the man ... I mean, these can't be the actions of a lone killer." The chief sighed. "The timing was too perfect, and everything points to a predetermined location."

"Right."

Aiden felt like shaking Criss to ask what she really believed. He needed her help. *Sure, she got the raw end of the stick, but I'm also getting tired of her act. I won't solve this thing alone, not this time.* "The Source-powered explosives indicate a wealthy backer," he added, hoping to stimulate a constructive response. Silence. "Your average Phaidrosians don't get their hands on such firepower on their own." Silence. "Agreed?"

"Agreed."

The one-word answer caused the chief to clench his teeth in frustration. *Not that kind of response.* They came upon a spacious corner office which was sparsely decorated, only a cheap Source-powered clock gracing its bare walls and a steel desk pushed near the corner. It too was barren, save a pencil and handwritten notes. A small door on the right led to a balcony with panoramic views of downtown Phaidros. Aiden settled behind the desk while Criss grabbed one of the two metal chairs.

She was the brightest mind in the Battalion, of that Aiden had no doubt. It should have been her sitting in his place, running operations and giving the commands. Several years older, she had shot up through the ranks, succeeding at each required stage in the Main Complex. And like every other woman working in Dominion institutions, her career path had met a ceiling. Criss was a role model to Aiden, and the misogyny made him uncomfortable. After all, she excelled at her job and solved the majority of her cases. *And her reward? To work for me? Her junior?* Had he been in her place, Aiden would have left. Criss stayed, a decision for which the chief respected her even more.

His second-in-command opened her notebook, a slim leather-bound journal with a thin white ribbon hanging from one end. Short auburn hair fell close to her shoulders, an underlayer of darker brown visible near the top of her head. She had a round face, and Aiden watched as her silver eyes darted back and forth, following the scrawl of her pen. *Pity's a dangerous emotion.* Criss was a strong and stubborn woman, one who resented any preferential treatment. In fact, she rejected the privileges he had bestowed upon her during his first days in office, only widening the perceived gap between them. Since then, the chief had managed to accomplish his original objectives more subtly, to the point where Criss essentially possessed Aiden's power. *Just not the title.* He sighed for what seemed like the hundredth time that morning.

Criss looked up at him momentarily and buried her head back into her notebook. She uncrossed her legs and crossed them once more, her loose fitting white pants moving like waves in an ocean as she changed positions. Aiden hated the outfit, it made her look like an Overseer. *Not like I'm on one side or the other. Overseers, Adepts, and Nobles, they're all the same.* The chief had a job requiring him to remain neutral and detached. And he had no problem doing so.

But Aiden felt purposeless. *What's the point?* As a child, he had always been curious, the inquisitiveness morphing into a full-blown existential crisis when he grew into a man. It came and went as it pleased, like a beast striking one day while ignoring him on another. The chief was embarrassed. He had a comfortable and secure employment, and one of the more prestigious titles in the entire Dominion. *There are people living in the streets, and I'm struggling with the meaning of life?* Aiden despised himself for it and often resorted to suppressing his feelings altogether.

"Chief," Criss said a second time.

"Umm ... yes?"

"You wanted to talk about motives?"

"Oh, right," he replied, adjusting his glasses. Aiden was born with heterochromia and was known for his disheveled appearance, a permanent two-day beard and messy brown hair. It had almost kept him from being promoted to his current position, though the members of the Noble Assembly had neglected aesthetics in favor of his stellar record and successful crime-solving skills. "Who would cut down those Council members?" He was now hunching in his chair, thinking out loud. "Who, who, who."

Criss remained silent and flipped back a few pages in her notebook. "There are multiple possibilities."

The chief sat up straight. *Okay, here we go. Once she starts talking ...*

"The most obvious suspect is some high-ranking official at the Academy, if not the preceptor himself. It was done with explosives which are Source-powered and developed by the Academy under supervision of the major source manipulator. And we know Adepts and Overseers wouldn't be caught dead sharing shadow time together. The two dead Council members were the commandant himself and his greatest Noble ally. So they have every reason to do it."

"Doesn't seem to fit the preceptor, does it?" Aiden was eager to feed into what he could foresee turning into a very beneficial brainstorming session.

"Right," she replied. "And it's too obvious. Unless they misjudged the backlash, doesn't seem like the Adepts have gained much from it. Still possible nonetheless."

"Because?"

"Because the Council is about to undergo a shift in power, one that could benefit the Academy in the long run."

"Disastrous short-term damage for long-term gain?" asked the chief.

"Sounds more like the preceptor, doesn't it?"

"It sure does."

"Which leads me to our second suspect," Criss continued, "someone else known for her long-term vision."

"Najara." Aiden realized he was whispering. "The confidante?"

"Yes. Support for her and the Temple has never been higher following the murders, especially with what's going on out in the countryside. That should be the focus of our attention, by the way."

"Yes, I know, I know."

"If we could send out a force," she pursued, "and—"

"This case first," the chief interjected. "And they're connected, anyway."

"Perhaps."

"I know they are."

"Perhaps."

Aiden sighed. "Go on."

"Najara has a track record for shady activities, and—"

"Nothing like this."

"That we are aware of."

Aiden said something under his breath, tapping his fingers on the steel desk and making a sound that echoed throughout the office.

"And let me add, her new commandant is no God herself," said Criss.

"She sure looks like one, though."

This time, the chief's second-in-command was the one to say something under her breath.

"It doesn't matter, we have no proof showing the Temple's responsible," contended Aiden.

"Well, we can't arrest the Temple. We need proof someone did it."

"Yes, fine. What I'm saying is we know the Academy and the Temple, as institutions, have the resources to execute this. Ergo, we just need to narrow down the culprit within."

"Right, but—"

"But what?" cut in the chief, frustrated.

"Aren't we forgetting the Nobles? A lot of those families could have pulled this off."

"What would any of them have to gain?"

"Lord Lester was the richest and most powerful of them all," Criss explained. "Someone must benefit from the fortune he left behind."

"No, this isn't financial. Doesn't make sense. If you do it for that reason, you do it at night with a knife, not in broad daylight with a suicide bomber and expensive Source-powered explosives." Aiden sighed. "This was a statement kill."

"Money is a statement."

"And what, the late Commandant Rex Quintus was just collateral damage?"

Criss nodded.

"What else?"

"It could have also been a common citizen," she suggested.

"Not a chance, already disproven. Weren't you listening to me just now? Source-powered explosives cost too much for a common Phaidrosian to afford."

"I'd say, right now, nothing's been proven or disproven."

The chief stared out the window. "It's not a random citizen."

"When we know that for sure, then you can cross it off the list." Criss slammed her notebook shut. "Along with the Nobles you seem so eager to discount."

"Okay, I get it. Everyone has motives to kill the most powerful men in Phaidros." Aiden stood up. "That's why we need to focus on the guy's looks, figure out who he was. It's our only chance of connecting the dots."

"Well, there's not much left for us to focus on."

"Yeah, I get that." The chief's face lost some of its color. He had been one of the first to arrive at the scene of the crime, and the bits of flesh scattered about the street were still keeping him up at night. "Hopefully, the team finds something at the flower market."

"And if they don't?" asked Criss.

"Then the greatest crime in our history may go unsolved."

CHAPTER FOUR

Elias had risen through the ranks of the Academy despite his meek disposition. Streaks of gray ran through his otherwise dull black hair, and not a trace of a beard could be seen sprouting on his unremarkable face. In fact, the Adept was so unassuming, people would often overlook his presence in a room. Rather than holding him back, the cards life dealt him played in his favor. By lurking in the background, Elias stayed out of the spotlight. He was promoted often, if only because Academy officials had no reason not to. And one day, he became right-hand man to the preceptor himself.

But now, the unimposing physique that had helped Elias climb the ladder was causing him grief, as he failed to prevent the much taller and stronger Edvon from attempting to strangle his younger brother. "Please, step back. This is no way to handle the situation." Kyran struggled to free himself from Edvon's lethal grip, and the officer noticed the younger brother's smirk had yet to dissipate. *He's actually enjoying this? I should step away and let Edvon teach him a lesson.* Before Elias could make a choice he would come to regret, the older of the two backed off on his own free will.

"You're such a geegabrain, Kyran!" Edvon yelled. "What is this now, your fourth trip to the preceptor's office this month? Don't you ever learn? Can't you be more—"

"Like you?" spat Kyran. "Why can't I be the perfect little Auralus running along the halls of the Academy, teachers fawning over my talents and girls gazing into my beautiful green eyes?"

"That's not what I was going to say, and you know—"

"That I'm not calm and collected, like you?" Kyran asked.

"No, and stop interrupting me while I speak."

"Only when you stop comparing us."

"I'm not comparing us!" Edvon shot back.

There was a pause, and Elias attempted to add something yet failed to get anyone's attention.

"What are you getting at then, huh?" pursued Kyran. "That I'm always getting into trouble? Well, there's only room for so many suck-ups at the Academy."

Edvon took a step forward. "Just because I work harder than you doesn't make me a suck-up." They stood there for a moment, until Kyran dissolved into laughter. Were Adepts graded on their ability to provoke and aggravate, the younger brother would have been at the top of the Academy.

"Look, your bickering will solve nothing," said Elias. "I think this is best left to—"

As if on cue, the door to the preceptor's office swung wide open. Kyran cringed in anticipation, while Edvon felt relief at the sight of a man he had come to value as a mentor and friend. Marrek was standing still, a calm look on his aged face. He considered the siblings with an unrevealing demeanor and beckoned them to follow him in. The young men obliged, with Kyran requiring a slight push by Elias. Swiping the hand off his back, the Adept took in the familiar sight. Manuscripts overflowed from shelves and books were stacked on an assortment of smaller tables scattered about. The office was lit naturally through skylights and a dozen large Source-powered crystals hanging from the ceiling. Marrek's desk took up half the room and was stacked with tomes, most notably all ten volumes of Ikbar's Chronicles of the Dread Shepherds, handwritten notes, as well as modern technological tools and objects. Most unique to the office was a sweet aroma emanating from the small indoor garden. It was replete with a growth of vegetables and wild flowers, a testament to the preceptor's favorite hobby. As soon as Marrek had settled into his comfortable leather chair, Edvon spoke up.

"Sir, I want to apologize for the scene outside your office, and—"

"That's quite enough," interjected the preceptor with a wave of his hand, his deep and soothing baritone voice overtaking Edvon's. "We have much to discuss, and brotherly love is the least of our concerns."

"I'd hardly call it love," muttered Kyran.

"And what would you call it?"

The young man was taken aback by the question. *How in the Gods did he hear me?*

"If you think Edvon has ill-intentions toward you," Marrek proceeded, "then let's hear what they might be."

The preceptor spoke in a manner which had the effect of dispelling much of Kyran's anger. *How does he do that? I was so angry walking in here and now, I'm … not.* "Well … umm … he just yelled at me without even knowing what I'd done."

"You're definitely not up here for something good," Edvon replied in defense of his own actions.

"And why not?"

"Elias was giving you an earful when I walked in. If that's not enough of an indicator, I don't know what is."

"Yeah, well … I … well …" stammered Kyran. "I still didn't do anything wrong."

"Oh, you were the victim again? If I—"

"Enough," Marrek declared.

Suspended above them, a Source-powered kinetic sculpture rotated upon itself.

"Anyway, maybe I'll get going," said a voice in the back of

the room.

Kyran jumped from his chair, while the startled preceptor clutched his chest. Edvon spun around, bracing himself for the worst.

"By all the Gods!" Marrek exclaimed.

"I ... wh—what's wrong?" asked Elias.

"We didn't realize you were still here. You frightened us."

Elias held up his arms in confusion. "You were, like, facing me directly, sir."

"Right, right, of course," said the preceptor. "Thank you, I'll handle it from here."

Elias opened his mouth yet said nothing. He then bowed and vanished from the office.

There was another moment of silence, and the young Adepts made a concerted effort not to laugh. Marrek stared at them with his brown eyes, he too suppressing a chuckle. Edvon caught the slightest trace of a strange emotion, one he had never seen manifested by the preceptor. *Apprehension?* He looked again, but it was gone. *Anxiety? Too difficult to tell.*

The brothers had been living at the Academy as long as Edvon could remember. Most Adepts joined at a young age, separated from their families as soon as Source manipulation capabilities were discovered, unless the child was born in East Phaidros in which case the only way to join the Academy was to run away. By the time one was old enough to make that conscious decision, his or her powers would have already disappeared. Without proper practice and refinement within the walls of the Academy, Adepts turned into nothing else than common citizens.

Students were sometimes allowed several days to visit their families. *If the family even wants to see them. Not that it matters.* The preceptor himself had taken in the brothers during one of his visits to an orphanage. With a bald head and traces of white hair around the edges of his ears, Marrek was the closest they had to a parent. Edvon considered himself lucky because he doubted very much he would ever meet an individual as clever as the one sitting in front of him.

Older teachers would often tell stories of the preceptor's youth, when he excelled in his studies and rose to the top of the Academy's ranks. Perhaps most impressive was Marrek's unrelenting desire to remain active. Early mornings, he could be seen walking the grounds of the Academy, garbed in his usual sand-colored robes and often accompanied by students or younger teachers picking his brain on various matters of academia.

"Kyran, I know you find your courses boring," the preceptor said. "But they are a foundation, a bedrock as you begin to venture out into the Dominion."

"Why does it matter how many lords form part of the Noble Assembly? Or what affairs the Council of Five has jurisdiction over? Whether salt is sold in cartons or in barrels. Where Lutigas met the hermits. I don't care about any of that stuff. It has no significance in my life."

"Are you not curious about how the Dominion functions?" asked Marrek.

"No, not unless it's practical and useful to me," Kyran replied. "And in any case, what will I do with this information? As an Adept, I seem destined to live the rest of my life within the walls of the Academy, at best venturing into the streets of West Phaidros. There's no future for me, other than becoming a Source refiner or a professor, to pass on useless information to the next generation of Adepts. So they can pass it on to the next generation after them."

The preceptor sighed. "There are many things you have yet to learn, Kyran. And there are many things you do not yet know." The young man opened his mouth to respond, but as he was about to speak, Marrek continued. "And remember, with the absence of the mundane, the exciting ceases to exist."

"What does that mean?"

"Without white, there is no black. And without black, there is no white. We can only conceive such simple concepts because they differentiate and add meaning to each other. If everything in life were exciting, the concept of excitement would cease to carry any significance. Don't you see? We should relish the boring moments of our existence. They are a platform through which the exciting points come to life."

Edvon nodded in agreement.

"You're still skeptical Kyran, and I understand," said the preceptor. "What excites you most in your studies?"

* * *

The bale of hay erupted into flames.

"Try to hit the target, not make the whole thing explode."

Kyran took a deep breath. "I'm trying."

"You're trying too hard." The major source manipulator put an arm around the young man's shoulder. "This isn't about pulling in as much energy as you can. Our preceptor often says any Adept can do that. It's about learning how to control it."

"But how?"

"Stop trying to grasp at the Source, Kyran. Instead, focus on manipulating the energy it emits." He turned to the rest of the class. "Adepts tend to forget that, yet it's critical to your development. We don't use the Source itself, and candidly, we don't even know what or where it is."

"Huh?"

The Academy's most skillful member clapped his wrists and launched an immaculate beam that drilled a hole into another stack of hay. "I didn't reach for the Source. Rather, I collected all the energy I could sense around me and re-directed it toward my target."

"Doesn't that weaken your strike?"

"On the contrary, it strengthens it. Think of the Source as a a candle. The light emitted is what we are interested in, not the object itself. Alright everyone, we'll try again next week." The major source manipulator ended the lesson.

* * *

"When we are practicing drawing energy from the Source. That's pretty fun, I guess."

"Well, imagine every day here at the Academy, you were only allowed to do that. Instead of taking your usual array of academic subjects, you were told to show up at the training field and practice drawing Source energy. I can tell you that in a matter of weeks, the activity would become monotone and tedious, and you would lose your enjoyment." Marrek smiled. "I've worked with addicts in the slums of Fisherman's Bay. And even they reveal that after a while, the drug becomes boring and loses its edge. Then they seek a stronger, more potent fix. And before they know it, they've spent all their money at the Saryn plates. So the plunge begins. In life, one must learn to live in moderation."

Another moment of silence swept through the room, and Edvon snuck a look toward his younger brother. Kyran appeared to be in deep thought, pondering over Marrek's words of wisdom. *He's not stupid, if only he could harness his vitality.*

"Which brings me to a second point, one we've been discussing for several years now," said the preceptor.

"Yeah, yeah, I get it. Controlling my emotions." Kyran was spitting the words out, frustrated with Marrek, or perhaps even himself, for once again breaching the topic.

"As I've explained, the rage you often experience can be overcome. I recognize it seems you're in control, that's why one resorts to rage. It makes you feel strong and powerful. When it builds within you, Kyran, it's because you are displacing helplessness." The preceptor paused. "You know, there are other ways of dealing with this. When one's at peace, there's no need to feel helpless. Peacefulness is a virtue that overcomes rage, subdues it, sending it back to the depths where it belongs. There is no need for rage when peaceful individuals have learned to live with themselves. Don't you see?"

"Yeah, but ..." Kyran turned to Edvon, and in that split second, his older brother caught a glimpse of the sly smile he had seen so many times prior. "Applying your earlier logic, with the black and white ... Without rage, how can there be peacefulness?"

Edvon sighed. *Clever little cholee.*

CHAPTER FIVE

It was midday, and the sun was shining through the skylights in Marrek's office. As the preceptor leaned back in his chair, rays of light illuminated the top of his bald head. This amused Edvon, and his thoughts wandered. *Does his dome ever get burned by the sun? He must wear some kind of protective balm to prevent that from happening, right?* With Kyran in one of his combative moods, the meeting had taken a twist, and Edvon knew he might be there for a while.

"I admire your resourcefulness in attempting to use my argument against me," Marrek said. "Very ingenious indeed. Yet you miss the point I am making." The preceptor stood up and paced behind his desk. He picked up a piece from a Mira board, twirling it around. "I'm not telling you to ignore your anger but asking you to learn how to control it. Anger is a normal emotion, one that is even, dare I say, healthy. In essence, it's nothing more than the natural manner in which we respond to threats from the outside. Anger inspires us to act aggressively, and it can mean the difference between life and death when we're attacked or forced to defend ourselves. Anger is necessary to our survival, Kyran."

Edvon felt like he was sitting in a morning lecture.

"When it gets out of control and turns destructive, that's when the problems arise. By allowing anger to turn into rage, you put yourself at the mercy of an unpredictable and powerful force, one that isn't easy to tame." Marrek turned his attention to Edvon. "You've been rather quiet. What do you make of this?"

"I don't know," the older Adept replied. "Philosophical

considerations aside, I don't have a problem with my brother just ignoring his anger."

"Really!" Kyran blurted out. "So you would have me live with blinders covering my eyes? Like a balbak with its head in the marsh?"

Marrek shook his head and chuckled. "Such a strange myth, one that's not grounded in reality. If the balbak stuck its head in the marsh every time it saw a predator approaching, well … there wouldn't be many balbaks left in the Dominion, would there?"

Amused, the brothers joined the preceptor in a hearty laugh.

"Tell me, Kyran," asked Marrek, "has the swimming helped?"

Edvon was perplexed. "What swimming?"

"You haven't told anyone?" the preceptor whispered, to which Kyran shook his head. "Very well, we can speak of it another time." Marrek stretched his arms above his head and returned to a more serious tone. "Kyran is right. Ignoring the fact that he has a problem coping with his anger is equivalent to denying the problem exists in the first place. And living in denial can be a dangerous path to follow. It has the consequence of trivializing feelings necessary to our well-being."

"Right," Edvon replied, still unsure why he was there.

"More importantly, it causes us to neglect solutions to potential dilemmas that may arise down the road. That's why I reopened the Court of Grievances, despite the growing number of protesters coming to our gates. An action I'm sure you question, correct?"

Edvon was stupefied. *How did he know I'd ask him about that?* "Well yeah, I'm a little skeptical. But I'm sure you have excellent reasons, sir."

"I appreciate the diplomatic answer, though it is unnecessary," said the preceptor. "I value constructive feedback from my peers."

Kyran glanced at Edvon, expecting to see his brother's typical smug look. *Peers? What a couple of cholees! But seriously, why was that dread court re-opened?* His reflection was promptly answered.

"Providing demonstrators with an outlet through which to express their complaints puts the Academy in a position of control," Marrek explained.

"Why?" inquired Edvon.

"Letting them choose their own means of protest could lead to violent behavior, putting our students and faculty at risk. Establishing the Court of Grievances as a reliable forum not only allows us to safely channel any potential resentment against the Academy, it also displays our respect and recognition for differing viewpoints."

"Doesn't it make us look weak?" Kyran asked. "If protestors trekked up Mount Kilda to challenge the Temple's practices, they would be thrown right back down the hill."

"That's why so many within Phaidros hate the Temple."

"I haven't heard many people say that."

"Because people fear the Temple and fear to speak out against it," continued Marrek. "A regime of fear is supported by a questionable foundation, a foundation that in time will come crumbling down. Since it's difficult to be both feared and loved, it is much safer to be loved than feared. Fear gives rise to resentment, and when the leader ceases to instill fear, he's left facing an angry and vengeful populace. Leaders who embrace love, however, receive the trust, respect, and support of their subjects."

"Yeah, but isn't it easier to take advantage of the leader who loves as opposed to the one who is feared?" Kyran responded.

"How so?"

"To be loved, one has to give something up, right? What prevents people from wanting more and more from loved leaders until there's nothing left to give?"

"A question scholars have been discussing for centuries, Kyran. Why do people always assume the loved leader is one who is weak and capitulating? A logical fallacy. There are other ways of gaining love than through generosity."

"Yeah, but I feel like fear is much more predictable. It doesn't wear away as easily."

"I disagree," interjected Edvon. "The strongest groups are the ones held together by the power of friendship and loyalty. And in any case, this argument seems pointless. Why can't a leader be both loved and feared?"

Kyran, irritated by the comment, stared at his brother with disgust. "That wasn't the premise of the argument."

"An argument we can always debate again another day," Marrek said, glancing at the intricately carved clock adorning the back of his office door. The preceptor sat in his chair. "Unlike our balbak, I won't live with my head in the marsh. I want to know what people are thinking, how they're responding to the forever changing tides. And we'll never bring ourselves down to the Temple's level because we are a bastion of knowledge and hope. We bring people up to our level. This is important to remember, these being dangerous times."

"The attacks on the villages," Edvon muttered.

"And the Council members," Kyran added.

The preceptor nodded.

"Sir, I can't believe I'm asking this. The rumors are false, right?" asked Edvon. "We have nothing to do with those things, do we?"

"Even if we did, do you think he'd tell you?"

Marrek peered at Kyran with pursed lips, and after several uncomfortable seconds, refocused his attention on the older brother. "Rumors are the least of my concerns. These troublesome attacks are peculiar."

"What do you mean?" questioned Edvon.

"I can't say for sure, I need more evidence," the preceptor responded.

"Evidence of what?"

"If it's what I think it is ... well ... I don't know. I think ... I think I need more proof ..." The old man looked up to the skylight as his sentence drifted away, an aging face filled with concern. Edvon was confounded, for he had never witnessed his mentor stumble through words, much less entire sentences. "If it's what I think it is, a lot will change," Marrek said.

"What will change?" Kyran asked.

"In time. Everything in time."

"Wait, what do you mean?"

"You will know in time."

"Wh—what?" stammered an impatient Kyran. "Well, what do you think it is? At least tell me what you think it is."

"In time, you will know."

"Really? Why won't you just tell us now, what's the big deal?"

Edvon could sense a growing degree of disrespect in Kyran's language, and he felt like hitting his little brother. By the same token, he was content to sit back and listen, hoping the pressure might lead to concrete answers from the cryptic preceptor.

"There are matters I must share with you, a discussion we're bound to have. Granted, one I would have preferred to delay a while longer." Marrek took in a deep breath, as the perplexed brothers held on. "In the next days, I'll know more. And if my intuition is correct, we'll have that discussion, I promise."

"What matters? What discussion?"

The preceptor looked at Kyran with a compassionate smile. "In—"

"Time," Edvon finished. "In time, am I right?"

"Yes."

"Why in time? What's this in time, anyway?" Kyran formed quotation marks in the air. "What does it matter when you tell us this ambiguous yet crucial information?"

"You're not ready," Marrek answered. "And unless my hand is forced, I'd prefer to wait until you are."

"This is ridiculous!" Kyran pushed back his chair, causing it to make a loud screeching sound on the hardwood floor. He glared at the preceptor and stormed his way out of the office.

Edvon shook his head. *So much for controlling your anger.*

"I didn't expect him to take it any better." Marrek grimaced. "Speaking of time, we're running short on it. I called you to my office because I need you to go on a mission, Edvon."

"What type of mission?"

"Elias will tell you more. You'll be going to the Noble District together and meeting with a candidate for the Council vacancy. He requested to speak with students. Normally I'd come with you, but—"

"Don't worry, I'm on it, sir."

"Excellent. And I want you to bring your brother."

"What?"

"I said I want you to bring Kyran."

"No," replied Edvon with a shake of his head. "No way."

"He needs to explore outside the Academy. It will do him good to see Phaidros, walk its streets."

"But—"

"It's not up for debate," cut in the preceptor. "Carry out this mission, keep an eye on your brother, and by the time you come back, I'll have more information. And we can have that discussion."

"Discussion? That's no longer on my mind, sir. I have a mission to accomplish."

"Edvon, you'll find what we have to discuss very interesting."

"How can you be so sure?"

Marrek gave him an intense look. "It concerns your father."

CHAPTER SIX

They showed up around the same time every morning. First, the fanatics, with the sunrise, hoping to enter the Temple ahead of anyone else. Next, the pious locals, making a quick stop on the way to their various places of work around the city. The last wave, comprised of Pilgrims from around the Dominion, was always the largest and lasted the entire day. They lined up for hours, awaiting their turn to enter the Inner Sanctum and worship those same Gods who had sentenced them to the harshest of punishments, as the Book of Provenance explicitly described. From atop her quarters in the Temple's largest tower, Rex Ruga would sometimes watch the crowd amass, impassive and unconcerned for the long waits they had to endure. "Fools," she mumbled to no one in particular. Rex Ruga spun around to face her bed and considered the burly naked man half covered by the sheets. *Why do I keep doing this?*

He sensed her scrutiny and cocked his head. "You know you shouldn't call them that."

"I can call them what I want because I own them."

"You only own them because they're blind, like Lutigas."

"And who will open their eyes?" There was a pause. "Will it be you, Gorgios?"

"Hmff. How perverse of me to do that, as it would only lead them to the tip of my sword."

Rex Ruga smiled. *That's why.* She turned back to the window, disregarded the throng of pilgrims, and gazed at the Bay of Alboran. *And I wouldn't put it past you either. As much as I dislike men, there's something to be said for their virility. A necessary change of pace from those sweet girls I toss around.* Her divertissement was now sitting up, running his fingers through his thick dark hair and stretching out his sinewy muscles. "You should leave," Rex Ruga said dryly.

"Already?"

She turned around. "Who do you think you are? My lover? Dress yourself and go do something productive!"

Gorgios laughed. "Nothing is productive until you tell me it is, Ruga." Hoping the comment had succeeded in flattering her, the large man swung his thick legs off the bed and onto the wool rug, digging his fleshy toes into the fibers. He then crept toward the commandant, but she put an end to his lustful aspirations.

"And I told you to put on some clothes, did I not?" The question silenced Gorgios. Her back still turned, Rex Ruga listened to him snatch his tunic from the ground. Seconds later, the door slammed shut. *How long before his ambitions get the better of him?* The commandant realized she was still naked. *What ambitions? He already holds the power he craves.* She looked at her bare legs. *And more. He's not going anywhere.*

Grabbing a robe and pulling it atop her shoulders, Rex Ruga looked back to the blue ocean on the horizon. Although she still hoped undiscovered land existed, she was well acquainted with the reality. The Great Expedition leaders had been methodical in their quest, one which yielded conclusive and grim results. The commandant remembered the contagious excitement that spread through the Dominion two decades earlier, when the major source manipulator had announced the development of new Source-powered vessels capable of traveling the sea for days on end. The Noble Assembly had commissioned a fleet, hiring the best boatsmen to navigate it. Many aspirants also joined the crews, promising to return with wild tales of adventure and riches lining their pockets. Rex Ruga, then just a cadet at the Temple, had attended the send-off ceremony along with thousands of other Phaidrosians. Their collective enthusiasm was matched only by their disappointment when the fleet came into sight in Portown a week later, empty-handed and having crossed the entire ocean. They went out again, each time on a different trajectory, returning to Dominion lands having encountered nothing but open water and agitated geegas.

Rex Ruga stared at herself in the wardrobe's mirror, contemplating her tight stomach and muscular limbs. *What a small place we live in.* The morose woman's short bleach-blond hair was matted as a result of the engaging night, though her aquamarine eyes were crisp as ever. She dipped her index and middle finger in a small container, applying the gel to the terse strands of hair near the top of her head and creating little upward spikes. *Some, like me, might even call it an island.* Rex Ruga reached for her white pants. *An island filled with filthy Nobles.* Slipping into them, she snatched her coat. *And presumptuous Adepts.* One last look out the window. *And a bunch of morons.*

Najara was waiting for her in the hallway. "You slept well, Commandant?"

The confidante, as she was called, was an elderly woman who had been at the Temple for an eternity. Like every other Overseer, she wore white robes, though hers had taken on a shade of gray, making them look like those of an initiant. This bothered Rex Ruga, but she had yet to convince her closest advisor to commission new ones. "I never sleep well, and you know it."

"Perhaps you need to clear your thoughts."

"And how do I go about doing that?"

"You can start by getting more rest."

"What do you think I do at night?"

"You mean who you do at night?" Najara's purple lips

contorted into a venomous smile, her sharp eyes contrasting with the lines of age marking her face.

Rex Ruga clenched her teeth. *What do you care?* For a moment, she felt an urge to shove the confidante, knocking her onto the cold floor. *Hopefully her dread head wrap falls off.* Everyone wanted to know the shade of the old woman's hair. *Most likely the same color as her withered robes.*

"The Senate's waiting for us," Najara remarked.

So they made their way to the Great Staircase serving as the main access to the Temple's multiple floors. *Why do I keep trusting her?* The one person Rex Ruga was supposed to feel comfortable sharing her secrets with elicited the opposite sentiment. *Doesn't that defeat the whole point of a confidante? To confide in her?* Najara was too conniving, it was an impossible task to ascertain her numerous and shifting ulterior motives. Few denied she was one of the cleverest individuals in Phaidros. A woman rising through the ranks of the Temple or any Dominion institution was becoming more commonplace, yet during Najara's youth, it was inconceivable. She had muscled her way to the top, using her wits to secure a position on the Senate which she held for several decades. Though commandants had come and gone, the confidante remained, lurking in the shadows, whispering in their ears and forever scheming.

Rex Ruga was no fool, she knew far too well Najara orchestrated her nomination following Rex Quintus's murder. In a matter of hours, the confidante had garnered sufficient support from the voting lieutenants, despite the stronger and more capable candidate, her opponent Tibon. They continued down the stairs. *Why didn't she take the title for herself?* Rex Ruga knew the answer. Being commandant would have exposed Najara to new responsibilities and, more importantly, thrown her into the spotlight. She performed best in the background, controlling the true decision-making while a manipulable figurehead sat in office. *A figurehead like me* ... And the Temple was divided into a structure that allowed the confidante to do just that.

Overseers belonged to a class, one which bestowed upon them varying levels of power. At the lowest tier were the initiants, most of them sent to the Temple by their families. Discernible by the gray robes they were required to wear, the initiants spent much of their time studying the Book of Provenance. One gained the privilege to don the white when he or she had graduated and been inducted into the ranks of the general Temple population. These cadets, as they were called, made up the largest class of Overseers. A small selection rose to become lieutenants, a prestigious status that enjoyed voting privileges. Even fewer would join the Senate, a group of five nominated to serve a lifetime appointment to the Temple's highest authoritative echelon. Upon the death of a senator, lieutenants voted for a replacement, with none more important than the commandant, their de facto leader. What Rex Ruga had discovered was that a senator could sometimes have more power than the commandant. And she feared she was looking at one in that very moment.

Najara exhibited nimbleness as she clambered down the final steps, always a surprising sight given the plumpness she had accumulated over the years. There were those who said the confidante had been a great beauty in her youth, though Rex Ruga hardly believed the gossip. While age played a role in masking beauty, the latter never disappeared. On the contrary, it could always be seen frolicking behind the wrinkles, caged by the morbid yet unavoidable reality of elderliness. Nothing spectacular was perceivable underneath Najara's wrinkles. *Probably just a rumor she made up herself.* Rex Ruga smiled at the irony. The confidante cared little about her image, certainly not at the expense of her power. *Or does she?* Gorgios often asserted all women were in tune with their personal appearance. *Maybe he's right.* The neatness with which Najara tied her headscarf caught Rex Ruga's attention. She observed the old woman's simple yet elegant necklace, the eye shadow she was wearing, the two rings on her left hand, the subtle polish on her fingertips ... *She is! She's still trying to be beautiful.*

They were the last to enter the grandiose hall that served as the Senate's meeting point. Limestone statues, depicting notable Overseers from centuries past, surrounded an immense pentagon-shaped marble table. High ceilings gave way to a round skylight allowing for a single ray of sunlight to descend into the middle of the room. The effect was symbolic, but it was also a practical disaster as senators found themselves squinting at each other during the clear summer months. If Rex Ruga had any say in the matter, she would have long ago covered up the hole with a plank of wood.

"You're late." An older man with a white goatee and thin wire-rimmed glasses was speaking to them.

"And we appreciate your patience, Tibon," answered Najara.

Rex Ruga settled into the largest of the two remaining empty chairs.

"Even my patience has limits," Tibon shot back.

"From what I hear," said the commandant with a nasty smile, "patience is only one trait of yours which has limits."

"How dare you! Do you know—"

"Who I am? Yes, I am your superior. And if I want to joke around about your impotence, you will accept it."

Tibon slammed his fists onto the table, alarming Gorgios, who until then had been disinterested in the conversation.

"That may well be true," answered Vasant, the fifth senator at the table and Tibon's closest ally. "But procedures do exist for the deposition of insolent and foolish commandants."

"Are you threatening me?"

Vasant did not pause. "Yes."

Rex Ruga was unnerved. *Not the answer I expected.*

"That's an expressed defiance to her authority," noted Najara. "Perhaps you misspoke?"

"No, I did not." Vasant turned toward Tibon, as if to confirm the appropriateness of his next comment. "Tibon may be … ahem … impotent, but he is not perverse. And there are rumors circulating within the walls of this great institution—"

"Enough!" Rex Ruga exclaimed.

Gorgios, entertained by the exchange, was now paying full attention.

"It is far from enough," persisted Vasant, undeterred. "It is my duty as senator of Overseer affairs to bring to light these allegations."

"Not if those allegations are false."

"Girls have approached me whispering of blasphemous acts." Vasant looked around the table, bearing a sinister frown. "Unthinkable things."

"You are wrong, and you will retract these words," warned Rex Ruga.

"Not two days ago, a young Overseer was thrown in the dungeons, without so much—"

"Gorgios, as your Commandant, I order you to arrest this man."

"That's not an order I'm allowed to follow," replied her Master of Arms. "You know very well senators carry immunity."

Rex Ruga shoved her chair back onto the cold stone floor. "Fine. I'll do it myself." The commandant took several menacing steps toward Vasant, prompting Gorgios to leap to his feet. The giant man pulled from under his belt a long broad sword.

"Enough!" hissed Najara. "We don't have time for this. There are more pressing matters."

"Are there?" Tibon asked the woman he hated.

"Yes."

"And why should we trust you? After what you did to me, never mind the Temple, when you gave the power to this … this fool of a girl."

Najara stood. "Why should you trust me? Do you doubt my loyalties to this Temple, Tibon? I find that to be an insulting remark to the person who's transformed this institution into the strongest in Phaidros. Was it not I who consolidated the support of the population after the failure of the Great Expedition, by launching a propaganda campaign blaming it on the Academy's brazen promises? Was it not I who insisted on investing in the smoking lounges, despite their illegality? A decision that has refilled the Temple's coffers to amounts we could not spend in an entire lifetime. Was it not I who—"

"Yes, fine," interjected Tibon. "I don't doubt your loyalties."

"Was it not I who spread the recent rumor that our own commandant was killed by militant Adepts? Senators, there are attacks going on in the countryside, as I'm sure you're aware. And they correspond with the narrative we've been building throughout these years."

"Which is?" asked Gorgios.

"That Adepts are a threat to the peace. Terrified villagers are flocking into the city in droves, at a time when the Temple has never been stronger. They're pounding on the gates of the Academy, demanding accountability and blaming them for these horrid events. With our help, they could succeed in bringing down those gates. Senators, this is too good an opportunity to miss."

Vasant looked at Rex Ruga. She turned around, picked up

her stray chair, and returned to her place at the table.

"Whatever these accusations against our commandant, I give you my word they will be handled," promised Najara. "Internally."

Tibon gave a slight bob of the head. "There is an even greater matter, one you have yet to address."

"The vacant Council seats?"

"Right."

"I was getting to it." Najara paused and readjusted her head wrap. "From my sources, it looks like Lord Hanstun is in line for the Noble Assembly's open seat. The Academy will have heard the same information, and Marrek is surely sending his Adepts to make overtures."

"Then I'll go talk to the Noble as well," Gorgios declared.

"Yes," concurred the confidante. "Try to gauge the direction he might be leaning so we may plan ahead."

"Don't worry, I'll make sure to show him the benefits of the Temple's patronage."

"Very good. Which leaves us with the Overseer seat. Our seat."

"What must we discuss?" asked Rex Ruga. "The Council representative is always a commandant, and I intend to keep it that way."

"No."

Rex Ruga swung around to face Najara. "What does that mean?"

"It means that Tibon will sit on the Council, not you."

CHAPTER SEVEN

A massive wave battered the hardened walls of the Sea Tower, crashing into the rough stone with vengeful force. It dissipated and retreated to the security of the ocean, ceding to a new series of waves preparing futile strikes of their own. Through the endless assault on its foundation, the Sea Tower stood tall, as it had for many centuries. Legend asserted the building was the first Academy structure, erected in the bay to protect Adepts escaping persecution. As the Academy's territory expanded together with its influence, the Sea Tower's purpose waned. Now it remained abandoned, though many students found the relic to be a popular destination for late-night escapades.

In one of the tower's highest chambers, a lone figure stared at a rising wave from a balistraria. Eyes glazed, Edvon watched as it picked up speed and came slamming into the stone below in a cloud of foam and mist. *Failed again.* He walked toward a large armchair in the middle of the room. As the Adept sat down, he brought his hands up to his head, massaging his temples and letting out a heavy sigh. Edvon had been there on many occasions. The quietness and seclusion of the Sea Tower, a satisfying getaway from the Academy's commotion, appealed to him.

At that moment, any rational thought was unattainable. After his meeting with the preceptor, Edvon had found his way out of the Ivory Spire and across the narrow bridge leading to the Sea Tower. He had followed his feet, oblivious to where they were taking him. His instinct had him hold the guardrail, and the Adept trudged along, sluggishly climbing the numerous stairs to the room. *My father ... My father?* The Adept's mind swirled with uncertainties. *Who was he? What did he look like? Is he still alive? Does he have something to do with the village attacks?* Most puzzling to Edvon was Marrek's timing. *Why not wait until I get back? It just makes no sense.* As the sun set, he remained seated, succumbing to a deep sleep.

Edvon woke up with a startle. He looked around in confusion, rubbing his sore neck. The Adept took in a deep breath and his expression changed from one of self-pity to one of determination. There was a mission to accomplish, and the young man realized he was wasting time moping around. *The quicker I get this done, the quicker I can get back to the Academy for an explanation.* With newfound conviction in his step, Edvon marched to the door, slamming it shut on his way out.

They were waiting just inside the main gates of the Academy. Elias was irritated, as his less than subtle body language indicated, hands on his hips, left foot tapping, and neck twitching. The officer tilted his head to the side as Edvon approached, the young man's disheveled look taking him by surprise. Kyran was smiling, delighting in his brother's untidy appearance.

"Hardly an appropriate time for a late night," announced Elias.

"I—"

"That's his kind of behavior," cut in the officer, waving a hand toward Kyran. "Instead, he was here five minutes early. The Dominion has turned upside down."

"I—"

"Come on, let's go." Elias spun around, shaking his head. "And don't get lost on the way."

As they followed behind, Kyran turned to his brother, never missing an opportunity to taunt. "Left her alone in the Sea Tower?"

"You know I don't do that," Edvon replied, too tired to be

annoyed.

"Probably not what she—"

"And keep up!" shouted Elias, putting an end to what was becoming a contentious exchange.

During congested times, it took Adepts several hours to walk to the Noble District. Built near the salt marshes, where the nobility acquired a substantial portion of its wealth, the district had systematically encroached into Phaidros, with Nobles buying out precious land upon which to expand their growing estates. The massive compounds, flush with sumptuous gardens and lavish villas, differed from the packed and simple buildings found throughout the rest of the capital.

Elias hated the chaotic nature of the city. The narrow streets and dense crowds gave him headaches, and he avoided those at any cost. A passerby bumped into him. *Gods! Again?* As they approached the market, the streets narrowed, and the mass of citizens thickened, making it difficult to move unimpeded.

"I can walk first for a bit," offered Edvon. The tall Adept stepped ahead and cleared a pathway.

Pinching the bridge of his nose in frustration, Elias cursed his short height. *It should be Marrek in my place. Going to the Noble District will just make me jealous.* He imagined himself in his room back at the Academy, its quaint terrace high above any commotion. *What could the preceptor be doing that's more important than this? Could it have to do with …* Elias shook the thought from his head. *No.* It was something he should have never stumbled upon. *And I promised never to speak of it.*

"Why are we going again?" Kyran asked.

"I already told you," replied the officer.

Edvon was hoping for a more telling answer. He knew it was related to the Council of Five. *The loss of two members threatens the Council's pro-Temple majority which they've held for more than a decade. If the nominee from the Noble Assembly supports the Academy, then a shift in the balance of power can be expected.* And for whatever reason, Marrek had picked him and Kyran to make first contact with the likeliest replacement. "Wait, why isn't the preceptor coming to this meeting?"

Elias looked at him with a raised eyebrow. "Didn't I tell you why yesterday?"

"Umm ... I don't think so," lied Edvon.

"Gods. Well, the reason ..." Elias tried hard to conjure an answer to the question he was also asking himself. "I don't know," he said. "So let's just keep going."

They came upon an open square, and Kyran turned to his older brother. "Why am I, of all people, going?" he whispered.

"It's what you were told to do."

"Yeah, whatever." The younger Adept pulled from his pocket a small wrapped package. "I'm supposed to give the lord this stupid thing."

"What's that?" Edvon asked.

"No idea, Marrek handed it to me this morning."

"You saw the preceptor this morning?"

"Yeah, right before you showed up."

"Did he ... did he say anything?"

"Regarding?"

"Umm ..."

"What do you mean? Obviously, he did. He told me to give this package to the Noble. What's wrong with you?"

Kyran turned away, annoyed, and Edvon breathed a sigh of relief, as Marrek had urged him not to mention the reference to their father.

The Adepts crossed a square, launching themselves into another alley. They walked in silence, Elias laboring to keep up with the siblings' long strides. As they traveled further east,

Phaidros adopted a more commercial feel. With the residential districts behind them, the group made its way through street bazaars that had cropped up in recent years and become the ultimate destination to purchase Source-powered technologies. The market's proximity to the majestic Albai Bridge made it accessible to all residents of the capital, and because it was still within the limits of West Phaidros, merchants could confidently avoid any Temple persecution. Citizens of every class were bartering a variety of items with merchants, from household appliances to trinkets and decorations. A handful of Overseers in their conspicuous white robes haggled with shopkeepers.

Kyran watched as one agreed to buy a self-vacuuming Source-powered cleaner. *Hypocrite. Wipe your own floors.*

"Hey mister!" A group of children was pointing at a small widget that had collided with Kyran's feet. "Pass it back here!"

The Adept picked up the little toy and flung it back in their direction. It hovered through the air, glowing. As it was about to reach the children, the toy shook and crashed into the ground. The small reserve of Source energy had emptied. *Time to replenish.*

"Kyran!"

Elias and Edvon were waiting for him a block away. He raced toward them and felt his heart leap at the sight of the Albai Bridge. It was swarming with people traveling in both directions, a chaotic mass of bodies and fast-moving SPCs that flowed in harmony. The Apex rose high in the background, and Kyran realized he had never seen it from so close.

"We need to get to the other side," said Elias.

The brothers stepped out of West Phaidros for the first time in their lives.

CHAPTER EIGHT

Soothing sounds drifted from the music maker, floating around the lounge. They eased their way across the striped rugs, twirling around the plush sofas and meandering up the red velvet curtains before teasing their way through the elegant tables and glasses filled with rare liquor. Ending their pleasant stroll in the musky air, they penetrated many ears in the room, loosening up well-dressed spectators and making them smile. The player could sense this effect and drew from it, using his delicate fingers to produce a stream of tranquil, down-tempo music. He was hunched over, sleeves rolled and glasses almost tumbling off the bridge of his nose. Occasionally, he would look toward center stage, making sure his notes remained in sync with the main act.

"Wait, it's right here!" exclaimed a performer, the taller of the two. He wore tight pants over his long legs, a tailored coat around his broad shoulders, and a buzz cut uncommon in a capital whose citizens liked to showcase their flowing locks.

The music stopped, and a murmur of delight ran through the audience, punctuated by a few claps. The tall performer returned to a woman her shiny necklace, then beckoned her to leave the stage. "And that's why you never trust an Adept with anything valuable." The crowd laughed. "Or with your lady," he added, winking.

The laughter continued as the second performer smiled at the volunteer and blew her a kiss. His short and portly physique juxtaposed his partner's, and a large mustache sat on his upper lip. It was black and twirled upward at both ends.

"Because I don't exactly adhere to the Recital Supreme, if you catch my drift," the taller performer announced. He was leaning over, his hand cupped around his mouth as if confessing a secret, a subtle bit of acting that earned him more chuckles. But Pluto was getting weary. They were close to the last act, around the time he felt like jumping off the stage, walking up to the nearest Noble, and punching him in the face. He sensed a nudge from behind. Joss was his best friend, never mind the second half to their two-man act. Never uttering a word, he often expressed himself through body contact or hand gestures. And Pluto had grown to learn a nudge in the back meant he was losing focus. He watched as Joss pointed at another volunteer, waving him up to the stage for a trick they had practiced hundreds of times since their days together at the Academy. "What's your name, sir?" Pluto asked.

"Romon."

"Romon, if I could guess in which hand you're holding a coin behind your back, would you call that impressive?"

"No, umm … I think that would just be luck."

"What if I did it twice?"

Unsure of what to say, Romon turned to the audience for support. "Uh … I'd say it would still be luck."

"And what if I did it ten times in a row?"

There were gasps of disbelief.

"That would be pretty impressive," admitted Romon.

"Go ahead then, put your arms behind your back and place this coin into either hand." Once the volunteer had completed the instructions, Pluto beckoned him to hold forward both his closed fists. "The coin is in your right hand," he called out. A couple of tentative claps came from the audience as Romon revealed the coin. "Again!" shouted Pluto. The volunteer echoed the movement, and once more, the performer guessed the correct hand. "Again!

Again! Again!" Pluto never failed to pick the correct hand. Audience members were now standing, disregarding their initial skepticism and holding their breaths in anticipation.

"Again!" someone shouted.

In frustration, Romon brought the coin behind his back and endeavored to trick the magician just once. Pluto sighed as he watched the shuffling hands through a mirror concealed in the stool placed behind the participant.

"I think the coin is in your left hand ... but," Pluto paused for maximum effect. "Before we check ..."

Joss wobbled over to Romon, reaching into the volunteer's vest pocket and pulling out a paper. He took his time unfolding it, as the suspense in the hall grew.

"Well, this is very interesting," announced Pluto.

"What?" an audience member cried out.

"This paper Joss just found in Romon's coat tracked exactly what happened here." Pluto held it up for everyone to see, then read the big black letters. "Right, right, left, right, right, left, left, right, left, left."

When Romon displayed the coin, a collective glee overcame the spectators. They cheered and whistled as the performers bowed. Joss struggled to keep the other forty papers safely tucked in the pockets of his coat.

"And now, for our grand finale." A curtain lifted behind them, revealing three small tables, each with a chair pulled up to it. Off to the right, the audience could see three plates covered by stainless-steel domes. "For this act, we'll need yet another volunteer." He scanned the crowd and chose a man who started making his way to the stage. "No, wait. You can assist us better from where you are."

"Umm ... okay." The new volunteer took a few steps backward.

"And your name?"

"Marvis."

"What you can do for us, Marvis, is pick three random members from the audience here today."

"Okay. You ... you ... and you," the volunteer said, pointing his long index finger.

Three Noble-looking men rose to their feet.

"Alright gentlemen, come on up here. And what are your names? Clasius ... Ruan ... and Ziatte. Excellent." They were grouped on the side of the stage, and Pluto turned to Marvis. "In my hand here, I have three envelopes. One red, one blue, one yellow. You tell me which one to give to each of these gentlemen."

"Uh ... sure." Marvis scratched his gray beard. "How about the red one to Ziatte. Umm ... I think the blue one should go to ... what was your name again?"

"Ruan."

"The blue to Ruan, then. And that leaves the yellow one for Clasius." Pluto distributed the envelopes. "Marvis, now please assign a table to each of these gentlemen. As you can see, each table has a little card on it with a number. Number one on the left, number two in the middle, and number three on the right. So what's your choice?"

"Well, this is fun," said Marvis, getting a laugh from the other audience members. "Let's put Clasius at table two, Ziatte table one, and ..."

"And," Pluto interjected, turning to Ruan. "I think you get the drill, no?"

The three volunteers sat down at their respective tables, and Joss picked up the first plate.

"Marvis, to which table should Joss bring this?" asked Pluto.

"Umm ... well, how about table ... uh, table three."

"And that one?"

Joss had already set the covered plate in front of Ruan and gone back for another.

"Table number one."

"Are you sure?" Pluto prodded

"Actually, change it to number two."

"That's what I thought. Don't you worry, Ziatte, we still have one last plate for you."

Joss brought it over and waited near the tables while Pluto stepped off to the side. "Now gentlemen, I'd like you to open those envelopes and read them so everyone can hear what they say."

Ziatte was the first to act. "Sitting at table number one, someone named Ziatte will be eating baked geega with rice."

Joss removed the cover form the plate, and the crowd gasped.

"And you?" Pluto asked Clasius.

"Sitting at table number two, someone named Clasius will be eating a delicious tart." He looked down in shock as Joss uncovered a fruit-filled pastry.

"Dig in, my friend!" urged Pluto.

The audience was too shocked to laugh.

"Sitting at table number three," said Ruan. He stopped and turned to the crowd.

"Come on, read it already!" someone demanded.

"Someone named Ruan will be eating a vegetable soup."

Pluto unveiled the meal. "We would have gotten you grilled balbak, but the kitchen boy burned it all."

The standing ovation lasted several minutes. Instead of relishing the moment, the performer found it irritating, only thinking of the pay waiting backstage. With one final bow, he followed Joss behind the curtain.

"How about some enthusiasm, maybe an encore, huh?"

asked Slivar, the performance hall's manager.

"Don't you hear that clapping?" fired back Pluto.

"I don't care. You looked like a Source-powered machine out there."

"A Source-powered machine who made you lots of ticket sales."

"Doesn't matter, that sort of behavior won't be tolerated in this venue."

"Why don't you just give us our money then, and we'll be on our way."

"Fine." The manager pulled from his pocket a small cloth sachet filled with coins and tossed it to Joss. "Take it. But if that ever happens again, it's the last one you'll see."

"And I'll be having my share of that before you spend it at the smoking lounges." Marvis walked up, still struggling to unglue the fake beard he was wearing.

"Gods," sighed Pluto.

"What's wrong, kid?"

"I hate paying you."

Marvis held out his hand. "Don't care. Without me, the tricks don't work."

"Yeah, whatever." Pluto dumped four coins into the mole's outstretched palm.

"You know, it's funny you fellas don't use your magic for those tricks."

"Idiot. They'd see our eyes shine if we did, wouldn't they?" The two Adepts walked toward the exit and stepped into a blinding sun. Pluto hated the matinee shows. "Lucky Roach?" Joss winked with enthusiasm.

As they left, a pretty woman accompanied by a strapping young lord came around the corner. "Excuse me," she said.

"What?"

The pair was taken aback by the patent annoyance in Pluto's voice. "Could you tell us how you did the trick with the disappearing coin?"

"Sure, do you have a coin?"

"Yes, right here." The Noble pulled a solid gold piece from his vest and handed it to Pluto.

The magician smiled and pocketed the coin. "There, now it vanished." He spun around, leaving the dismayed young couple behind. Joss chuckled. After crossing through several squares and streets, the companions arrived at their destination. Pluto entered the Lucky Roach, grimacing as he caught a whiff of musty air. The ground floor of the establishment disgusted him, and he hated walking through it.

"We have a table in the back, sir," said a tired waitress. She had materialized out of thin air and was crowding them into the wall. "And what will it be today? I'll get your order started."

Pluto, still irritated, was eager to answer. "I'll have two eggs, runny on top and burnt on the bottom, five strips of balbak, well done on one end and still raw on the other, a stale piece of bread, and a lukewarm glass of water."

"Hey!" the waitress exclaimed. "We don't serve that stuff here."

"Funny. That's what I had yesterday."

Offended, the young woman strutted away.

"Hmff." Joss grabbed his mustache, twirling it between his thumb and index finger.

"Come on, it was funny."

They made their way through the busy eatery to the back where a colossal man sat in a chair, picking at his fingernails with a shard of metal. He looked up, total apathy gracing his enormous face. The man brought his attention back to his nails, giving them in the process a slight nod. The two performers shuffled around, turning the corner to a dead end where rungs of a ladder had been fixed into the wall. They led to a trapdoor in the ceiling. Pluto clambered up, pushed the hatch, and disappeared through it. Taking a second to draw in the fresh air, he turned around to give Joss a hand.

"It's like emerging into a wonderland, my friend."

They were standing on a rooftop terrace, one of Phaidros's many well-hidden smoking lounges. Patrons could be seen chatting, relaxing, and partaking in the prohibited activity. A variety of potted leafy plants gave off the aura of a small garden, with an overhanging lattice and vines growing all around. The vegetation embellished as well as concealed the Lucky Roach's secret business, since the Noble Assembly had yet to recognize the legality of such establishments. The hypocrisy was evident, as everyone knew they existed, and most lords and ladies joined in the fun. Pluto and Joss walked toward an elevated bar at the far end of the terrace, giving an occasional thumbs up to familiar faces on the way over.

"And what will it be today, gentlemen?" inquired the convivial barman.

"Anything new?"

"Same as yesterday, I'm afraid. New shipments coming in the morning." As he spoke, the man pulled from behind the counter several terra-cotta plates containing different strains of herbs.

Joss pinched a bit of each one, smelling the various options with long and exaggerated sniffs. After a moment, he pointed at one dish. "I'm pretty sure you picked the same thing yesterday," muttered Pluto. Joss shrugged. "And the day before." Joss rolled his eyes. "Fine, fine. We'll take a pouch." Joss grinned, and Pluto handed the barman several of the coins they had recently gained. The two performers then plopped themselves down on one of the pillow-top benches, and Joss pulled from his inside vest pocket a little glass pipe. In one effortless motion, he packed some of the herbs into it and cracked a match, inhaling deeply and passing the pipe. As the euphoric sensation coursed through his body, Joss hummed. He surveyed the terrace while Pluto coughed beside him. That's when the mustached performer spotted her, and he grabbed his friend's elbow. "I know, I know. I inhaled too much." Joss kept nudging him. Pluto put the pipe on the table and followed the direction of his companion's finger. And then he saw her, too. The most beautiful woman he had ever set his eyes upon.

CHAPTER NINE

A sweet fragrance floated around the parlor, pungent enough to please, yet delicate so as not to become overwhelming. Edvon could make out hints of citrus in the scent. *And Tecaupylus oil? No, not quite right. It smells fruitier than that. Perhaps some kind of herb*? He continued to speculate while taking a moment to admire the luxurious room.

The main opening through which they had entered caught his attention. Intricate geometric shapes had been carved into the marble, and they surrounded colossal double doors towering to at least twice Edvon's height. They had been painted with vibrant blues and yellows, lending elegance and gentleness. *Imposing and graceful at the same time. Like that mystery aroma.*

From his new vantage point, Edvon realized the entire entrance resembled an oversized keyhole, circular at the top and narrow as it descended, before opening back up to accommodate the colorful work of art. He smiled, thinking of the Academy teachers who stressed the importance of symbolism in the works they read. *I'm sure they'd come up with something pertinent for this.* One door was cracked open, and through it Edvon could see the pristine gardens.

Upon their entrance into the palace, an attendant had beckoned the three Adepts to wait in a sunken seating area. It was a square pit, enclosed by the flooring of the elevated main level. Along the inside walls were built-in armchairs of a soothing milk color, matching the lush white rug and round table where servants had placed gold goblets for tea and water. Kyran gazed at the crimson pillows adorning his chair, then the small set of magnificent mahogany steps. "I feel stuck in a hole."

"A spectacular hole, one that must have cost a fortune to construct," answered Elias. "These sunken sitting rooms? So in vogue throughout the Noble District, I heard all about it." The officer looked around, mesmerized.

"It's in vogue to put your guests in a hole in the floor?" asked Kyran.

"Yes!" snapped Elias. "And if you keep complaining, you'll regret it. So you would do best to keep your limited aesthetic tastes to yourself and let the experts decide what's art."

"Why do they get to decide?" Brief silence followed the exchange, and Kyran counted the seconds it would take for his brother to jump in and voice his opinion. *It's inevitable, he always does.* Six seconds passed, then seven … eight … nine …

"I actually like the whole sunken idea," Edvon declared.

Kyran clapped his hands, delighted. "And why's that?" he asked, pretending to be interested.

"It makes the entire room feel more expanded. If the sitting area hadn't been lowered, the furniture would break up the space. It wouldn't feel as open as it does now."

"How fascinating."

Edvon caught onto the sarcasm. "Whatever. It's clever, and you know it."

"Whoa!" Kyran broke the whisper they had adopted. "So now, you're also an architect?"

"If you think that was technical architectural talk, then you clearly have no idea what an architect does."

"An interior designer, then."

"Shh," whispered Elias.

"But sir, we might have found Edvon's one true passion."

"Could you two please just …" Elias's eyes were closed,

and he was massaging his temples. The brothers turned back to their thoughts.

The walk from the Albai Bridge to the Noble District had been less exciting than anticipated. Kyran, expecting another setting to materialize before his eyes, was disappointed to find much of the same lifestyle he had grown accustomed to in West Phaidros. The streets were similar, as were their inhabitants. However, once within the Noble District, he had struggled to contain his astonishment.

Sumptuous palaces boasting immense gardens rose high into the air around a series of lakes and ponds. Smaller villas surrounded each palace, used to lodge guests or serve as entertainment for the lords and ladies, and there were sprawling verandas along the outside, generally level with the ground floor. During the hot summer months, an enthusiastic Elias had explained, many Nobles would sleep out on the porches, taking advantage of the cool air that drifted from adjacent pools of water.

As they sat, Kyran reached for a goblet and gulped the tea down, wishing he was also resting in one of those veranda hammocks, enjoying the cool breeze. For once, Kyran and Elias shared the same aspirations.

"Someone's coming." Edvon was pointing a finger toward his ear. "Listen."

Faint footsteps could be heard off in the distance, growing louder with each stride. Kyran felt his anticipation increase, when a door near the back of the room swung open, revealing a strange looking attendant. The man wore the same black tunic as servants in the palace, yet his was embellished with a sparkling hemline, a belt made of pure gold, and flashy arm cuffs. The man smiled, exposing a set of immaculate white teeth. His hairstyle featured undercut sides with textured length on top, and as he walked toward them, Kyran noticed a grotesque scar running from the side of his temple to his jaw.

"Welcome, dear friends." The man bowed, greeting the visitors. He wore a subtle streak of dark-teal eyeliner under his bottom lashes. "My name is Ruan, I am the personal attendant to Lord Hanstun. Thank you for your patience, I trust you have enjoyed the refreshments?"

"Yes, thank you," replied Elias.

"Good, very good. Now, if you would please come this way, Lord Hanstun is ready to meet with you."

They followed Ruan into a long and dim corridor, the end of which Kyran could barely discern. The young Adept looked up instead and noticed an indoor balcony that ran the entire length of the hallway. *Why is there a balcony with a view on such a boring corridor?* Its railing was made of wrought iron, extending a third of the way up to the domed ceiling. *And Elias was mocking my aesthetic tastes.* Kyran returned his gaze to their usher and noticed a long scimitar hanging from the back of his belt. *A personal attendant carrying a sword that size?* He gave Edvon an inquiring look but found his older brother scrutinizing the end of the hallway. Kyran coughed once, and then twice, hoping to catch his sibling's attention. *Can't he hear me? What's he staring at?* Then, the younger man caught sight of them. *That's what.* From behind Ruan, Kyran saw a group of six or seven Overseers advancing in their direction, white robes fluttering as they marched in unison.

"I didn't know you had other guests," said Elias.

"Of course, you didn't," Ruan replied. "How could you possibly know the lord's schedule of affairs?"

"Don't be coy with me, boy."

The hostile remark startled both brothers as well as Elias.

"I mean ... umm ... we're not here for any kind of trouble," the officer added.

"Quite on the contrary, they're just leaving." Ruan grinned.

"There will be no trouble."

"No trouble at all, by Auralus!" The group of Overseers had stopped a few paces ahead. Speaking was a gigantic man with long bushy sideburns extending down to the corners of his mouth. Yet he lacked any whiskers on his chin or upper lip, lending him the characteristics of a Fisherman's Bay sailor. His long black hair was pulled back into a slick ponytail, and he glared at the Adepts.

"Gorgios."

"Elias."

"Look, we have nothing to say to these people," Elias said to Ruan. "Can you just get them on their way, please?"

"You know you're wasting your time," taunted Gorgios.

"Okay, we're going now." Elias moved forward, but the gargantuan senator impeded his path with a small step to the left.

"We just had a very, shall we say, fruitful meeting with Lord Hanstun," continued Gorgios. "Dare I say, I think he's made up his mind on his preferences."

"Here's a little hint," said another Overseer, a short woman with bangs covering her square forehead. "It's not the Academy."

The Temple's delegation broke into laughter, causing Kyran to clench his fists. "You can't prefer something when you don't have anything to compare it to."

Edvon cringed. Apparently his brother had been listening during Marrek's lectures, though he was picking the worst time to showcase his newfound knowledge. The laughter ceased. Edvon put his hand out, hoping to prevent Kyran from uttering another word. It was too late.

"But given that a balbak rivals the brain capacity of an Overseer ... we'll give you a pass."

"What did you just say, runt?" The Overseer standing nearest Gorgios was a tall and thin man with gaunt cheeks. He appeared eager for confrontation.

"Do you have trouble hearing too?" asked Kyran.

The man took a step forward.

"Wait!" interjected Elias. "Uh … let's just … let's …" He looked to Ruan for help but found none.

"We should go our separate ways," offered Edvon.

Gorgios shook his head. "Not so fast. Your little friend here insulted us, and we want an apology."

"Well, you're not getting one," Kyran answered.

"Yes, we are." The senator shook his finger. "Or else …" His intimidating physique bolstered the threat's credibility.

"Okay, fine. To whom should I offer my apologies?"

"To me, you should offer them to me," said the lanky Overseer, delighted to be witnessing the upcoming humiliation. "Do it now."

Kyran looked at Edvon and shrugged. Then, to the older brother's horror, he broke into his notorious and mischievous smile. "That's what your mother said to me last night."

"How dare you!" shouted the Overseer.

"She said that, too. Right when I tried—"

The Overseer lunged at Kyran. With no time to react, the Adept braced himself for the inevitable impact. It never came. A deafening bang echoed through the corridor. The tall Overseer soared into the air, slamming hard into the wall with a sickening crunch. After what seemed like an eternity, his limp body collapsed to the ground. Kyran turned and looked at his brother in awe. Edvon's arms were extended out in front of his body, wrists joined and hands cupped. His eyes were shining brightly, knees bent in a fierce position.

"Matthias!" Gorgios approached the lifeless body of his fallen associate and attempted without success to reanimate him.

Elias twirled toward the brothers, gesturing at them with an agitated look on his face. "What have you done?"

Blood-curdling howls echoed through the hallway, and Gorgios rushed at Edvon. A bolt of Source energy hit the immense Overseer in the abdomen, but the giant ran through it, unharmed. Edvon launched a second anemic blast, missing to the right. Before a third try, the senator barreled into him.

The other Overseers approached Kyran and Elias, brandishing small blades.

"Stop this!" Elias appealed to Ruan.

The personal attendant was nowhere to be seen. Kyran dodged to the right, narrowly avoiding a first swipe. Another Overseer stabbed out, almost catching the young man in the thigh. He looked for his brother. Gorgios was crouched on top of Edvon, his thick fingers choking life out of him. Closing his eyes in anger, Kyran drew as much Source energy as he could.

A wave blasted down the corridor, knocking everyone to the floor. The dazed Overseers were stunned to have witnessed such a display of force from a young student. Kyran felt faint, and he dropped to one knee.

"He's depleted!" Gorgios yelled. "Get him now!"

Taking advantage of the distraction, Edvon scrambled to his feet, followed by the burly senator. The Overseer swung his left fist into the young Adept's gut.

"Ough!" yowled Edvon, writhing in pain.

Gorgios kicked the older brother in the chest, sending him sprawling onto the ground. Edvon managed to launch a crack of Source energy, a sharp little barb that grazed the side of the Overseer's cheek, leaving a thin laceration in his skin. Gorgios brought a hand to his face. Seeing blood at the tip of his fingers, he roared in outrage and lunged once more at Edvon.

Another Overseer struck Elias, hitting him on the side of the head. The officer slapped back, connecting with the side of her face in a loud clap. Elias was kneed in the lower spine, and he let out a yelp.

Kyran looked up, desperate, as he saw several more Overseers closing in on him.

"Enough!"

The booming voice froze everyone into place, and they looked up toward the balcony. Leaning on the railing and contemplating the scene with delight was the palace's master, Lord Hanstun.

CHAPTER TEN

The effect was never immediate. *Actually, nothing happens in the first minutes.* Novices were left wondering whether they had done it the correct way. And then, a tingle of anticipation, in the most pleasant manner possible. The gentlest flourish, skirting the corners of the mouth and drizzling down from the temples. Senses enhanced, music sounded sweeter, air felt lighter, and bliss permeated the Dominion once more. *Out of nowhere, it hits you like a stack of bricks.* Like water rushing through a broken levy, accompanied by an inundating flow of ideas, realizations, and desires. *One second you're fine, and the next, you're flying high.*

Neeta closed her eyes. The rules were clear and forbade Adepts from patronizing the smoking lounges. Being seen by the wrong person would most likely lead to a long conversation with Marrek, one that might set her promising career back by several years, if not derail it altogether. For someone so focused on her own success, Neeta often wondered why she took such a risk. *Because it feels dread good, that's why. So unfair. I'm sure the preceptor sampled herbs in his younger days. Bet he still secretly smokes in his Ivory Spire.* Neeta chuckled at the thought of the old man getting high and babbling on about the latest book he had read. *Perhaps Elias joined him.* She brought a hand up to cover her mouth, the notion making her laugh out loud. *That dweeb? He would never.* She detested her puritan colleague, or at least, pretended to. Neeta thought about it, and she realized pity better described her emotions toward him. Elias was incapable of making the difficult decisions his position required. *And he's not even good at manipulating Source energy. He'd have made a good Noble. Sitting around in his garden, listening to the birds chirp and sipping his tea, shielded from worries and responsibilities.* Neeta shook her head.

To his credit, Elias somehow gained access to Marrek's ear, though she still had no clue how that happened. *It's not going to last. One slip-up, and he'll be replaced. And the slip-up is coming, I'm sure.* The Academy needed leaders with a tenacious temperament, capable of standing up to the likes of Rex Ruga and her band of thugs. And Neeta was ready to step in. *All I have to do? Patiently wait my turn.*

On the other side of the terrace, the Adept caught sight of two men ogling her. *Those clowns again?* Neeta turned her head away, not wanting to give them the wrong impression. This was the third or fourth time she had seen the pair since frequenting the Lucky Roach, and on each occasion they had acted just as unsubtly as the last. *Like a pair of dopey balbaks.* While most would find the obstinate behavior to be annoying, and Neeta did, she also considered it interesting. She had never thought of herself as the epitome of beauty, a sentiment deriving from her disdain for relationships. Given her unequivocal reputation for spurning potential lovers, men stopped pursuing Neeta. As a result, she had no idea what others thought of her looks, which ironically enhanced her attractiveness.

Out of the corner of her eyes, she saw the two men had shifted their focus to a little glass pipe, refilling it from a dwindling pouch of herbs. One fumbled the pouch to the other and dropped it. The men quarreled over the incident, and Neeta giggled. The one on the left was lanky, with strange short hair and bold sideburns. His companion was short and pudgy, sporting an absurd mustache twirling up along both sides of his nose.

The men spotted Neeta scrutinizing them and stopped

moving, their breaths held in anticipation. They both grinned at her, the smaller one making a clumsy little wave with his fingers. Realizing how ridiculous it must have looked, he blushed and retracted his hand under the table. For some reason, Neeta felt an urge to talk to them. *No. I got better things to do.*

The Adept stood up briskly, long dark hair falling onto her face. With a hand, she brushed it away, tucking it behind an ear. Neeta pulled out a little tube from the front pocket of her dark-brown pants, and bringing it up to her mouth, she applied another layer of dusk-red lipstick. She swung open the latch, disappearing down the ladder much to the chagrin of Pluto and Joss.

After making her way through the dining room, Neeta stepped out onto the street. She loved Phaidros, and it never ceased to amaze her how much the city offered. Though it was not the architecture that attracted her, nor the history or culture. What drew Neeta to the urban sprawl were the people. *The massive amounts of people, of different shapes and sizes.* She knew many of them, taking great pride in building her network of connections. Neeta had a talent for talking to others, and she routinely got what she wanted with her sweet rhetoric. That this rhetoric was often accompanied by threatening insinuations, the Adept ignored.

Neeta crossed the street, intending to take the quickest route back to the Academy. Only a few steps later, she spotted him. *No ... it can't be.* He was standing on his left leg, right foot planted against the wall, hands in pockets. His silky blond hair glimmered in the sun. The man flashed a dazzling smile when his ice-blue eyes spotted Neeta, and he pushed himself off the wall.

"What in the Gods are you doing here, Lecarn?" hissed Neeta.

"Same as you. The Lucky Roach always has top shelf herbs."

"What - are - you - doing - here?"

"I just told you."

"Do you think I'm a fool?"

The man smiled. "You haven't seen me in ten years, and this is the love I get?"

"You don't need anymore love, from what I hear," snapped Neeta.

"I can always use more love."

"Why are you here, Lecarn? Seriously."

He sighed, running fingers through his long hair. Something else had replaced the look of guiltlessness. *Something much more difficult to ascertain.*

"I need a couple Adepts," he admitted.

"Get lost."

"They'll be paid well. I promise."

"I said get lost."

"Come on," pleaded Lecarn. "Don't make this hard,"

"No."

"You wouldn't want people to know about your little secret, would you?"

"What?" Neeta asked. "That I smoke some grass along with seventy percent of the Phaidrosian population?"

"Yes."

"Go ahead, tell anyone you want."

"You're bluffing."

Without hesitation, the Adept turned toward the street. "Attention everyone, attention!" she shouted. "I just smoked some herbs in the Lucky Roach. My name is Neeta, and I'm an Adept." People stopped, then went along their way, indifferent to her admissions. "There, I did it for you."

Lecarn paused. It was an unanticipated turn of events for a man who usually succeeded with his threats. "Fine," he conceded. "Have it your way. We both know I could destroy your career. I have connections with people in higher places than the street."

"Then do it."

"No, I think not." Lecarn smiled once more. "I'll have better luck with Elias."

Neeta let out a laugh. "Of that, I have absolutely no doubt." She turned and blew him a kiss over her shoulder. "See you around, old friend." Making sure not to walk too hastily, the Adept fought the urge to look back and check whether he was still there. Once she had turned the corner, Neeta broke into a sprint. She raced as fast as she could, zigzagging her way through side alleys. After a reasonable distance, the Adept stopped, leaning forward against the nearest wall and resting her head on the back of her hands. Panting, she reflected upon the events that had just unfolded.

If an official from the Academy had walked by during her outburst, the consequences would have been different. In fact, Neeta had been incredibly fortunate. *Lecarn was truthful. Spreading the rumor I frequent the Lucky Roach to the right people? Might as well have my bags packed.* The Adept chuckled nervously. She had never been one to shy away from taking a gamble. If the alternative entailed Lecarn exposing her, Neeta was more than willing to lay bare any vulnerabilities. Her former friend acted like the master manipulator, though she understood his ways rather well, having spent years witnessing him in action. *Lecarn follows one rule. Act only when it brings personal gain.* Despite the apparent bluntness of his menaces, destroying Neeta's career would net him zero benefits. Lecarn made an empty threat, and she had called him out on it.

A few minutes passed, after which Neeta straightened her back and found her bearings. The Adept pulled out her little lipstick tube from a pocket, and twisting the bottom, she watched the dark-crimson stick rise. *I need to learn to trust my intuitions more often.* Neeta reapplied the color onto her lips, smacking them together to ensure proper distribution. She then remembered something that made her smile. *Lecarn was right about one thing. Elias will surely cave.*

CHAPTER ELEVEN

"What a spectacle!" Lord Hanstun clapped as he leaned back in a fauteuil. He smiled, looked up at the ceiling of his office, and shut his eyes.

The awkward silence gave Kyran an opportune moment to scrutinize their host. He was dressed rather ordinarily, wearing a simple brown button-down coat and an unremarkable beige cravat. With a plain goatee and wavy curls, the Noble looked like a street laborer. *Definitely not the richest man in Phaidros.* His receding hairline gave away his age, despite the absence of any gray streaks on his scalp.

"Ruan," he said, eyes still closed. "Have our guests from the Temple been escorted off the premises?"

"Yes, my Lord."

"Excellent. That was, indeed, quite a … spectacle." Hanstun opened his eyes upon uttering the last word.

"My Lord, if I may," said Elias. "What happened … was … uh … it was just an accident. Yes, just an accident. If you would find it in your heart to … umm … pardon these young men, I can assure you they will be reprimanded, severely reprimanded."

"Accident?" asked the Noble. He exploded into a roar of laughter. "This was far from an accident."

Confusion flooded the Adepts' minds.

"Do you think it was a coincidence those Overseers were in my hallway? No, no, no. You see, it was part of the plan. And it worked out better than I could have possibly imagined." An animated Hanstun rose from his chair. "Don't you understand?" he rejoiced, arms extended and a malicious grin on his face. "I wanted you to bump into each other, to see what would happen. And what better place to stage a genuine confrontation than a dull hallway." Pleased with himself, Hanstun sat back down. "All of you were so unsuspecting, it worked out magnificently."

"How so?" asked Elias.

"I needed to see for myself who the Overseers and the Adepts actually are. How you react under real pressure. Did you expect me to throw my support to whichever delegation brought me the nicer gift?"

Kyran reached into his pocket and ran his fingers alongside the edges of Marrek's wrapped present. *Should I even give this to him now?*

"These young men," continued the Noble, waving his arm at both Kyran and Edvon, "should certainly not be reprimanded. On the contrary, they should be commended."

Edvon was unsure whether to be relieved or concerned with the direction of the conversation. He stole a glance at Elias but found the officer's expression useless in solving his conundrum.

"What courage!" proclaimed Hanstun. "More importantly, what a fascinating display of pure power." He leaned forward, resting his elbows on the railing and peering in a manner that made both brothers feel uncomfortable. "Tell me, how long does it take to build up energy like that?"

"I ... I ..." bumbled Edvon.

"Can you control the force of your blast?"

"Yes sir ... I mean, my Lord ..."

"How do you aim it?"

"Well ... we can't—"

"My Lord," intervened Elias. "We at the Academy—"

"Silence!" Hanstun barked. "I'm asking them the questions, not you. Interrupt again, and I'll have Ruan escort you outside."

"Oh!" piped Elias, turning red from humiliation.

The Noble carried on as if nothing had happened. "You were saying?"

"We're … we're not really fit to answer your questions, my Lord," lied Edvon. "We're only just learning the techniques."

"Hah! What a bunch of rubbish. Neither of you are novices. If Marrek sent you here, then you must be some of his best students."

Edvon cringed. Not because Lord Hanstun had outed him, rather because Kyran had been called a good student.

"It's very interesting, the Source seems to sap you," the Noble said, pausing to scratch his chin. "Your first strike killed a man, whereas the second caused no wound. And you," Hanstun pointed his finger at Kyran, "I've never seen such a strong manifestation of Source power. I always thought Adepts had roughly equal capabilities, but that's clearly not true."

They were breaching a topic always avoided at the Academy. Some Adepts were subpar despite their best efforts to master the Source. And nowhere was this phenomenon more evident than in the varying lifespans of different Source-powered machinery. The strength of a Source blast and the resulting transfer of energy from individual to machine directly correlated to that machine's power. On one hand, the strongest Adepts of this generation had produced engines capable of lasting months at a time. On the other hand, there were those Adepts only capable of making a trinket buzz through the air for a short hour. It was a well-kept secret. By branding all innovations as works of the Academy, generations of Adepts had been able to avoid the truth from slipping out.

"No answer?" prodded Hanstun. He was met by muted faces. "Fine. It doesn't matter now, we'll have more time to talk. And I've seen what I needed to see." The Noble leaned into his guests. "Tell me, though. You've been testing Source-powered technology in those poor villages, haven't you?" Before any of them could deny the allegation, he brushed aside his own question and winked. "You don't have to answer. We all know, right Ruan?"

"Right, my Lord."

"Don't you worry, I like the direction your preceptor has picked. No, in fact, I love it. And with my funding, the Academy's full potential will be realized."

Kyran raised an eyebrow. *Full potential?*

"You don't agree?" the Noble asked, having caught the dubious look.

"No, I—"

"Not so quick with your tongue anymore, are you? Words only get you so far, their abstraction only means so much. You think I acquired my power by taunting people? Hah!"

Kyran gritted his teeth. "No, I think you gained your power when you were born."

Ruan unsheathed his scimitar in a swift motion, but Hanstun waved him away.

"I could kill you for saying that," threatened the Noble.

"I thought words were abstract, that they only mean so much."

Hanstun peered at Kyran for several uncomfortable seconds, and convulsed with laughter. "I like you!" he exclaimed. He then addressed Elias, setting aside their previous exchange as if it had never occurred. "Go back and tell your preceptor I'm inclined to lend him my support. Together, we will forge a stronger Academy, one that won't bend to the will of others. Based on what I saw today, the possibilities are endless." The exuberant Noble walked behind his chair and paused. "This is truly exciting," he added before vanishing into the depths of his palace.

The stunned Adepts remained still, until Ruan spoke. "This

way, please." They followed the scarred personal attendant as he accompanied them out of Lord Hanstun's office. The dead Overseer had disappeared, though there was a trace of smeared blood on the wall where his body had struck. Walking around the sunken pit in the waiting room, past the large and colorful doors, and out into the welcoming garden, the three Adepts left the property.

"We need to talk," said Elias.

Foregoing benches along the walkway, they cut to the right and followed the edge of a pond toward a secluded grove.

"I don't even know where to start," mumbled the officer.

"How about with my brother's big mouth almost getting us killed?"

"Are you blind as Lutigas?" Kyran snapped back. "Didn't you listen to a single thing that clown said? My big mouth is the reason he's supporting the Academy. He wanted to see which group would win his little game."

"Game?" shouted Edvon. "Is that what you think this was?"

"No, that's what he thought it was."

"Whatever it was," threw in Elias, "those Overseers were holding real knives."

Kyran sighed. "There's no way Lord Hanstun would have let it go that far, watching the whole scene from his stupid balcony."

"It did go that far!" exclaimed Edvon. "And even so, did you know any of this when you decided to inflame the situation?"

"Well ... ahem ..."

"Exactly what I thought," the older Adept concluded, satisfied by the small victory. "Just because it worked out doesn't change the fact that you acted like a cholee in there."

"At least I stood up for us," Kyran proclaimed.

"By doing what? Making a joke about a mother?"

"Stop … arguing, please," interjected Elias. "What was he saying about the Academy?"

"Sounds like he wants to militarize Adepts. Push for the development of more Source-powered weaponry."

"Nothing wrong with that," muttered Kyran.

Edvon glared at his brother. "So it's easier to blame us for the annihilation of those villages?"

"We're already being blamed for that."

"Doesn't mean we should be building an Adept army."

"Might be exactly what we need."

"You're so immature."

"And you're—"

"Will you two just shut up?" said Elias. "By the Gods, keep acting like this, and you'll end up killing one another." The officer massaged his head with his soft hands. "And now, I have a massive headache."

As Elias spoke, a large object came crashing atop his head with a deafening crack.

"Maybe this will help!" Gorgios hollered.

The senator's hand was grasping the end of a long branch, and the brothers watched in horror as Elias's numb body fell to the ground.

"You punks are coming with us."

CHAPTER TWELVE

When viewed from a distance, the Apex was a preposterous sight. The column rose so high into the air, it stuck out like a sore thumb in an otherwise vertically challenged city. The palaces found in the Noble District averaged five stories, the Academy's Ivory Tower was estimated to be double as much, and the Temple's largest spire climbed to a remarkable twelve. These structures were significant architectural accomplishments in their own right, only embellishing the incredible fact that the Apex reached eighty stories. Even more impressive, the feat of engineering had been accomplished by none other than a coalition of common citizens, with no help from any of the Dominion's predominant institutions.

Sunlight glistened off its smooth white stone, bestowing upon the Apex a surreal glow. On bright days, the tower became difficult to stare at without causing a temporary glare in the viewers' eyes. But it served quite a practical purpose by acting as a giant sundial for the citizens of the capital. As the Apex's massive shadow progressed over neighborhoods, residents were reminded of the time. In fact, districts around the city had constructed entire schedules according to the Apex shadow's diurnal commute. Some restaurants only opened once it had gone by, others would close upon its onset, and workers took breaks from their jobs for what they liked to call shadow time. What had initially been created as a testament to the Phaidrosian work ethic spawned a daily sabbatical.

The long shadow neared the Academy, an indication that the day was moving too fast for Aiden to follow. *I need answers. Now.* His team had come back from the flower market empty-handed, leaving him irritated and in charge of an investigation getting colder by the hour. As he leaned on the railing of his modest office balcony, the chief contemplated the small statue at the very top of the Apex. *Man or woman?* A question all residents of Phaidros had asked themselves at one point or another. The androgynous figure was staring up at the sky, legs close together and arms outstretched. *A symbol of our longing to return to the Gods. Or something like that.* Aiden was still a believer, most Phaidrosians held the Book of Provenance in high regard and trusted its words. *But I have neither the time nor the desire to care, especially when Overseers use the text to their advantage.* The chief turned around and went back inside, closing the door behind him. *Not like the Adepts are any better, in their secluded Sea Tower.* Grabbing his coat from one of the two chairs, Aiden left his office and made his way down a flight of stairs. He walked through a set of adjoining rooms, saluting his men as he exited the building. *Would be nice if we could all control It.*

Source manipulation was gained at birth, something Aiden had come to accept. *You either have it or you don't. And I was one of the unlucky ones.* Though extensive research had been carried out, it was still not well understood why some gained that ability, while others retained ordinary faculties. Several years back, a rumor had circulated that everyone was born with a form of Source control capability, but only those who went to the Academy learned to refine it. For the rest, whatever innate skill they possessed was quickly lost. Aiden winced. *Probably a conspiracy theory floated by that conniving Confidante Najara.* He knew the Adepts, major source manipulator or not, had neither the luxury nor the desire to pick and choose their brethren. The Academy, making up only one in a hundred, perhaps even less, needed every man and woman it could get its hands on. *Especially now.*

Chomping on the skewer of roasted geega he had picked up

on the way, the chief crossed through a narrow courtyard and walked under the archway leading into the gymnasium.

"Shouldn't you be at work?" said a voice behind him.

Aiden spun around. "You must be kidding me ... Lecarn? I was just thinking about you the other day."

"Oh! Of me?" Lecarn exaggerated his astonishment by bringing his hand up to his forehead.

The chief laughed and pulled his old friend in for a warm embrace. "It's been too long."

"I know."

"So why don't you come to Phaidros more often? You must miss it."

"You know why."

"Yes ..." *What a gaffe.* For a moment they remained quiet. "What are you doing here, then?"

"Come on, let's talk inside," answered Lecarn.

Aiden raised an eyebrow. "You want to lift weights? Now?

"Sure. For old times' sake."

"Hold on. You were waiting for me here, weren't you?"

"And I timed it well, it would seem."

"How do you know I still come to this gym?" asked Aiden.

"Some things never change."

"No, you're up to something, I can tell. What're you really doing here?"

Lecarn smiled. "Can't we talk about it inside?"

Aiden sighed and entered the gymnasium. They changed into the required tunics and made their way onto a main level filled with grunting men. Over the years, a majority of the workout facilities in Phaidros had become mixed-gender, except for the one Aiden frequented since he was a teen. *Just my luck, of course.* The chief smiled. *At least I know I won't stumble upon Criss here.* "Let's start with the press."

They walked to a wood bench, one of several along the wall. An iron bar was suspended on a rack. Lecarn lay down while Aiden stepped behind to act as a spotter. With his feet flat on the floor, Lecarn grabbed the bar, pulling it off the rack and toward his chest. He thrust the weight back into the air, repeating the motion ten times. "Ah!" he exclaimed, standing up from the bench and rubbing his pectoral muscles.

"Looks like you haven't stopped exercising either." Aiden took his turn on the bench.

"Got to keep fit for the baqua courts."

"They have baqua in the countryside?" Lecarn looked the other way, and Aiden regretted his remark. "You won't believe it, they're building a gym in the Main Complex," added the chief, trying to change the topic.

"Oh, yeah? Did you commission it? I hear you're the big boss, now."

"Something like that." They switched exercises. "So have you seen your friends at the Academy?"

"I don't have many friends left there, I'm afraid."

"Doesn't … surprise me … the way … you left …" huffed Aiden in between repetitions. He wiped the sweat from his face with his forearm. And only then did the chief notice how little his friend had changed. Lecarn's hair was still long, its golden shine contrasting with his piercing eyes. The square jaw and strong features that had made him such a handsome youth had faded ever so slightly.

"How are the girls, anyway?" asked Aiden with a wink of his blue eye.

"As beautiful as ever."

"Yeah, that's what I assumed." Lecarn had always been good with women, frustrating Aiden to quite an extent back in the day. *Now, I don't even care.* Just like everything else in life, the chief accepted some were better or luckier than others.

For an hour, they progressed through a number of athletic motions, alternating muscle groups. On one hand there were those who liked to spend an entire afternoon in the gymnasium, exercising in leisure and socializing with friends. Aiden, on the other hand, wanted to get in and out as quickly as possible. The time he spent there was one of his only releases, and he had come to find the shorter he hung around, the sweeter it was to return the next day.

"So why are you here, Lecarn?"

"Coming back and saying hello to an old friend isn't a good reason?"

"It's a reason, just not a valid one for you."

"You know, you're the second person to tell me that today."

"Then, it must be true."

"By Gods, I've got one rotten reputation," lamented Lecarn. "One I don't deserve, you know?"

"Doesn't matter whether you deserve it. No one shows up ten years later to say hello to people they've supposedly been missing."

"And why not?"

"Because, well …" Aiden paused, unsure how to drive home his point. "I don't know," he said, sighing. "People just don't do it."

They got to the final contraption in their routine, a large tree stump carved hollow. Inside it was an iron weight connected by a rope and a pulley at the top. The other end of the rope was attached to a handle which Lecarn seized with both hands. He pushed down, lifting the weight inside the stump.

"My triceps are already too tired for this," he whined after several repetitions.

Aiden ignored his friend, stepping forward and grasping the

handle.

"So what do you think about these attacks in the countryside?" asked Lecarn.

"Ah!" The chief dropped the weight with a slam and turned around. "That's why you're here."

"No, I ... I was just making conversation."

"You're not even subtle anymore."

"About what?"

"Come on, it's too late. Who's paying you?"

"No one."

"You may be a good liar with others, but with me?" Aiden winked his brown eye. "You can forget about it."

Lecarn chuckled. "I can't tell you. Client confidentiality and all."

"Tell me, and I'll give you the Battalion's dossier on the attacks." Aiden was serious. "The entire thing, it's back at the Main Complex."

"That," murmured Lecarn, "I didn't expect."

"So come on, who is it?"

"Obviously someone whose identity might help you solve the case, given how much value you've placed on the information."

"Perhaps, or perhaps I'm just making conversation."

Lecarn laughed once more. "No," he decided. "I'll find out what I need on my own."

"You'd throw away an opportunity for inside information?"

"Yes. Your dossier's still empty."

Aiden winced. *What a cholee.*

"Remember that whole thing you were saying about detecting lies? Well, it's a two-way street, my friend."

"Fair enough."

They walked to the exit.

"It was nice seeing you, Aiden."

"Good luck," the chief responded. He extended out his hand. "You'll need it."

"I can always use some luck."

"I'll see you in another ten years?"

Lecarn looked over his shoulder with a grin. "I have a feeling we'll be seeing each other much sooner."

CHAPTER THIRTEEN

The glob of saliva came flying at an impressive speed. With a stable trajectory and ideal composition, it flapped through the air before splattering onto Edvon's cheek. The young man wiped the spit off his face, scanning the crowd for the perpetrator.

"Nice aim for an old granny," quipped Kyran, having identified the culprit.

"Shut up." Edvon locked eyes with the woman. Her spine curved by age and her scalp dotted with clumps of white hair, she stared back with a hatred that made him shudder.

"Nasty Adepts. You soiled, repulsive Adepts. You disgusting, abominable, repugnant Adepts. You vile Adepts. You dreadful, stinking Adepts!" As she screeched one insult after another, the old woman's face morphed from a light pink to a deep purple. Running out of air, she coughed, gasping for air and stumbling. "You think …" cough "funny?" squawked the woman. "Wait till you …" cough "what they do to" cough "those who disobey the Recital Supreme." She tried to inhale, but it only made the hacking worse. "They'll …" cough "send you to the …" cough "you belong." In a last-ditch effort, she brought her head up and spat toward them once more.

This time, Edvon dodged the oncoming projectile, despite the cumbersome platinum collar on his neck. "You'll have to do better than that, cholee!"

"How dare you … that name …"

Her response was hardly audible as the wagon moved ahead, bringing them one step closer to Mount Kilda. Kyran fiddled with the small lock keeping his collar fastened. Scarce and hard to find, only platinum suppressed an Adept's Source drawing capabilities, and rumor had it the Overseers hoarded any amount of the material they could get their hands on. Some even whispered that the walls of the Temple were lined with the precious metal. Kyran could feel the platinum weighing him down. *I'm nauseous.* The young man had trouble deciding whether the substance itself was making him sick, or whether it was the simple realization he had no ability to access the Source. He lurched forward as they hit a bump in the road, much to the delight of the growing throng of people following behind. "Where did these losers come from, anyway?"

"What do you—"

"Make way for the murderers!" shouted Gorgios. "Make way for the murderers!"

"—care?" finished Edvon.

The delegation of twenty Overseers was advancing, its two captives confined in a caged wagon.

"Well, I've always wanted to visit East Phaidros," said the younger Adept.

"You don't get the trouble we're in, do you?"

"That's precisely why I'm trying to enjoy it as much as possible." Kyran pointed at the crowd. "I'm not going out the way they want me to, crying for mercy."

Edvon had no answer, so he looked around instead. As they traveled farther east, the metropolis gave way to a more rudimentary habitat. Simple thatch homes, many spewing gray smoke from their mud chimneys, replaced brick and mortar structures. *How depressing.* Edvon remembered the bazaars of West Phaidros, the laughing children and bright colors, a stark contrast to the bleak stares they were receiving from citizens trudging by. Some continued along their way, while others joined the procession, as if it presented the only excitement they had witnessed in months. The wheeled vehicle tilted backward and launched a steep climb. *A point of no return.*

The Adepts sat in silence for the remainder of the journey along the winding road up Mount Kilda. They passed trekking pilgrims, many holding the Book of Provenance and muttering verses to themselves. Edvon took in the scenic view of Phaidros that grew more stunning the further the wagon ascended. It was shadow time west of the city where he could discern the Academy, its Sea Tower jutting out into the Bay of Alboran. The Apex caught his attention, as well as the Noble District with its hundred shimmering lakes. *We were just there.* He spotted the gloomy walls of Crain Prison. *And we may end up there.* He shuddered and looked the other way, only to take in the vast city cemetery just to the south of Mount Kilda.

"There!" Kyran prodded his brother in the ribs.

The peak revealed the Temple in all its glory. Constructed of white stone, the massive building was a sight to behold. An enormous central spire rose high into the sky, surrounded by seven similar erections of lesser height. Golden statues glimmering in the sunlight graced the top of each one. The heptagonal structure was enclosed by thick walls, similar to a fortress rather than a place of worship. The Overseers came to a full stop and unlocked the cage.

"Tie their hands!" ordered Gorgios.

The brothers were paraded toward the entrance. They walked across a big drawbridge and into a main courtyard where hundreds of pilgrims were standing in line, waiting to enter the Inner Sanctum. The Temple's most sacred chamber marked the precise location where the Gods had exiled the Dominion's forefathers, or such were the writings of the Book of Provenance.

"Can we make a quick stop to pay our respects?" asked Kyran.

"Shut it!"

A congregation had already gathered, clapping en masse and cantillating spiritual verses in a disorderly fashion. Gorgios pushed his way forward, clearing a path as they got closer to one of the smaller spires. The brothers were shoved inside, and the last Overseer closed the door, preventing the curious crowd from following them into the edifice. They marched up a stiff helical staircase, leading to a room with no furniture or decorations, save a long raised desk near the rear wall. The senator disappeared through an opening behind it and resurfaced with three elderly Overseers in tow whose white robes had multiple gold stripes adorning the sleeves. They settled at the desk.

"Marshals of Justice, these men are accused of murdering cadet Matthias," announced Gorgios.

"Witness for the prosecution?" asked a marshal, his eyes peering overtop thin wire-rimmed glasses.

"I, Master of Arms of this Temple, present myself as a witness."

"Very well. And—"

"What is the meaning of this?" exclaimed Rex Ruga as she barged into the room.

"Commandant," hissed Tibon, "you are interrupting a trial."

"A trial I have every right to attend."

"In case you have forgotten, I tend to the judicial matters of this Temple."

"Perhaps," Rex Ruga replied, walking to the marshals' desk. "But not if I invoke the Gods as witnesses."

"What?"

The commandant was facing the brothers and the group of Overseers that had assembled behind them. In desperate need of a victory, she could sense one within her clutches. "We do this the old way."

The gathered Overseers looked on with anticipation, and Tibon tried to stall her. "Commandant this is—"

"We do this by way of the Gods!" Rex Ruga shouted, scoring several grunts of approval. She pulled from her pocket a large coin, holding it out for everyone to see. On one side was a skull and on the other a star. Flicking it up into the air, the commandant caught the piece of gold on the back of her hand. "The Gods will guide this coin!"

The audience cheered, and Rex Ruga approached Kyran, grabbing his collar. She kicked the young Adept in the shins, making him drop to his knees with a scream, then leaned in close. "If it lands skull up," she said, tossing the coin once more, "then the sentence shall be death."

"And if it lands skull down?" Kyran groaned, struggling to pull himself away.

Rex Ruga brought her lips to his ear. "It doesn't matter."

With a clink, the coin hit the cold stone floor. Edvon watched as it rolled around, losing speed at every new turn. The coin fell flat, skull face up. Overseers roared in unison, while the Adept closed his eyes in despair. *This can't be happening.*

"The Gods have spoken." Rex Ruga spun around and left, satisfied with the success of her act. Word of the judgment would soon spread throughout the Temple, and best of all, Najara was nowhere to be seen. The spoils were the commandant's reaping. She would be lighting the pyres, front and center for any Overseer to witness. The execution of two Adepts, the first such event in years, would define her regime. Naturally, partial credit would need to be attributed to her Master of Arms. Had Gorgios not sent an Overseer ahead to warn Rex Ruga, Tibon might have brokered a diplomatic arrangement with the Academy and received all the praise.

Meanwhile, Gorgios led Kyran and Edvon out of the room

and down the spiral staircase. Rather than stopping on the main floor, they kept descending until they felt a wave of cool air. The stunned brothers had penetrated the Temple's dungeons. Gorgios grabbed a torch from the wall, leading them along a tenebrous and narrow passageway. Secured cells with iron bars lined both sides. Approaching one on the left, the brothers watched with dismay as two Overseers pulled open a heavy door.

"In you go!" roared Gorgios.

PART II

CHAPTER FOURTEEN

The Book of Provenance's verses included many tales. Although each had been analyzed and dissected by Overseer scholars throughout the ages, one stood out as the public's favorite. It took up less than a couple pages, and rather than depicting the life of the Gods in their Red City or the piousness of a Noble lady from centuries past, the verse told an altogether different story.

Following the infamous Exile from the Heavens, an episode of prolonged misery known as the Dark Age arose. Marred by conflict and death, the period's anarchy ended only when Auralus, the very first Overseer, climbed atop Mount Kilda and laid the foundation for a Temple. He succeeded in uniting the population under a new theology, one revolving around an acceptance of and reverence for the Gods' punishment.

While constructing the Temple's fifth spire, Auralus suffered a grievous injury, a gash across his chest that festered. He was rushed into the newly built Inner Sanctum, his followers praying with all their might for the Gods to save him. They applied ointments, crushed herbs, geega blood, nothing would help. Days passed, and Auralus grew weaker. At his request, the dying founder was brought in the courtyard to once more breathe fresh air before his impending departure.

That night, a drunkard ascended Mount Kilda from the fledgling town below, captivated by the sight of the Temple's new spires. Clinging to the fresh-laid stone, he pulled himself up, swinging wildly in the air and shouting incoherent words. Those awakened by the commotion were convinced the man would fall.

Instead, in his intoxicated state, the drunkard managed to drop his pants and urinate. The golden shower, caught by the breeze, trickled right onto an unsuspecting Auralus.

They never found the man, and the next morning, to everyone's amazement, Auralus's gash was healed. The urine's alcohol content was so high it had disinfected the wound, allowing the Overseer to recover and live out the rest of his long life. Many argued the drunkard was in fact a God, sent to ensure salvation for the Temple's founder. Never debated, however, was the merit of alcohol as a disinfectant, the main reason why the amusing tale also made it the favorite of modern day medical practitioners around the Dominion. And one of them just happened to be using a dose of the liquid on a squealing Adept.

"Ouch!" shouted Elias.

"Will you be quiet," Gaston pleaded. "And stop squirming around so much." The doctor dabbed his rag in a small vial of rubbing alcohol and applied it once more to the cut on Elias's head. "How did you say this happened again?"

"I … I ran into a doorway."

"Is that so?"

Gaston gave the Adept a suspicious look. "It seems more like an object struck you, not the other way around."

"Well … the doorway struck me."

"Fine. Say what you want. All I can conclude is you suffered a concussion, and you're lucky the blood coagulated fast enough. Otherwise, you'd be lying dead under some …" The doctor paused, and raised an eyebrow. "Doorway." He finished cleansing the injury and bandaged it with a beige dressing.

The color reminded Elias of something, though he had trouble placing it. *Why does that feel familiar? Beige … the color of robes … the color of Marrek's robes.* The officer closed his eyes. Returning to the Academy was unthinkable, not after what had happened.

"Done," Gaston announced.

Elias picked himself up.

"And duck next time you walk through doorways."

"Yes, yes." The Adept tossed him several well-worn coins. He staggered toward the tapestry hanging from the ceiling and pulled it aside to expose the busy street. A sensory overload compounded Elias's searing headache, from loud passersby, children shouting as they played, merchants calling out to sell their wares, bright sun reflecting off the stalls of the market, and smells both pleasant and rancid. He wanted to throw up.

The boys were probably dead, there was nothing he could do to change that. *I guess I'll have to leave Phaidros, find somewhere to live in hiding.* The officer stepped into the street, scenarios playing out in his head, hundreds of them, with different endings. Elias envisioned himself in a rotting shack in Fisherman's Bay, or sleeping in a barn out in the countryside. He shuttered. *Wait. Maybe they won't blame me for this, and I can stay at the Academy. After all, it wasn't my fault.* The Adept imagined the pleasant patio back in his quarters, the sweet sound of water trickling from his little fountain, the soothing sunlight warming delicate plants placed along the railing. Suddenly, the rays became brighter, to the point where Elias felt his skin burning. The water evaporated from the fountain, the plants erupting into flames. He shook the image from his head. *Of course they'll blame me for it.* The officer's nausea intensified, and he stopped to take a breath. *I could follow Lecarn's treacherous ways to get out of this. Should I just do what he did to Marrek?*

Conflicted, Elias resumed a mindless pace, trudging his way through a crowd that never seemed to end. It was estimated more than half the Dominion's population lived in Phaidros, an urban sprawl that continued to grow. The Noble Assembly knew it to be an unsustainable rate and a few years back had attempted to alleviate the problem by developing new neighborhoods on the outskirts of Portown, as well as forcing the displacement of several important industries to the south. These included the city's largest breweries, employers to thousands of workers. However, the plan, initially instituted to encourage citizens to relocate, had backfired. The workers stayed, finding employment at other factories seeking to add to their pool of labor. And with a gradual shortage of ale, one by one the taverns went out of business. Rather than admitting its mistake and remedying the problem, the Noble Assembly did nothing, wagering instead that the lack of alcohol would drive thirsty citizens southward. But Phaidrosians lost interest in the drink altogether, new vices replacing old ones. Enterprising growers seized the opportunity, opening smoking lounges throughout the city where one could puff on a variety of herbs. It was like Marrek had always said. "The citizens don't make Phaidros. No, Phaidros makes the citizens."

A convoy of heavy-duty SPCs cut in front of Elias, forcing him to jerk back. As the Adept waited for it to pass, he considered one such lounge off to his right. *The Lucky Roach. Hmm …* Fortune had smiled on him today. Phaidros was an overcrowded mess, yet the best medical practitioners resided there. If the officer had been struck in Fermantis or Portown, perhaps he would have survived. *Anywhere else and I'd be dead.* For a hypochondriac like Elias, there was no place to live but Phaidros, and he knew it all too well. The road cleared, and the Adept was about to take a step when he felt a hand on his shoulder.

"My friend, what have you gotten yourself into?"

To Elias's chagrin, that was a voice he instantly recognized, despite persistent efforts to erase it from his memory. After all, he had spent a good part of his youth within earshot of it, time he only recently acknowledged as not entirely wasted. The officer turned to face a man with long blond locks framing his chiseled face. "Lecarn, you're back in the city."

"Only for as long as I need to be. And not a second more."

"And then? Back to your band of rebels?"

Lecarn flashed his patented pearly-white smile. "A band you are more than welcome to join, as I've told you many times."

Elias paused for a moment. It was too great a coincidence to envisage blackmailing the preceptor and to be facing the man who had done just that only minutes later.

"Problems at the Academy?" Lecarn asked, picking up on the hesitancy.

"No, and it's time for me to go back."

"Fine. Before you leave, I need a favor."

"I stopped doing favors for you long ago."

"Through no fault of your own, I'll be the first to admit."

"I don't care what you have to admit." Elias turned away. "I've got nothing more to say to you."

"I'm afraid you do."

The officer stopped in his tracks, and Lecarn sighed while stroking his long hair. "I didn't want it to come to this."

"Come to what?"

"Remember our personal matter?"

"Which one?" asked Elias.

Lecarn rolled his eyes. "It's irrelevant, I'd hate for either to become public knowledge."

"Are you … blackmailing me?"

For a moment, the sound of zooming SPCs was overwhelming. "Yes."

"You must be kidding."

"Look, I need this," insisted Lecarn, "and you haven't even heard me out."

"I don't care what you need, you only think about

yourself."

"Will you or will you not listen?"

"Seems like I don't have much of a choice, do I?"

"It's not a big ask, all I want is—"

"You appear out of nowhere," said Elias, "threatening to expose my personal matters, after I haven't seen you in a decade?"

Lecarn nodded. "Fair enough. Well, tell you what. The sooner you listen to me, the sooner I'll get out of your way."

"What do you want?"

"Two Adepts."

"No way."

"You don't understand," replied Lecarn. "I need them on my side, to help track something down."

"And what is that something, exactly? You know what? I don't even care. How long do you need them for?"

"A month. Maybe longer."

"A month?" Elias snickered. "Are you out of your mind? What Adept would leave the comfort of the Academy for that long?"

"I never said anything about the Academy."

"Oh, you want dropouts, huh?"

"Yes," said Lecarn. "I'll take dropouts as long as they can manipulate the Source and do my bidding." He reached into his vest. "Here, two Ocean Star tickets. Give them these."

"This is ridiculous."

"Why?"

"I'm not some Adept trader."

"You have access to the Academy's archives, so you know the whereabouts of each one of them."

"I don't need the archives, you fool." *I definitely do.*

"Then, you'll find them for me? They'll be paid handsomely. Seven hundred gold coins each."

The officer exhaled, his headache worsening. *Lecarn will expose my secrets. Both of them. He has nothing to lose.* If that happened, then the option Elias had contemplated, one which provided an out to his predicament, would no longer be viable. He could already smell the village stables, visualizing his bed made of hay and the pack of balbaks crowded around him. *And this headache ...* "Okay. By all the Gods, I'll get you the two Adepts."

"Excellent!" exclaimed Lecarn. "Tell them to meet me in Portown. I'll be waiting up the hill in a green SPC, by Mirabel Crater."

"On one condition," Elias added, snatching the tickets.

"What?"

"This is the last I ever hear from you."

CHAPTER FIFTEEN

Edvon writhed in agony. Try as he might, the young man found it impossible to fall asleep. When crawling around the cell's dark corners, he had smeared his hands in a smooth and soft matter that smelled like feces. The platinum collar rubbed against raw skin each time he laid his head on the uneven stone, and drips of water fell from the ceiling at regular intervals, often striking the Adept in the face. *We're actually going to die.* He shuddered. *Not only that but burned at the stake.* The gravity of their situation was sinking in.

"So ... what did she say?"

"It doesn't matter."

Inhaling restlessly, Edvon rolled back and forth. *Will they be quiet?* The sequence of events had been ludicrous enough that he harbored no desire to hear it recounted, unlike Kyran who was narrating the proceedings in great detail to his newfound audience. There were three other occupants in the dungeons, and though it was poorly lit, Edvon had discerned to their far right a hairy old man with long locks flowing down to his chest. In the cell opposite the Adepts sat a bald prisoner with a goatee, and to their left, a woman concealed by the shadows, wearing what looked like the white dress of an Overseer.

"It doesn't matter," repeated Kyran.

"Huh?"

"That's what she said to me."

The elderly prisoner grunted before grasping the iron bars of his cell door and lifting himself up to his feet. "So what?"

"So what?" Kyran shook his head in disbelief. "So it means the coin flip was rigged."

"Yeah, obviously." The hairy man receded into the gloomy depths, and Edvon smiled. His brother had lost two-thirds of the audience.

"Sweet prince?"

Kyran scanned the narrow passageway. "Um … yeah?"

"I'd whisper things into your ear, too. You know, they don't call me Tickle for nothing."

"Uh … I—I think I'm okay," stammered Kyran. "Th— thanks."

"Oh, you're missing out, sweetheart." Tickle leaned forward, squishing his face between the bars. "Let me tell you a little story."

Annoyed, Edvon opened his eyes. "Can you please tell the story after I'm dead? I need to get some sleep here." There was a period of precious silence, alas, a brief one.

"So there's this joint called the Overseer's D-Light," Tickle said, "and once a month, they host—"

"Gods!" Snapping his head up, Edvon hit the wall hard. "I was almost asleep," he grumbled, rubbing the back of his skull. "Won't you all just shut up?"

"What about the story?"

"No one wants to listen to the story."

Kyran pounced, knowing there would not be many opportunities left to aggravate his brother. "I want to hear it. What do they host at the Overseer's D-Light?"

Edvon gritted his teeth. "By Gods, I'm going to murder you."

"Two kills in one day? Even for a star Adept …"

Tickle chuckled.

"And in any case," continued Kyran, now on a roll, "it

would only be a couple hours ahead of schedule."

"Next cholee who dares to speak," roared an infuriated Edvon at the top of his lungs, "I will massacre!" The final word reverberated in the dungeons for several seconds. Satisfied, the older sibling closed his eyes, relishing in the ensuing silence.

"He never said anything about whispering, right?"

Feeling defeated, Edvon cupped his hands over his ears. He could barely hear anything when Tickle began to recount the story. *They actually are whispering.* Drowsiness enveloped the Adept as his breathing steadied, temples relaxed, and shoulders sagged.

"The package!"

The shout jolted Edvon, and he again knocked his head on the stone. Kyran and the young woman were giggling, amused by Tickle's bombastic plot.

"So did he open it?" she asked.

"Pretty boy like him? Oh, baby … what did you say your name was?"

"Sabine."

"Well, let me tell you something, Sabine. We were in for a huge surprise." Tickle proceeded to describe the package's contents.

Edvon was left in the unenviable position of wishing he knew the backstory. *Package? What package? What are they …* "By Gods!"

"You see?" said Tickle. "I knew this would … ahem … tickle your fancy."

"I don't give a dread about your stupid story." Edvon leaped to his feet. "Kyran, do you still have Marrek's gift to Lord Hanstun?"

"What? Yeah, it's in my pocket."

"And you didn't think to open it?"

Realizing Edvon's pragmatic acumen, Kyran's heart rate

soared. He rotated the present in his hands, searching for the edges of the wrapping. Finding a seam he ripped the paper, and his fingers connected with what felt like a long ceramic object. The Adept held it up.

"What is it?" asked Tickle.

"I don't know." Kyran ran his thumb up and down the length of the present, eventually grazing a protrusion at its base. "Wait, there's a button." He pressed on it, lighting up the object and revealing a model of the Ivory Spire. The glow of the miniature tower was of a light-blue hue, and it carried enough power to illuminate the edges of Sabine's cell. And for a brief moment, Kyran saw what appeared to be violet eyes. Then, the tower went dark.

"It's just a Source-powered gimmick," Edvon muttered.

"Gimmick?" repeated Tickle. "I, for one, can think of plenty of good uses for that object."

"Like what, exactly?"

"Don't you know anything, little man?"

"As a matter of fact, I do. I've tested out of all core topics at the Academy, and I even did five M-level electives. So I know a lot, probably much more than you."

Tickle chortled. "Clearly not, or that tower would already be—"

"Hold up," interjected Kyran, "the Source works here?"

Sabine was the one to answer. "Regrettably, yes. Why wouldn't it?"

"Everyone at the Academy thinks the Temple's built with platinum."

"I can't believe you're actually Adepts," said the young woman. "By Auralus! You aren't what I thought you'd look like."

"Never met one of us?"

"Of course not. How and why would I do such a terrible

thing?"

The brothers laughed, and so did Tickle.

"You think it's funny?" Sabine retorted. "It's a good thing you're in these dungeons."

Kyran raised his eyebrows. "The same you're in, you mean? And why's that?"

"Because ... well, because you killed an Overseer."

"That's true," mumbled the Adept.

"And you use It," she continued, undeterred. "When the Book of Provenance strictly forbids it."

"Wrong." Edvon's fourth year thesis had been titled A Farce Uncovered: The True Meaning of It in the Book of Provenance. "The verses never tell us what It is, and you just assume It is the Source? It could be anything. On his ninth trip to see the hermits, Lutigas refers to It in a way that makes it seem like a material object. Baratna does the same thing when he speaks to the farmer in the Temple's second spire. And in Hubris 5, the Gods only weep after seeing It. Wouldn't they sense It in their presence, if It was the Source?"

"Ooooo ..." gibed Tickle. "Bam!"

Sabine was unmoved. "I don't care about any of that, you're reading it the wrong—"

"Way?" cut in Edvon. "As opposed to what? Have you ever thought there might be other ways to interpret your sacred verses?"

"Those are wrong ways, the Recital Supreme says so."

"Ah, typical Overseer fallback."

The prisoners remained still for a while, until Tickle broke the silence. "So anyway ... about that model tower."

All at once, the gate to the dungeons swung open, and a short Overseer carrying a torch rushed in. He hurried toward Sabine's cell while jangling a set of keys.

"Cyrus," she whispered. "What are you doing here?"

"Shh, don't say my name," the wheezing Overseer replied, glancing around. "I've come to help you get out."

"Why?"

"Sabine, you don't deserve this. I know you're innocent."

"You believe me?"

"Everyone is aware of Rex Ruga's perversions." Cyrus leaned in. "It's just that no one has the courage to do anything about it." The Overseer unlocked the door. "Come, you must leave Phaidros tonight."

"What about you?" Sabine asked.

"Many in the Temple have access to the dungeons." Cyrus pulled her toward the entrance. "Let's go, quick!"

"But …"

"Don't worry about me, Sabine. They'll never know who let you out."

"Unless I tell them," threatened Tickle. "Cyrus, was it?"

The Overseer approached the captive's cell. "Yes, an undeniable case of a violent, dangerous, and deviant being. I'll be putting in an immediate request to add you to the pyre tomorr—"

Cyrus never finished his sentence. The ceramic Ivory Spire came crashing against the back of his head, shattering into a thousand pieces and thrusting the Overseer to the ground, unconscious. Reacting to Kyran's stealthy throw, Edvon stuck his hand through the bottom of the iron gate, snatching the key ring from Cyrus's limp grasp before Sabine could seize it.

"What have you done!" she screeched in horror. The young woman knelt to the ground, gasping as she touched Cyrus's bloodied temple. Terrified, she looked up, only to find the two Adepts had already unlocked their cell and were in the process of releasing Tickle.

"Come on," said Edvon, "let's go!"

Sabine held firm. "Just kill me and be done with it."

"Kill you?"

The brothers looked at each other.

"I think she's being serious, boys," quipped Tickle.

"I know you will." A tear rolled down Sabine's cheek. "So just do it now. Please!"

"What in the Gods ..." Kyran trailed off. "We may be Adepts, but we're not killers."

The old hairy prisoner whose presence had been neglected voiced a plea. "Forget about her and let me out."

"Wait!" said Tickle. "The Overseers mentioned he was highly dangerous when they brought him in."

"Don't listen," replied the man. He brushed aside his long hair, revealing a platinum collar around his neck. "See? I'm one of you."

Kyran nodded. "We have to help him."

"He's tricking you," warned Tickle.

"We're helping him, why would he do that?"

"He's dangerous."

Edvon pointed at Cyrus on the ground. "That guy said the same thing about you, right?"

The Adept opened the cell, and the old man bolted out. Flying across the narrow passageway, he pounced onto Tickle and tackled him to the ground. The wild-haired man plunged a hand into his prey's gaping mouth. "Hayah!" Pulling back a bloodied tongue, he sprang up, grabbed Sabine by the wrist, and vanished up the stairs.

CHAPTER SIXTEEN

"Did you wash your hands?"

The young woman stared back at him, confused. She was naked save a thin strip of fabric hanging from her waist. "What?"

"I asked if you washed your hands."

"My Lord, I—"

"A simple yes or no, girl."

"No."

Lord Hanstun brought his fingers to his temple. "By the Gods." Grumbling, he pushed aside the head resting on his torso and sat up in the immense bed. Several arms reached for him to lie back down. The Noble brushed them aside. "You would think to join our soiree without having washed your hands?"

"No ... no, my Lord," stammered the young woman.

The newcomer scurried toward the door, and Hanstun watched her bottom wiggle from side to side until she disappeared from sight. "Don't take too long, either." The Noble fell into the pillows.

"You're such a germaphobe," Ruan whispered, leaning in and twirling his finger on Hanstun's chest.

Without warning, the Noble sat up and slapped his attendant's face across the scar. Ruan, with an expression of utter shock, let out a shout of indignation. Hanstun smacked him again, this time across the neck. Then across the shoulders, and the back. And then the waist. And right on the personal attendant's nude butt. Hanstun spanked it two, three, four times, each hit coming with greater speed. Ruan squealed in delight as the others on the bed joined in, grabbing and tickling him, while he feigned escape. They stopped when the girl came back, her hands still wet from the sink.

"You're dripping, dear," someone on the bed said.

"Imbecile," murmured Ruan.

"I ... I'm—"

"Go back and dry your hands."

"No, let her." Hanstun ordered, looking below his waist. "We can use a bit of wetness. Come here."

Stepping onto the bed and crawling her way to the Noble, the young woman accomplished the task being asked of her.

"Good," Hanstun said, pulling the fresh arrival by the hair. "Now, all of you stay on that side and leave us for a little while."

"Oh, he wants some alone time," Ruan whispered, and the others snickered.

Another man nipped Hanstun's feet, while several of the women seized the newcomer's arms and legs, pulling her in. Ruan lunged at the clutter of bodies, hoping to get his hands on the Noble. Shouts of ecstasy permeated throughout the chamber, when they were interrupted by a loud knock.

"Yes," howled a breathless Hanstun.

An attendant stepped into the room. "My Lord, we captured her."

"Very good!" the Noble exclaimed, rising to his knees. "Bring her in."

Two attendants entered, a woman between them. Her hands were tied behind her back, and she wore a white robe. Ruan signaled with his fingers, and the men threw her onto the edge of the bed.

"So, you thought you could escape to the Temple?" the personal attendant growled.

The captive remained quiet, and Ruan turned toward Lord

Hanstun.

"Strip her!" the Noble commanded. "And tie her down."

The participants fastened the young woman's wrists and ankles to the corners of the bed as she attempted in vain to get away.

"My Lord, I think there's only one thing left to do," said Ruan.

Hanstun smiled and, in that instant, his personal attendant knew he had succeeded again. The fabricated storylines were getting more inventive and difficult to manage, yet each seemed to satisfy his Noble's venereal desires better than the last. Ruan looked at the girl's frightened expression, and wondered whether she was actually in on it, as should have been planned. *Doesn't really matter.* He helped tear the white dress from her body. *Time to have some fun.*

It was late in the morning when Ruan awoke. He surveyed the area and found the group still in bed, tangled and fast asleep. Except one. Ruan cursed. *I should have been up first.* Just as he was about to scamper off the indulgent mattress, the personal attendant heard a whimper. He turned around, only to find it was coming from the Overseer girl. In the excitement, they had forgotten to untie her, and she was still lying there, under the mishmash of limbs. Not that Ruan cared. He had paid a handsome price to procure the entertainment, insisting on good quality performing skills. Perhaps the local brothel-keeper had taken his request too earnestly, for Ruan doubted very much there had been any acting involved throughout the night. The tired woman was looking at him, still laboring to unleash herself. He removed her gag.

"Please ..." she moaned.

Ruan smiled and leaned in, his scar rubbing against the side of her face. "If you think that was hard," he whispered into her ear, "you better hope the lord doesn't ask for some of the other things he's known for."

"No, wait, ple—"

The personal attendant stuffed the piece of cloth back into her mouth, cutting off her pleas for help. He pinched the woman's cheeks, making her squirm.

The movement awakened one of the men. "What's going on?"

"Not sure she's learned her lesson," Ruan whispered back.

"Is that so?"

The man crawled toward the frightened girl, and Ruan made his way off the bed. *Enough fun, time to go.* Scooping the clothes he had left on the ground the night before, he exited the bedroom, crossed an anti-chamber, and walked into a room built entirely of wood. The personal attendant turned a small knob placed on the wall, and water sprinkled from the ceiling. It felt cool against his skin, and as much as he wanted to stand there and let it soak in, Ruan kept the rinse brief.

After drying off and slipping into his usual tunic, he rushed through the hall toward the office where he was sure to find Lord Hanstun. As the personal attendant followed the palace's opulent corridors, he reflected on the prior night. If Dominion law was applied fairly, they should have been beheaded. Sleeping with a member of the same sex was forbidden, the Book of Provenance's verses stated this explicitly. *The law rarely applies to the one who enacts it.* Lord Hanstun and his Noble contemporaries could do whatever they wanted, and no one would tell them otherwise. *Oh, what a job I have.* There were certain comforts Ruan had grown so accustomed to, he could never again live without them. *The banquets. The matinee performances. The social functions.* Of course, his position was one that required a high level of sacrifice. If the Noble wanted something, his personal attendant had better procure it for him. The stress involved in such catering was negated hundredfold by the fact that money would never be a concern. *Even though it's not my money.* Ruan could buy all he wanted and often did so on credit throughout Phaidros.

There was more. He felt a personal connection to Lord Hanstun, one that existed with nobody else. Often assuming it was reciprocated, the attendant had yet to gauge the accuracy of his presumption. *I see the way he looks at me.* He knew there were other lovers and other advisors, he just liked to believe he was the best among them. In essence, the personal attendant enjoyed flattering himself.

Ruan arrived at Lord Hanstun's office and stopped. Throughout the years, he had learned the Noble detested mixing business and pleasure. *And unfortunately, I have a feeling the next hours will be strictly business.* Ruan knocked.

"Come in."

The personal attendant had barely entered the room when he was greeted with a loaded question.

"What do you know of Source-powered engines?"

"A decent amount, my Lord."

Hanstun pointed at the chair in front of his desk. "Tell me everything."

"Everything?"

The Noble raised an eyebrow. "Was I unclear?"

While irritated, Ruan kept his composure. "My Lord, I do not want to insult your intelligence with things you already—"

"No," interrupted Hanstun. "Explain them to me."

The personal attendant sat still. *Really?* Another of the Noble's annoying traits was manifesting itself, namely the desire to hear from others what he already knew. *Fine, you're going to get it all, then.* "Adepts are able to draw energy from the Source," said Ruan. "When they do so, the energy is stored within them."

"Yes, yes, go on."

"From what I understand, the storage eventually reaches a tipping point and gets released."

"And?"

"Generally, the release results in a force blast, the energy dissipating into the air. But those clever Adepts have designed machines that trap the released energy, holding it within them."

"Like engines."

"Exactly, my Lord. These engines, and other machines for that matter, use the released Source energy to function. Until the energy runs out, that is. The machine is then—"

"Sent back."

"Right, back to the Academy for what they call Source refinement. A recycling of sorts, if you will, overseen by the major source manipulator."

"The supervisor of the Academy's refinement facilities?"

"That's what they say," replied Ruan. "Though, if I understand correctly, he still reports to the preceptor."

"Who is it? I want to speak with him directly."

"No one knows."

Lord Hanstun sat back in his chair and sighed. "I should have put money into this a long time ago. Even my hypocritical rivals have been developing machines for the Academy to refine for years now."

Ruan looked at the floor. *It's never enough, is it?* The man sitting in front of him had made a fortune with the salt marshes, the greatest in all of Phaidros. *And he's still not content.* They sat in silence.

"If I may, my Lord, why the sudden interest?" Ruan asked. "You're thinking of those village attacks, aren't you?"

The Noble smiled. "Yes."

"I thought so."

"And what do you make of it, Ruan?"

"Well, I think it doesn't make any sense. The destruction is one we've never seen, like stories of the Dread Days."

"Precisely. This only leads me to believe the Academy has developed a super weapon." Hanstun frowned. "Though there's one problem with this theory."

"Which is, my Lord?"

"Who at the Academy would be capable of transferring energy into such a weapon? The major source manipulator?"

"Well, it might not be one person."

"Explain yourself."

"They could have collaborated. My inside sources tell me it's a common practice at the Academy. There's even a rumor Ocean Star's engines were created by a team of one hundred Adepts."

"Is that so? Are you positive?"

"Absolutely, my Lord."

"Then why haven't they made even bigger ones?"

"Machines can reach a tipping point as well. Just like the living body does."

"Interesting," muttered Hanstun. "Well, they've clearly made some developments, and I need you to find out what those are."

"Yes, my Lord."

"Go to the countryside, figure out whatever weapon they're hiding. I need ans—" A knock interrupted Hanstun. Annoyed, the Noble called out for the visitor to enter, and an attendant rushed into the office.

"My Lord," the man said, panting. "News from the Temple."

"Go on, speak."

"Last night, two Adepts were brought up Mount Kilda.

They were tried for murder, done in the way of the Gods. And sentenced to death."

Lord Hanstun jumped to his feet. "Was it those two boys?"

"What two boys, my Lord?"

"The two boys!" shouted the Noble. "The two boys!"

"The ... the two boys?"

"That were here yesterday, you fool!"

Disregarding his confused attendant, Hanstun turned to Ruan. "It was them, I'm sure of it. You'd better get ready. Now! Before the Academy changes its plans."

"Yes, my Lord." The personal attendant sprang toward the door.

"And Ruan," called out Hanstun.

"Yes, my Lord?"

The Noble paused. "Be careful out there."

CHAPTER SEVENTEEN

The eyes were spellbinding. They harbored a distinct yet unplaceable melancholy, their violet hue captivating Kyran just as it had earlier that night. *By the Gods. She belongs with, well … the Gods.* Her head tilted to the side, briefly uncovering ears pierced by small round gemstones. There was a certain shyness, detectible in her slight hesitations as she moved around. "Are you ok?" Kyran had been swift up the stairs, grasping Sabine's arm and engaging in a tug-of-war that only ended when the hairy old man let go and clambered away.

"Yes, thank you," she replied. "You saved me."

"Oh, it's nothing, I do it on the regular."

Edvon rolled his eyes. "Tickle's dead, in case anyone cares."

A spider crawled across the stone wall.

"We need to get out of here," continued Kyran. "Someone else might come down."

Sabine stayed still. "I'm not following Adepts anywhere."

"Wait, didn't I just save you?"

"It doesn't matter. You're still an Adept."

"Fine," said Edvon. "Go back to your cell if you want, we're leaving."

Kyran reminded himself that the last time he stared at a beautiful woman, it had ended poorly. *Oh well.* "Sabine, hold up!" She faced him, causing the Adept's heart to skip a beat. "Look, I don't know what happened to you. You're obviously in some kind of trouble, and this could be your one chance to escape."

"How do you know what I need?" she retorted. "What if I too killed someone?"

"With those eyes, I'm sure you've killed many."

Edvon exhaled and snatched the key ring from Kyran's hand. He walked toward the stairs, mumbling as he tested one of the smaller-sized keys on the lock of his platinum collar. Finding it did not fit, he tried another. And the next. Until the sixth and last one clicked into place. Edvon tossed the restraint to the ground and the keys to his brother.

"Nice!" Kyran exclaimed, also freeing himself. "Come on, Sabine, let's help each other get out of here."

"I can't leave Cyrus like this."

"Forget about that guy, we've got to save ourselves."

"No, they'll kill him."

Kyran knelt and shook the listless Overseer. "Out cold. He's not going anywhere."

A bell tolled above ground.

"That … that's the morning ring," Sabine whispered. "They'll be coming down here any minute."

"Then it's time for you to make up your mind," said Edvon, and he ran up the stairs to the main level. The two others followed. Stepping ahead, the older Adept cracked open the courtyard door. To his dismay, the area was already filled with a number of pilgrims waiting to enter the Inner Sanctum for the sermons. "Too many people."

"Where can we go?" Kyran asked Sabine.

She frowned. "There's no other way out. These stairs only lead to the dungeons or up to the Court of Justice."

"Come again?"

"That's why we call them the Stairs of Judgment."

They weighed their options.

"Can't you Adepts just blast your way through?"

Kyran chuckled and shook his head. "Only the major source manipulator could do something like that."

"Wait a minute." Edvon snapped his fingers. "Now that I think about it, those judges walked in from the back of the courtroom."

"I'm not sure," replied Sabine. "I've never been behind that door."

"We don't really have a choice!"

Across the yard, Gorgios had come into view. He was making his way toward them, shoving pilgrims out of his path. Kyran shut the door. "Do you think he saw us?"

"I'm not waiting around to ask him." Edvon dashed up the flight of steps to the Court of Justice. Much to his relief it was empty. Without hesitation, he made his way toward the small opening behind the marshals' elevated desk. A corridor lay ahead, and the three escapees rushed into it.

"These must be the marshals' quarters," whispered Sabine.

A row of ornate doors graced the left side of the hallway, each revealing magnificent carvings depicting scenes from the Book of Provenance. Tainted glass windows were letting in a stunning array of color from the morning sunrise, bringing the art to life.

"Look! Reflections 24." Sabine was in awe. "And there's Conception 7."

Edvon pointed to a narrow passage at the far end of the hallway. It curved out of sight, in all likelihood leading to the Temple's main building. They tiptoed across the hallway when Tibon stepped out of his quarter, whistling a tune to himself and carrying a thick stack of papers. Startled by the sight of the unexpected visitors, he dropped the documents in a flurry of confusion. Edvon pummeled him with a vicious Source blast. The old man was sent sprawling onto the floor like a newborn balbak, his bleeding nose likely broken and glasses shattered beyond repair.

Sabine gasped. "He was just ... he ..."

"He was just in the way." Kyran pushed the young woman out of the corridor, his older brother following close behind. They came to a large square staircase.

"Which direction?" asked an agitated Edvon.

Shocked by the aggression she had just witnessed, Sabine remained silent.

"We should go down," Kyran said, "and hope there's a way to sneak out."

"What if—"

"Help me!"

The two brothers looked at Sabine in horror.

"Hel—"

Kyran covered the young woman's mouth with his palm as she struggled to push him away. "What are you doing?" asked the Adept. Sabine's panicky eyes stared back at him. "I promise we won't hurt you. Plus, there's no way out of this now, if we get caught, you're as much to blame as we are. Listen, I'm going to remove my hand, and we're going to find an exit together. Okay?" Kyran lowered his arm.

"There ... there's a route to the gardens one floor below us," murmured the young woman.

They were about to descend the staircase when they sensed approaching footsteps.

"Someone must have heard the shout," Kyran whispered.

Edvon nodded. "That leaves us only one choice."

The escapees spun around and went up instead. One floor above, another hallway led to a set of closed doors behind which faint laughter could be heard.

"That's the dining hall," revealed Sabine.

"We need to keep going, then." Edvon took a step up but stopped, a fraught expression on his pale face. "Someone's coming down."

With nowhere left to escape and the sound of footsteps drawing nearer, they ran down the corridor toward the dining hall. Edvon spotted a possible exit to their left. "What's that?"

"The kitchens," answered Sabine. "We can't go in there, they'll see us."

"We're about to be seen, anyway." He shoved his frantic companions into the unknown.

They were hit by an array of pungent breakfast smells, ranging from cooked eggs and brined geega to baked beans and burnt toast. An Overseer chef was barking orders as initiants bolted in all directions, a complete and utter mess. The confusion played out in their favor. Though they were in plain sight, no one paid attention to them, and the three fugitives looked at each other astounded.

"Just act normal," said Edvon.

They crossed the vast kitchens, as oblivious initiants carrying trays to and from the dining hall bumped into them.

Kyran walked through a side door and let out a sigh of relief. "I can't believe that just happened. No one even noticed—" A series of clanging bells resonated throughout the Temple with ferocity. "Never mind."

Edvon sprinted to the end of the hallway and shook his head. "It's a dead end. Is there any way out of here?"

"I don't know," Sabine replied.

They were standing still, unsure where to go, when Kyran noticed a hatch in the wall. Opening it, he discovered a hollow shaft, complete with a pulley system designed to bring up food for the kitchens. "Here, maybe we can climb through."

"Are you crazy?" Sabine interjected. "There's no way I'm

going in there."

"Have it your way," replied Edvon, squeezing his large frame through the hatch and positioning himself onto the platform. "Lower me."

Kyran untied the rope and carefully let it glide between his hands until Edvon hit the bottom. He pulled the platform back up and turned to Sabine, but she shook her head.

"I don't want to."

"Doesn't matter, I'm not leaving you here."

Sabine looked at him with wide-eyed apprehension.

"I won't let you fall, I promise."

The young woman slid through the hatch, and as Kyran monitored her, he felt a funny feeling wash over him. Seconds later, a knock on the shaft signaled Sabine had safely reached the base. When Kyran pulled up the platform one last time, the door sprang open, and a group of Overseers stormed in.

"They're here!" one of them yelled.

Kyran scrambled through the hatch and onto the platform, bringing the loose end of the rope with him. Straining to prevent his weight from pulling him down too fast, he looked up to see an Overseer glaring at him from above. The man grabbed the rope, yanking it toward him and stopping the Adept's descent before he could exit the shaft. Closing his eyes, Kyran let go of his grip.

"Ah!" The Overseer screamed as the weight pulled the rope through his hand, the friction burning his skin raw.

Crashing to the bottom uninjured, Kyran climbed out of the portal. "They found us."

Shouts could be heard in the distance.

"We need somewhere to hide," said Edvon. "Now."

"I … I think I have an idea." Sabine rushed off, steering the trio through a series of narrowing passageways.

They reached yet another steep staircase, one with stone

steps that vanished below into darkness.

"Where are we going?"

The young woman turned to face them. "The Crypts."

CHAPTER EIGHTEEN

The yellow pip, baqua's bounciest ball, first rebounded off the ground, then the smooth wall. It took a high arc into the air, and those in the small crowd that had gathered held their breaths in anticipation. One of the four catchers jumped from his corner, arms extended and eyes fixed on the target. The ball landed just out of his reach, and he fell into the water with a spectacular splash.

"Yes!" shouted Pluto. He high-fived Joss. "That's five points, with no outs."

"No, it's four," shouted one of the opposing players.

The performer turned to his friend, who gave him a wink. "Yes, fine, my fault."

The wet pip was thrown back to them, and the team huddled together.

"It's your shot," Pluto said to one of the two players with whom they had joined forces.

"Right," she answered as she tightened her baqua gloves. "What are we thinking?"

"I'd say a short one, we've gone long a few times now, and they'll be expecting another."

"Good idea, I'll go with a left-handed curve."

Having made his last shot, Pluto took his place in the scoring box, while the teammate grabbed the ball and positioned herself in front of the wall. As she ran toward it, the catchers shifted around the edges of the pool, in an effort to confuse her. The plan worked. Hesitating mid-throw, the woman lobbed a weak toss. The pip rebounded pathetically off the wall and right at a catcher's awaiting glove. Rather than flipping the ball to a teammate for the extra out, he played a low-risk strategy and held onto it firmly. "One out."

Pluto exhaled, frustrated by the ineptitude he had just witnessed. "Come on, we still have three outs to work with."

Joss clapped his hands, and the opponents passed him the pip. Without pausing, he sprinted toward the wall, making a long swooping underhanded throw. The ball skidded against the ground and off the smooth stone, ricocheting toward the open water. Unfortunately for Joss, his drive throw was met by an outstanding defensive effort.

One of the catchers jumped out and diverted the ball with her foot. Anticipating the save, a second catcher snagged the pip and threw it to a teammate as he too fell into the pool. The third catcher, clutching the safety railing with one hand, leaned out and snatched the ball. "Triple out!" she exclaimed. The jubilant opposing players roared, slapping the water excitedly like geegas with their fins. "Our turn to throw. That's four outs."

The teams switched positions. They had achieved four points in the first frame, a decent score despite having stranded a thrower in the scoring box. There were only three frames in a game of baqua, and every toss mattered.

They opted for a traditional defensive formation, with one catcher at each corner of the square pool. This left a vulnerable spot in the center of the water, though aiming the ball there would require impressive accuracy. The first opposing player succeeded in exhibiting just that. A splash, and he went to stand in the scoring box, making a fist pump.

Pluto jumped in to fetch the pip. "Stick to your spots," he ordered. "They won't hit the middle twice."

The second thrower wound up and launched the ball at the wall. It rebounded and curved wildly before hitting the same point in the middle of the pool.

"No way …"

"Yes way," the second thrower retorted, loosening her gloves and taking her teammate's place in the scoring box. "One point and no outs."

Pluto looked over to Joss, who pointed at another zone on the defensive railing surrounding the pool. "Okay. You, stay put. You, cover the middle of the pool instead, and I'll slide there to cover the front."

They shuffled around, leaving a weak point in the back right corner. The opposing thrower zeroed in on it, but the ball sailed above the water, landing on concrete instead.

"That's an out!" exclaimed Pluto. He turned to his teammates. "Shift two steps to the left as he winds up."

The fourth thrower kept his concentration, arcing the pip toward a vulnerable location in the square. Joss jumped backward, catching the ball mid-air. As he fell into the water, he threw it back up, hoping someone would grab it for the double out. Or even divert it for a triple out. The plan failed, the closest catcher letting the ball slip through his glove.

"Another point," shouted the thrower. "And you don't get the first out since the pip hit the water."

Pluto brought a hand to his face before walking around the edge of the pool and helping his friend. "Listen, these two we're playing with aren't exactly the fittest balbaks in the pack, if you catch my drift. And we're using a yellow pip, not a black one. So let's just play the easy outs and forget about turning doubles or triples with them."

"Hey, I heard that!"

"Good, use it as motivation."

The disgruntled teammates took their respective places along the edge of the pool. More runs were scored, and they managed to get the required four outs. They were tied four to four going into the next frame.

Neither side netted any points during the second set of tosses, with miscues by each player preventing any scoring output. Pluto kicked off the third frame, however, with a beautiful spinning effort that landed into the water with plenty of space. He walked to the scoring box. "Come on. Bring me in!"

The second thrower did just that, driving a hard line drive which bounced off a catcher's outstretched glove. She took Pluto's place in the scoring box. An unforeseen double out resulted when Joss threw, emptying the box, though the fourth thrower filled it once more with a solid trajectory.

Pluto came up to the wall and fired a strong shot. But the opposing team had positioned someone at the front center railing. He caught the ball with his glove and flipped it to the nearest teammate. "Double out."

"Nice try," Pluto shot back. "But that was a catch, not a flip. You only get one out."

"No way, I never held possession of the pip."

"Yes, you did! That was a clear catch."

"Let them have it," one of the opposing players said. "We'll get the next out."

The bitter catcher tossed the ball back, and Pluto watched his teammate loop a high curve right into open water. "No, you won't!"

The fourth out did come with the next throw, however, and they went to the defensive position with a slim six-to-four lead.

To Pluto's surprise, the first attempt came flying at him. Against his better judgment, rather than catching the pip, he flipped it toward Joss, making sure not to maintain possession as his opponent had done earlier. Joss was ready, and he tapped the ball to their third teammate. She jumped forward, cradling and throwing it to the last catcher before falling into the water. Pluto closed his eyes. Peeping ever so slightly, he watched as their fourth teammate dove head first, stretching out his right arm and making the catch.

"Baqua!" exclaimed Pluto. "That's a baqua!"

The rare quadruple out, after which the game was named, ended the match. Pluto tossed his gloves and jumped into the pool to congratulate his exuberant teammates.

After shaking hands with the losing team, the performers dried off. They walked past a dozen courts, walls painted in vibrant colors and pools uniform in perimeter and depth. "Gods, I love winning. And we got a baqua." Joss grinned. "Lucky Roach?" He had no reason to double-check his companion's answer, Pluto knew. They left the athletic complex, traversing neighborhoods at a leisurely pace. As they arrived at their favorite locale, the two friends were stopped by a very ordinary looking man.

"Are you Pluto?" he asked.

"Yours truly. Who's asking?"

"I was told I might find you here," said the man, pointing to the Lucky Roach and ignoring the question.

"Oh, yeah?" Pluto replied. "And who told you that?"

Elias hesitated. It had been an arduous mission to sneak back into the Academy and access the archives while steering clear of Marrek. The officer felt he had betrayed the preceptor. Divulging that the Academy kept a file on every single Adept in Phaidros, complete with a sketch and common whereabouts, would only add to his guilt. He just needed to convince the two men to meet with Lecarn. "Um, one of your … friends."

"Which one? Is this about the baqua we just scored?"

"What?" asked Elias. "Look, it … it doesn't matter. I have a job for you, if you're interested."

"And if we're not?"

"Then, well … I'll move on to the next names on my list."

"Wait. How long have you been waiting here? And how did you know what we looked like?" Pluto frowned. "Have you been asking everyone walking in if they're us?"

Joss pointed to Elias.

"Yes, you're right, you're right," conceded the tall performer. "What's this job?"

"Well, I'm actually not too sure, uh … I think he's tracking something down, and—"

"Who's he?"

"Mister, umm … Lecarn."

"Lecarn? What kind of a name is that? Did you just make it up?"

Elias grimaced. "Why don't you just ask him yourself, alright? What I know is that he asked me to find some Adept—able … adaptable people for some type of job."

Pluto walked away.

"Wait!" shouted Elias. "It's paid very well. Seven hundred gold coins."

The performer stopped in his tracks and spun around, giving his best effort at a genuine smile. "Seven hundred?"

"Each."

Pluto and Joss glanced at each other. "When can we start, my friend?" They made their way back toward Elias.

"Immediately, he's waiting for you at Mirabel Crater."

"Yuck!" yelped Pluto, bringing a hand up to his mouth. "That's in … Portown."

Elias attempted an encouraging smile. "Only for a few months."

"A few months?"

The performers turned to leave. Once again, the officer begged them to reconsider. "Wait! How much do you want?"

"Double."

Not caring in the slightest for the state of Lecarn's wealth, Elias readily agreed. "Done."

"Excellent." Pluto rubbed the palms of his hands together. "And you've arranged for transportation, I presume?"

"Yes," replied the officer, pulling Lecarn's tickets from his pocket. "On Ocean Star, leaving tomorrow morning."

"Ocean Star? Why, my good man."

"Mhmm." Elias stepped away.

"Hold up!" called out Pluto. "Don't we get part of the payment up front?"

The officer stared back at them, his eyelids drooping dramatically. After a moment, he looked like a dead balbak, and Pluto felt genuine concern. "Did you, uh … are you okay?"

Elias disappeared into the flow of SPCs, and Pluto raised an eyebrow. "What a weird little man. So, should we do it, then?" Joss nodded. "Are you sure?" Another nod. "Yes, you're right. Some kind of job? Nothing we can't handle." They opened the door to the Lucky Roach. "Let's go make more coins, so we can smoke them all away."

CHAPTER NINETEEN

The skull glared back at her with a chilling scowl, a dim light from the torches flickering in and out of the dark orbits. Bereft of a lower jaw as well as most upper teeth, the head was melancholic. *Who were you?* Along the top of the corroded cranium, a large crack could be seen extending toward the nasal cavity, perhaps evidence of its owner's demise. *Yikes.* Sabine turned away, taking in the eerie sights. The four small interlocking rooms were made entirely of bones, organized in a macabre fashion that verged on a majestic display of artistry. In one, femurs were stacked horizontally, with a row of skulls zigzagging its way through the pile. In another, pelvic bones arranged in spirals encircled several full-size skeletons, their arms positioned outward. Sabine shivered, opting to altogether ignore the contents of the two remaining rooms.

Edvon was examining an elliptical display of thoracic vertebrae. "What is this place?"

"The Crypts," the young woman answered, as if she had visited many times. Sabine was terrified. Only the highest-ranking Overseers ventured into the sacred catacombs, and many within the Temple held the chamber in superstitious awe. "They'll never think to look for us here," she added.

"Because it's just like another dungeon."

"It's better than being caught and killed."

Edvon grunted.

"Did you have a better idea? As soon as the bells start to ring, they seal every entrance. So there's no way out." Sabine stomped to the base of the steps. She sat down, bringing her hands to her face and longing for her favorite place. Thick shag rugs mantled its hickory hardwood floors, faded tapestries hung from the brick walls. A crackling sound emanated from the massive fireplace which bestowed warmth to the space. Sabine's favorite sofa was nearest the grand bookcase. She could sit there, cuddled in her blanket for hours on end, reading or gazing out the arched windows at the panoramic view of Phaidros. Thinking of the warm common room high in the Temple's fourth spire was dispiriting, especially as she felt the frigid Crypts' air run up the base of her spine. *What am I doing?* The escape happened so fast, there was no time to think it through. *I should have kept screaming for help.* If the Adepts had been captured, the commandant would surely have forgiven her. Sabine just wanted her life to go back to what it had been, for everything to be normal once more. *After what happened, I'll … I'll never be welcome here again.* Edvon kicked a skull lying on the ground into the wall, shattering it into several broken pieces. *By Lutigas!* Sabine closed her eyes, shivering once more. *I can't trust them. They'll kill me as soon as we get out of here. Or worse, bring me back to their Academy.* The Book of Provenance was clear. Their ancestors had been exiled from the heavens for using It, and now, Adepts were making the same mistake. They were threatening everyone's life. *If only platinum weren't so rare. Then we could really keep them away.* The young woman wished that when her eyes opened, she could be on her sofa, a book in hand, surrounded by friends.

Kyran walked back into the chamber. "You need to come see this." They followed him through the Crypts, and he pointed at the far wall.

Sabine examined it and shuttered, nauseous. Hundreds of little skeletons, miniature in size, were stacked in a disorderly fashion.

Edvon too was perturbed. "Next time, I'll pass on seeing the dead babies."

"Just put your hands up to the wall," said Kyran.

"Are you out of your mind?" Sabine shook her head. "What is it? Just tell us."

"There's a flow of air."

Edvon examined the wall to verify the validity of his brother's claim. "He's right."

"So?" asked Sabine.

"It means there must be a passage on the other side," Kyran explained.

They scanned for a way through, but the bones, stacked tight from floor to ceiling, would not budge. Edvon suggested a more radical approach. "Let's blast these things."

Shoulder to shoulder, the defiant siblings faced their target. As Source energy rushed into him, Kyran directed the flow through his core and into his extended arms toward the stack of bones. Feeling the intensity grow, he strove to master the fine line between steady grip and complete loss of control. Kyran released the surge from his fingertips, savoring the transience of power cascading within him.

Sabine, huddled in a corner, watched in horror as the two bright-eyed Adepts clobbered the wall with a deafening explosion, sending bones flying around the room. When the dust settled, a large gap had sprung up, leading to an obscure tunnel.

"That was very loud," the anxious woman said, hands still cupped around her ears.

"Then let's not wait around." The shine in Edvon's eyes was fading. "Kyran, grab that torch over there!" The older brother ducked through the cavity.

They ran through the desolate tunnel, winding their way down a steep incline. In minutes, the three escapees stood at a crossing, with several paths extending in various directions.

"Oh no …" moaned Sabine.

Edvon held up a hand. "Let's stick together. If these passageways splinter off even more, we might never reunite again."

The Adept was proven right. For an hour they raced through the tunnels, stepping on scattered bones, taking different turns, and losing any sense of orientation. They paused at another intersection and caught their breath.

"I feel like we've been here before," said Sabine. "Look. Isn't that the same skull we just saw?"

"I have no clue." Kyran took notice of the fading torch. "It wouldn't surprise me if we're running in circles."

"Hold on, I have an idea." Edvon ripped a piece of cloth from the bottom of his pants. "I'll put this on the ground, and if we somehow come back here, we'll know not to go this way again."

"Looks like you'll be executed naked." Kyran's deadpan remark elicited a giggle from Sabine. Twenty minutes later, they found themselves back at the same intersection. "I think this maze has no exit."

"Of course it has an exit." Edvon tore another piece of fabric. "Otherwise, what's the point of building the maze to begin with?" He placed it at the mouth of another tunnel and froze. "Did you hear that?"

"Hear what?" Kyran whispered.

"There were voices."

Sabine gasped. "They must have heard the explosion in the Crypt."

The three rushed into another tunnel but soon hit a dead end. Kyran waved around the dying torch. Only walls looked back at them. "Okay, we're done for."

There were no replies.

"Just like him," continued Kyran, pointing at a skeleton hunched against the side of the tunnel. "Probably got stuck down here, too."

Edvon frowned. "Got stuck down here?"

"Exactly, and—"

"Come to think of it, what was that person doing down here in this tunnel?" The older Adept took a moment to ponder over his own question, stroking his chin between his thumb and index finger. Then, coming to an astonishing realization, he snatched what remained of the torch from Kyran's hand. Edvon pointed it toward the ceiling, eyes darting back and forth. "There!"

"What?" asked Sabine.

"The stone. Don't you see it? There's a stone up there sticking through the ceiling."

"So?"

Edvon smiled. "This isn't just a tunnel. It's a grave."

"I don't understand."

"When Kyran and I were in the wagon going up Mount Kilda, I noticed a cemetery to the south of the Temple. These tunnels, they're under it, I think. I mean, why else would a skeleton be sitting here?"

"Why would there be tunnels under a cemetery?" asked Sabine.

"Escape routes for high-ranking Overseers?"

"Wait …" Kyran pointed upward. "You mean that's actually the underside of a gravestone?"

"I think so."

The younger Adept looked at Sabine, unsure whether the theory was the figment of tunnel fever induced imagination.

"Fine, don't believe me," Edvon said. "But let's at least find out if I'm right or not. What do we have to lose?"

"Nothing," muttered Sabine.

"Exactly. Kyran, I'll lift you up. Try to wiggle the stone and see if it will push out."

Above ground, a widowed grandmother was making the weekly visit to her beloved husband's grave. The shock was unmeasured when, out of nowhere, a headstone erupted, flying high above her head and smashing in a cloud of dirt. Confusion only grew as a young man, eyes shining, popped up where the headstone had lain. "And we shall be castigated once more for ignoring the Recital Supreme," she shrieked, "and They will punish us for our sins!"

As the old woman scurried away, convinced the Temple's prophetic messages were materializing, Kyran surfaced into the daylight. He took in a whiff of fresh air. "You see? That was much easier than displacing it by physical force."

"Yeah, whatever. Just give us a hand up."

Reaching for Kyran's outstretched arm, Sabine emerged from the tunnel. She brushed dirt off her dress and gazed up toward Mount Kilda, overcome with sadness. *Will I ever come back?* With a heavy heart, the young woman faced the brothers.

"What now?" asked Kyran.

"I ... I don't know."

"Come with us."

"Where are you going?"

"Back to the Academy. You'll be safe there, I promise."

"Not a chance," interjected Edvon. "Don't you hear those bells? There's no way we make it back through the city without getting caught."

"Oh yeah? And what do you suggest?"

"I say we hide out in the countryside, wait for this to blow over."

"Are you crazy?" Kyran shook his head. "The Academy is the safest place right now."

"You seem to forget that the Academy is brimming with Overseers," his brother replied. "Our presence there could cause an all-out conflict, and we can't put other Adepts in jeopardy. The right thing to do is wait for the commotion to die down. We'll follow Merchants Road south, and—"

"No, we can make it, we can—we ..." Kyran realized the futility of his proposed actions, and his voice trailed off.

Sabine weighed her options. *And I don't have many.* She could either follow them on their journey or venture out on her own and hope not to get caught.

"Fine, you're right," conceded Kyran. "Forget the Academy."

"Good." Edvon straightened his back. "As I was saying, we can follow Merchants Road south and seek refuge in a village along the way."

Kyran turned to Sabine. "Are you coming?" He extended his arm.

The young woman hesitated, feeling the urge to distance herself from the Adepts and take heed in the lessons from the Book of Provenance. She grabbed Kyran's hand. "Yes."

CHAPTER TWENTY

The long table was filled with nutritious options. There were bowls of steamed rice, various legumes, fresh diced fruits, and vegetables. In the middle of the buffet, trays sitting over Source-powered burners held an assortment of meats. Criss drowned her food in chunky yellow sauce and placed a heavy dish on the cashier's scale. The Battalion's second-in-command paid and found a spot to sit near the large windows.

Cases came and went. A longtime agent of the peace, Criss had handled all types of situations. Many were straightforward, easy to deal with. Only a handful required closer attention and revealed in the end an unexpected motive. *Or a surprise culprit.* This investigation was different. Something about it made her uneasy, if only for the sheer magnitude of the act. Aiden kept his focus in the wrong direction, and her frustration was mounting. *I know the suicide bombing was brutal.* Though to Criss, the murders came second to what she considered to be the pressing matter, the abhorrent one more deserving of their energy.

Not since the barbaric Dread Days had there been anything like this. The Battalion needed to be stalking the countryside, predicting the next attack. In due course, they would find the person responsible for the deaths of Commandant Rex Quintus and Lord Lester, of that Criss had no doubt. The evidence pointed to a conspiracy, rather than a lone act. *And conspiracies always have too many loose ends. Too many mouths to keep quiet.* The destruction they were witnessing was incomprehensible. As far as Criss could tell, there was no logical reasoning, in that no one stood to gain from such death and carnage. *Entire villages.* It reeked of pure cruelty, and it was disturbing.

"Then, she called out to the Gods themselves."

Criss observed a group huddled around Mira boards.

"And what happened?"

"Auralus Himself appeared, and—"

There was a slight pause in the conversation.

"And?" one of them inquired.

"He guided the coin."

"And?"

"The Adepts were sentenced to die."

Their eyes widened upon hearing the insane anecdote. Criss, who had already gleaned several versions of it, was finding this particular one amusing.

"But then, listen to this." Leaning in, the storyteller lowered his voice. "They managed to escape."

"Wait, they got away?"

"Yep."

"How?"

"I heard they killed several Overseers."

"Monsters."

"It's what they're saying. They've become vicious beasts, destroying anything in sight."

"I even heard one of them was shooting It out of his eyes."

Criss's chuckles attracted the group's attention.

"What is it, ma'am? You don't believe me?"

"No, I don't," replied the agent. "They can't do that."

"And how would you know?"

Gulping her last spoon of rice, Criss got up to leave. "I used to date an Adept. And he didn't know how to shoot much of anything."

The group laughed, then one of them decided to try his

luck.

"Well if you want a real—"

"Save it," snapped Criss, and she walked out. *Just incredible how smooth men think they are. What a bunch of geegabrains.* The agent had shared parts of her life with a few of them and would invariably grow tired of catering to their needs and concerns. She glided through the food district, dodging the masses and taking in the smells that delighted her. *Before eating. After a meal, they become overwhelming and difficult to bear. Just like a man.*

Criss had important matters to deal with. It was indeed a strange story, the one about the Adepts that she heard repeated in the eatery. A crime had yet to be reported, meaning it was the Noble Assembly's problem, not theirs. *Gods, I hate them.* Hatred concededly derived from jealousy, as the agent was first to admit. Lords and ladies, living in their lavish estates and doing nothing more than attending pointless social functions, made for an easy target. *It's so unfair to blame individuals. They're just products of the system, right?* An oft-repeated narrative Criss was tired of hearing. *Who changes a system if not the individual?*

The agent tried to make sense of her sporadic thoughts. Then she remembered her last conversation with Aiden, and how wrong he had been. *Not everything has to always be connected.* The village attack, the bombing, and the growing tensions between the Academy and the Temple, even the escape of two Adepts suspected of killing. Though strange, those were events that could have arisen independently of each other. *Just because they may influence one another doesn't mean they're connected.* She had mentioned it, but no one else at the Battalion agreed with her. *They always want a perfect answer, something they can tie up with a nice little bow.*

At the Main Complex, Criss cleared the security checkpoint

and raced up the stairs, entering her office and closing the door before anyone could see her. The half-finished report detailing a previous case sat on her desk, though it would have to wait a while longer. *I have no desire to think of past crimes.* She sat down, tapping her fingers on a stack of papers. They had been unable to collect any valuable information from the bombing scene given how ferociously the fire had burned. "Making it that much harder for us to get our guy," mumbled Criss, imitating one of her many off-putting colleagues. *Did they even consider the possibility that the bomber might have been a woman?*

Nothing would ever get accomplished sitting in her office. *There's only one place to start.* Soon, the agent was taking in the dazzling colors of the flower market. A great variety of plants had been set out in front of the stalls, some hanging from pots fastened to overarching poles. It felt wonderful and enchanting, until Criss imagined what it must have been like for the suicide bomber walking through the aisles. She shuttered.

Hurrying down the infamous alley, the agent arrived at the crime scene and stopped in her tracks. Aiden was examining something on the wall. *What in the Gods is he doing here?* Criss backed up and ducked behind the nearest corner. The chief looked tired which enhanced his attractiveness, and it bothered her tremendously. *What is it? His intellect perhaps? His different colored eyes? Or is it his well-built physique?* She cursed herself and shook the questions from her mind. The agent lusted after Aiden, though when she was his superior, the desire had been more pleasant and fleeting. Now she was the one looking up. *And my perspective's been altered.* Criss was preparing to leave when the chief turned around.

"What are you doing here?" he asked.

"I could ask the same of you."

Instead of firing back at her, Aiden sighed. "Did you hear

the news?"

"Yes."

"All I need right now is another drowning in a baqua pool," mumbled the chief. "Anyhow, do you think those two Adepts are still in Phaidros?"

"I don't." Criss paused. "Chief, if I may, it might be a good idea to spread out your team. Taking advantage of our resources to relieve stress. Put a junior on the Temple case, and—"

"Send a small independent task force to Portown? Have them investigate the village attacks?"

Criss stepped back, annoyed, and she stared into the distance.

"And perhaps you would be interested in leading that expedition?" Aiden knew there would be no reply. "Look, I need you here."

"What's going on out there is—"

"Save it," snapped the chief, giving Criss a taste of her own medicine. "I said I need you here, sorry. Can't we discuss this later?"

His second-in-command kept gazing away.

"Now come check this out, I think I've found something." Aiden was pointing to potted flowers underneath a window.

"From the market," Criss said in a dry mechanical tone.

"Not the flowers, the decorations above them." Several strands of fabric graced the side of the wall, in a dainty display that complemented the floral arrangement. "Don't you see?"

She eventually noticed the anomaly. "This one doesn't belong." Criss removed one of the strands which was wider and of a different texture. "And?"

"And how did it get there, then?"

"The bomber ..."

"Right," answered Aiden. "It must have been part of his

clothing, a shred that somehow survived the explosion. Do you recognize it?"

"Sailor's stripes?

"Precisely. Our suspect's a boatman …" Aiden sighed once more, much to Criss's displeasure.

"So what?" she retorted. "Let's head to the docks and figure out who wears these stripes."

"Yeah, I already know which ship he's from."

"And how's that?"

"I was on its crew twenty years ago."

CHAPTER TWENTY-ONE

"The voice guided him, further still. And Blind Lutigas ascended the tepui. Higher and higher, until he could feel but only mist. To its summit he climbed, with the courage of a thousand men." The preacher paused, glancing at his copy of the Book of Provenance. "Until he could walk not a step more. Then the mist parted. And the Gods Themselves arose before his crippled eyes. Bathed in a crimson light, in all Their glory."

The pilgrims assembled in the Inner Sanctum let out a collective gasp, much to Rex Ruga's annoyance. *Like they haven't heard this story a hundred times.* She remained stoic, not a trace of emotion perceivable on her cold face.

"'Noble Lutigas,' They said. 'You who have been so pious, and so faithful. Come forth, that you may hold Our hand.' And Lutigas did so, his tears …" cough "flow—"

The preacher coughed again, cutting short the verse. The commandant, known for her rash and impulsive decisions, resisted the urge to storm the altar and scream at the old man to wrap it up. Rex Ruga was well aware many in the crowd had their eyes fixed on her. *Appearances are key.* She represented the Temple, as Najara often reminded her, which was the only reason to attend such an uninspiring sermon. *I have real issues to deal with.*

"The Gods exclaimed 'Our children sinned! For that, they were punished, and now you must pay the price. But beware, Lutigas, for your brethren sin once more.'"

Rex Ruga tilted her head to the side. The Temple's bells had been tolling for close to an hour now, and she was dying to find out why. Only an archaic rule preventing the Inner Sanctum from being unsealed mid-sermon kept the commandant in her seat. *A rule about to be broken if this preacher doesn't get on with it.*

"Blind Lutigas bowed his head, and he repeated the Recital Supreme." The preacher looked up.

"Thou shall not use It," the pilgrims chorused.

"And when Lutigas raised his head once more," continued the preacher, "the Gods had disappeared."

There was a long pause, and Rex Ruga almost stood up, thinking the sermon to be over. An honest mistake for an Overseer who had read no more than a few scattered lines from the Book of Provenance.

"There shone a ray of light that guided him back. And he descended the tepui with a heavy heart. And once more, Lutigas sought out the hermits in the Cave of Dust and Bones."

By all the … there's more?

"'Fear not, blind Lutigas,' said the hermits. 'For your sons and their sons will one day build a glorious shrine where every one of Gods' children shall reside. And they will take heed in the words you have heard today.'"

Pilgrims applauded, many moved to tears. The story of Auralus's forefather was one of the most celebrated moments in the canon. Not only did it foretell the Temple's creation, the narrative also included a direct visitation by the Gods, a rare occurrence.

Rex Ruga got up and offered a polite clap, hoping it might speed up the proceedings. She was dumbfounded when the pilgrims followed suit and gave a standing ovation. The tribute lasted several minutes. Having unwillingly instigated a delay, Rex Ruga was ready to pull out her own hair.

"Thank you, kind Commandant," said the old preacher. "The moral of these verses is quite clear."

The pilgrims sat again. Rex Ruga remained standing, unprepared for the verbose address.

"Adepts are using It with greater impudence. This has caused death in villages, as well as in our very own city." Reciting words that had been hand-fed to him by Najara, the preacher went on. "Today is the time to be pious, today is the time to unite. We, as the Gods' chosen children, must make this Temple stronger."

Rex Ruga clenched her fists. *I'm the commandant, not you. Battle cries need to be voiced by someone who's fighting the war.* She calmed herself, taking solace in the upcoming execution and the attention it would bring to her.

"The Temple shall forever be your star, your guiding light. May the Gods look down upon you with love."

Another round of applause, one Rex Ruga opted not to join. Instead, she hurried to the Inner Sanctum's doorway, impatient for it to be unlocked. Under the commandant's intense scrutiny, a nervous initiant pulled the key from his robes. He accomplished the task in double time, unsealing the chamber only to witness Rex Ruga push her way out without a word.

The bells were much louder in the courtyard than within the impervious walls of the Inner Sanctum. The commandant surveyed the area. *No pilgrims? Strange, considering the sermons are to go on all day.* She spotted Najara waiting near the gates which had been closed shut. The two women walked toward each other.

"I trust the sermon was—"

"What's happening?" Rex Ruga asked, cutting short the confidante's pleasantries.

"Oh, you mean the bells?"

"You've already taken one seat from me. If you've also conducted the execution, there will be consequences."

Najara smiled. "Empty threats are useless, dear."

"I haven't made any empty threats."

"Do you seriously believe sanctions can be imposed upon me?"

"Political retributions? Perhaps not. But you, of all people, are not stopping me from wringing your neck like a balbak, should I so desire."

It was Rex Ruga's turn to smile, as Najara's expression turned from one of arrogance to something resembling fear. The commandant, still furious with her confidante for vesting upon Tibon the responsibility of Council member, took a step forward.

"Don't be stupid." Najara backed into a hedge. "I need you, and you need me."

"I'm wondering if that's true." The conversation had taken a dangerous turn, and Rex Ruga knew she was nearing a point of no return. *It's not time for this. Not yet.* "I'm sorry. The sermon … umm … was quite an emotional one, and hearing the bells … as well as thinking about the execution … I …"

"My dear, it is forgotten. And there will be no execution today."

"Why's that?"

"The prisoners have escaped."

"What!" exclaimed Rex Ruga. "How?"

"No one knows. We were able to catch one of them, but the two Adept brothers somehow slipped out through the Crypts."

"How did they find those tunnels?"

"It looks like they had inside help."

"From?"

Najara inspected one of the Temple's spires. "A certain girl with whom I believe you are familiar."

"What are you talking about?"

"According to your report, you had a run-in but days ago."

"Th … that foolish girl? I can't even remember her name."

"Sabine."

"Right, Sabrine. She ... uh ... assaulted me in the halls, and I was fortunate there were others to help me."

The confidante raised an eyebrow. "She must be a vicious girl to assault one who speaks so casually of wringing necks."

Rex Ruga had no answer. "You said you captured one?"

"Well, to some extent, yes. Gorgios's pack found him first, in the fourth spire's common room, so I'm afraid he had little time to tell us anything of use."

"I need to speak with Gorgios. Now!"

"Oh, he's already on the hunt."

"Of course, he is." The commandant gritted her teeth, unsure whether to be grateful for her Master of Arms' initiative or curse him for taking off without her.

"There's something else." Najara paused. "During their escape, the Adepts bumped into Tibon. Suffice to say, they left him grievously injured."

Rex Ruga's heart leapt at the news. "Is he dead?"

"No, but he has yet to awake."

"The Council seat?"

Najara made her way toward one of the Temple's entrances. "You should know there's more to life than Council seats, dear."

"A strange comment coming from you."

"There's a lot about me you don't know."

"Is that so?"

The confidante turned to face Rex Ruga. "Yes, and there's a lot about yourself you don't know, either. Now that there are only three functional senators present in this Temple, our work has gotten more interesting, and it's time for you to grow up."

"Two senators."

"Dear, you will not harm Vasant, under my strict command."

"I'm leaving to find the Adepts."

"No. That's what Gorgios is for."

"Gorgios will kill them just like the first escaped prisoner, he has no restraint. I want them here, alive."

"So you can be the one to kill them instead?"

Ignoring the question, Rex Ruga followed Najara down the Stairs of Judgment. *Obviously, that's why. Those Adepts are my prize and no one else's. If Gorgios slashes their throats somewhere in the Woods of Murcavis, I risk a significant loss.* Her plan had been perfect, with a coin flip so moronic, it actually worked. And, as always, details of the incident were already morphing into exaggerated tales, much to the commandant's delight. In fact, she had even made sure to leak several sensational versions of the events. Discord always made for more intrigue, Najara taught her early on. The old woman had employed her own tactics that very morning by opting to broadcast the Adepts' escape with a loud concert of bells.

A pair of Overseers was still in the dungeons surveying a cell when the women walked in. Behind them, a body lay underneath a sheet, and another Overseer was slouched on a stool with a pack of ice on his neck. Upon seeing their commandant, they stood at attention.

"What happened here?" asked Najara.

Cyrus spoke up. "I was on my routine inspection of the dungeons. Out of nowhere, I get hit in the head. Wake up, they're gone, and this one's dead."

"And your observations?" the confidante asked another. "Is this accurate?"

"None of the cell doors were opened by force. So the prisoners used a key to get out. And we found these ceramic shards on the ground. Given he's got the nasty bruise on the rear of his head, I think the story checks out."

"They used your keys?" Najara asked Cyrus.

He bowed his head. "I suppose."

"What terrible luck!" exclaimed the confidante. She paced back and forth. "If only you hadn't been in the dungeons." The old woman paused. "Again, what were you doing down here?"

"Routine inspection, ma'am," replied Cyrus.

"Is that so? I've checked past inspection reports, and not once was your name registered on any of them."

"I was covering for a friend."

"Who?"

"Uh … Matthias."

"Matthias was killed yesterday."

Cyrus cringed. "Um … that's why I was covering for him."

"By the Gods!" Rex Ruga stunned her subordinates with her brazen language. "You're lying."

"No, I didn't let them out, I swear it!"

"You did come down here to save her, didn't you?" prodded Najara.

He lowered his eyes to the ground.

"Save who?" asked the commandant. "Sabrine?"

"I think it's Sabine."

"Whatever!" It was starting to make sense to Rex Ruga. "And the Adepts somehow snatched your keys when you let her out?"

Appearing to be studying the floor, Cyrus kept silent.

"Commandant," said one of the Overseers. "We'll bring him straight to the Court of Justice and—"

Najara interrupted. "You will do no such thing." She handed them the torch. "In fact, we found no one down here, understood?"

They looked at the confidante, not knowing what was expected from them.

"You may leave."

The two men walked away. While going up the stairs, one of them glanced back, curiosity getting the best of him. He caught Najara say something about wringing necks, and there was just enough light to see Rex Ruga's hands wrapped around the traitor's throat.

CHAPTER TWENTY-TWO

Thousands of villagers trudged along the ravaged dirt path. Most were exhausted and restless, having likely walked for days from their small towns in the outskirts of the Dominion. Phaidros, their ultimate destination, was nearing.

"How far to the Temple?" yelled out one man.

The query prompted several grunts.

"Where are the Overseers?" someone else shouted.

The three fugitives watched a woman walking on Merchants Road. She wore overworked leather boots and a green dress tattered and washed out by the sun. Wrapped around her midsection, a gray shawl held what appeared to be a baby. The mother turned toward the woods. "Everything is fine, little Matthias. We're almost there."

Bringing a hand up to his mouth, Kyran averted his brother's sharp stare. He fought the urge to laugh. *Matthias, of all names?*

"We just need to get out of here," Edvon whispered.

"And go where?" asked Sabine. "Isn't Merchants Road the only safe way through these woods?"

"Yes, but there must be …" The Adept looked at the thick cluster of jakarhandas behind them.

"I'm not going in there."

"Those are rumors, ghosts don't exist."

"Actually," interjected Kyran, "I don't want to go in there, either."

The reply from Edvon was undiplomatic and rather

scathing. "No one asked you."

"Why can't we just wait for them to pass?"

"We're being chased, remember? We can't remain in hiding forever, at some point someone will see us. And if—"

The sound of a gong interrupted Edvon.

"What—" Kyran paused as the gong resonated a second time, "—was that?"

To their dismay, a large group of Overseers was waving and shouting greetings as it approached the refugees.

"Gods." Without another word, Edvon darted into the forest and disappeared from sight.

The abruptness of his departure stunned Sabine. "Where … where did he go?"

"We have no choice but to find out."

The young woman shook her head. Taking a deep breath, she too vanished among the trees, and Kyran followed close behind. They ran after Edvon for several minutes, dodging low-hanging branches and leaping over protruding roots. A narrow stream came into sight, and the escapees slowed down as they approached its banks. They took time to recover, listening to the sound of trickling water.

Edvon massaged his tired temples. The day had been long and exhausting, constantly hiding at the sight of other travelers. At one point, they had spent more than an hour behind thick bushes, waiting for a large caravan to move along. The forest was cold and somber, yet it provided for a quicker means of transportation. *If we don't get lost.*

"Now what?" Sabine's eyes were darting from tree to tree, as if she expected a monster to come careening out.

When her shifting gaze crossed Edvon's, it gave him a troublesome feeling. He had come to realize, granted only in the aftermath of their escape from the Temple, that Sabine was beautiful. *Quite stunning for a woman.*

"It's getting dark," she continued. "What are we going to do?"

"I think if we walk upstream, we hit the Wimau River." Edvon had earned a perfect score in Dominion Geography. "Which would then guide us to Fermantis."

And so for an hour, they followed the winding creek. In synchrony with the fading daylight, the temperature had dropped, causing the young companions to shiver. Mind over matter, they were trudging through the woods when a modest clearing came into view. An older SPC was parked along the trees.

"Wh—whose is that?" Sabine's teeth clattered as she spoke.

Edvon frowned. "Keep your voices down."

They cautiously approached, and a pleasant wave of warmth hit their faces. Sitting in front of a campfire, a lone man was reading from a well-worn parchment. He bolted to his feet. "Who are you?" His hand was wrapped around the haft of a knife fastened to his belt.

"Umm … Broque, sir," said Edvon. "And these are my friends. We mean you no harm."

Broque? Kyran grimaced.

The man pulled his fingers away from the weapon. Donning a thin beard that extended to his sternum and a round bonnet covering his ears, he could have been a merchant with his long vest and tight black stockings. "Name's Volos. What're you doing walking through the forest?"

"We … umm …"

"You what, huh?"

"We're hunters."

"Oh! Is that so? And what do you hunt?"

"Whatever we can catch."

Volos laughed. He turned around and walked back to the fire, kneeling and tending to it with a wooden stick. "Liars. You're Overseers from Phaidros, aren't you?"

"Well—"

"Yes, exactly," interjected Sabine. "Would you be so kind as to share your fire with us?"

Both Adepts prepared to object, but Volos was looking at Sabine with a salacious eyebrow. "Of course, my dear."

The young woman hurried to sit by the warm flames. "Thank you."

Volos broke the awkward silence. "It's incredible, just incredible, what's happening."

"Umm, what's happening?" asked Kyran as he and his brother sat next to Sabine.

"Another village wiped out last week. The one closest to mine, if you can believe it. All burned. No survivors."

The newly minted campers averted each other's gaze.

"Whole houses razed to the ground. No sign as to what's caused it!" cried out Volos. "There's mass hysteria out there in the countryside right now, let me tell you. That's right, let me tell you."

"That's … uh … crazy."

"I sure don't want to end up like the others. Fourteen villages destroyed."

Edvon remained composed and attempted to contribute to the conversation. "We saw some villagers when we crossed Merchants Road."

"Is that so? Is it?" The light coming from the fire engulfed Volos's long beard and pointed cheekbones, while the top of his head remained hidden away in the shadows of the night. "And where will they go?"

"They're going straight to the Temple," said Sabine.

"Where they'll be fed, given clean clothes, lodged, and—"

"Indoctrinated?"

The young woman turned to Kyran with a deathly stare and was about to respond, when Volos diverted their attention with a delayed laughing fit.

"Right on, boy!" he exclaimed between coughs.

The man was bizarre, Edvon had established that early on, but it was especially unusual for a villager to dislike the Temple. Outside of Phaidros, Overseers exerted more influence than Adepts, their many outposts and shrines ensuring everyone had access to the Book of Provenance's divine verses. Equally perturbing, though, was the substance of the conversation. *Are we going in the right direction?* If they were leaving Phaidros only to burn in a village, then Edvon would have entertained his brother's original suggestion. The Academy was without doubt their safest choice. *No, we'll be fine.* There were hundreds of villages in the Dominion, and only fourteen of them had been attacked. The odds were still stacked in their favor. *I mean, how could they not be?*

"You hungry?" asked Volos. He left no time for an answer. "Then, why don't we eat what you've hunted?" The villager laughed at his own joke. "I'm just kidding. And in any case, I eat from the earth. You, girl!"

Sabine lifted her head in his direction.

"Get up and walk to that tree."

She hesitated.

"Go on. Go!"

"Wait a second, she doesn't have to—"

"Trust me," urged the merchant. "Just go!"

Sabine walked toward the tree.

"You see on the ground there? Mushrooms. Why don't you get us some?"

The young woman bent down, and she returned with

several brownish masses in hand.

Volos took the mushrooms from her and selected the largest of the bunch, distributing the rest to the tired escapees. "Go ahead, take the first bite," he said to Sabine.

She shook her head. "Please, not me."

"Yes, you."

Closing her eyes, Sabine chomped on the mushroom. With a frown on her face, she swallowed the raw mouthful and sent Volos into yet another fit of obnoxious laughter.

"I can't believe you did that!" he exclaimed, flicking his own mushroom into the fire.

"Wh—what?"

Volos was laughing so hard, tears ran down his cheek. "Didn't think you'd actually eat that gross thing."

Sabine coughed twice and turned away from the group, gagging.

Kyran contemplated the mushroom he was holding and dropped it to the ground. Volos kept shedding tears. *Are we safe with this weirdo?* "Mister …? Are you still laughing? Or crying?"

"Both," said a voice.

A man had cropped up in the darkness, causing an already shaken Sabine to shriek. Volos instinctively sprang up. "Who are you?" he asked, a clumsy hand feeling for the knife's hilt on the side of his hip.

The visitor did not bother to answer and invited himself to sit by the fire. He wore gray robes and thick glasses over the bridge of a nose too small for his wide face. His scalp was visible under buzzed dark hair. "Want a drink?" He pulled a flask from beneath a fold in his robes.

Volos held out his arm for the receptacle and took a long, hard gulp. "Thank you, stranger. Excellent."

"Wait, who are you?" asked Kyran.

The peculiar man frowned. "I thought I told you to be quiet."

"Oh, that's right, sorry. He told me to be quiet."

"To be quiet!" Volos exclaimed.

"Quiet." Kyran mumbled the word again. "Quiet, quiet, quiet …"

The exchange was peculiar, and Sabine turned to Edvon for an explanation. She found him sitting still, a dumb look on his face. "What's going on?" The young woman pointed at the new arrival. "Haven't you only just gotten here?"

The man smiled. "I've been here for hours."

"Hah! Where have you been, girl?" clamored Volos. "Up with the birds?"

Kyran produced a sound to imitate a bird, eliciting a roar of laughter from the others. Sabine jumped to her feet, her heart racing. Everyone was acting strange. "We … we should leave," she whispered to Edvon.

"But y—you still haven't h—had a drink," the Adept answered, words slurring.

"In the name of Auralus … you too?" The young woman stepped away from the campfire, and the newcomer rose to follow her. "Leave me alone!"

"Only if you taste the drink." He held out the flask once more.

"No."

"Have some."

Sabine stumbled further backward. Her companions had yet to move, and even Volos was sitting still, gazing at nothing in particular.

"Have some," the man repeated.

"I don't want any."

"Yes, you do."

As he spoke, his head twisted, and his forehead rotated down and past his abdomen at a wicked angle. From around his waist sprouted a set of tentacles, shaking as they extended out. Sabine screamed.

"Have some." The man was distorting into a nightmarish creature. His clawed hind legs doubled in size, raising him high into the air, and he opened his mouth, revealing a foul and terrifying set of sharp teeth.

Sabine's scream got caught within her throat.

"You will have some!"

Unable to speak, she turned to escape yet tripped and fell to the ground. Spinning onto her back, Sabine found the creature on top of her, drooling and smacking its jaws. The young woman tried to move but was restrained by the beast. She attempted to catch her breath. And then, woke up in utter panic. *I … it … was just a dream.*

Sabine sat upright, rubbing her eyes. She was in a large and somber room with wooden walls covered by a tattered and decaying black material. *Where am I?* The young woman surveyed her surroundings and gasped at the sight of several small cages in a row, holding motionless bodies. *Are … are they alive?* Sabine felt sick. She spotted Edvon and Kyran lying on the ground and nudged them frantically. Both remained unconscious.

The young woman heard a creak. The man in gray robes had returned, and she fell back to the floor, pretending to be fast asleep. He was humming a simple melody, washing his hands in a sink. Only then did Sabine notice the smell of the putrid room exacerbating her nausea. Heart pounding, she cautiously opened one eye. The man was standing near the wall furthest from her. Sleeves rolled up, he bent over to turn an odd looking lever in a clockwise motion. Sabine watched in horror as a woman was lowered from the ceiling. Her hands and wrists were tied together, and she had been hanging on a hook attached to the end of a pulley, like a freshly killed geega in a market. The psychopath unhooked the poor woman and dragged her toward one of the cages.

"Now that we have fresh meat," he murmured, "you won't be needed for a while."

Sabine listened as the man lifted one of the brothers. Squinting and trying hard to ignore the odor, she watched Kyran get tied to a metal table, thick leather straps immobilizing him.

"Oh, I know, it's not time to wake up just yet. Dear me, it's hours too early. Your medicine wouldn't have worn off." The deranged man scratched his head with the tip of his index finger. "Maybe I know a way." Turning to a shelf on the wall, he perused a collection of sharp and pointed utensils. "If I could just find the right one ..."

In her own estimation, Sabine's heart was about to suffer a massive cardiovascular failure, precipitated by the vile stench permeating the place.

The man hurried to the corner of the room. "Don't go anywhere, I'll be back." He pulled up the bottom of his robes and proceeded to urinate into a big pit. Sabine started to move not fully aware of her actions. Darting toward the repulsive man, she aimed to knock him into the hole. He spun around, but it was a second too late. The young woman heard the anticipated splash.

"Ah!" the madman screamed from below. "Ah!"

Sabine crawled toward the pit and peeked over the edge. She jerked back her head, as it became evident where the horrid smell was coming from. Pinching her nose, she glimpsed once more. The man at the bottom was covered in a slimy substance. *Excrement, blood, and ... enough!* Sabine looked away.

"Let me out, let me out of here!"

Ignoring the man's pleas, the young woman raced to the

metal table, brushing the utensils to the floor.

"Throw me a rope. Help me, you must!"

Sabine sat Kyran upright, but he slumped to the side, still drugged.

"I'll die down here, there's no way out."

"Shut up!" screeched Sabine. She shook Edvon, finding he too was in a deep slumber. *Why did I, of all people, wake up before them?* None of it made any sense.

"It's too high, I can't reach. Please, let me out!"

Sabine clenched her teeth. She wanted to drop a brick on the man's head. Looking around, she noticed other crippling devices and many more ropes hanging from beams in the rafters.

"I'll die down here."

"I said shut up!"

"If you let me out, I'll tell you what I did to your friend. I swear I will."

Friend? Sabine was unsure whom he was referring to. Then it hit her. *Volos.* She brought a hand to her stomach and decided it was better not to know the villager's fate.

"Let me out!"

Sabine sat near Kyran, cupping her hands over her ears to mute the madman's shouts. And then she waited. And waited. Until the brothers regained consciousness.

"What's going on?" Edvon asked groggily.

"We need to leave," answered the young woman.

The psychopath heard the new voice. "Wait, let me out!"

"Who's that?"

"I said we need to leave!" screamed Sabine. "Now!" The two stupefied Adepts followed her through a dark hallway to a door opening onto the woods. Once outside, the young woman ran as fast as she could, stopping only when her legs would carry her no farther. The others struggled to keep up.

"You need to tell us what's happening," demanded Edvon.

"We were in some sort of room … some torture chamber," she answered, "and there were knives, and … and ropes, and cages, and … by the Recital Supreme!"

"What?"

Sabine gasped. "The others."

"What others?"

"There were others in cages. We left them there!" Without another word, she retraced her steps, the bewildered Adepts blindly following once more. The psychopath's cabin came into view. It was the second worst sight.

Gorgios and his band of cutthroat Overseers were standing by the entrance. The senator brought a leg up and kicked open the front door. "Search the house! They're here somewhere." He scanned the woods, sniffing for a scent like a mad dog.

PART III

CHAPTER TWENTY-THREE

Ocean Star's bright indigo rigging contrasted with a jet-black hull as the vessel rocked in the Bay of Alboran. Phaidrosians overcrowded the docks and streets or were looking out of their windows with great anticipation. It was a venture years in the making. A group of leaders walked down the steps of the wharf and into an awaiting rowboat. Several faced the throng and waved. Through a combination of accomplishment and luck, they were the ones chosen to crew the fleet's crown jewel. It was the opportunity of a lifetime.

Aiden glanced to his left and caught Lecarn's attention. They grinned and turned their gaze toward the approaching schooner. Ocean Star's collection of ropes seemed to run aimlessly, crisscrossing each other mid-air, curling up the masts, and looping around the boom. To an amateur, the tangled mess of hoops and knots was nothing less than complete chaos. But to one who had studied them, it represented a work of art. The faint hum of the boat's engines signaled an imminent departure, and Aiden's heart leapt. Grabbing the ladder strung down Ocean Star's hull, the young man lifted himself up. Within seconds, he was on board and making his way toward the ship's bow.

Lecarn followed close behind. "You ready?"

"Yeah, I think." The two of them had become friends, having trained side by side during the past months. For inexplicable reasons, Aiden believed he could trust Lecarn with his life. "And you?"

Laughing, Lecarn dashed to his assigned position, and

Aiden shook his head. They were part of a small class of leaders in a crew of one hundred hardened sailors, and their preparations had been strenuous. Constant exercise and dieting, combined with intense nautical studies, nearly pushed Aiden to the brink. All for a rather pedestrian task, sailing as far as possible in a single direction and stopping only when the engines would force them to turn around. The entire fleet was equipped with the newest Source-powered motors, products of years spent in the Academy's refinement facilities. Despite their power, the major source manipulator had warned they would only last for two months, and not a day more. It was a margin of error that often kept Aiden awake at night.

He looked back to shore. Everyone was there to see them off. Lord Lester gave a speech at the steps of the Apex, a rousing rhetoric about the glorious Dominion and its search for something Aiden soon forgot. In an uncommon show of solidarity, Preceptor Marrek and Rex Quintus jointly delivered the keys of Phaidros to the fleet's captain. Later on, Aiden walked near the Temple's delegation. The young women were stunning, their beauty enhanced by the buzz of a preposterous adventure that provided no guarantee as to anyone's survival. Not one fisherman in the Dominion ventured beyond sight of the shoreline, it had never been done. And now, a whole fleet was being sent into the unknown.

The sound of a horn resonated throughout the bay, prompting the captain to engage full speed ahead. The crowd roared, and Aiden took a deep breath. He watched as men on the ship in front of his moved around, yanking down on sets of designated cords. An assemblage of mighty sails made its way up the masts. Realizing his own vessel was undergoing a similar transformation, Aiden spun around and was met by a flurry of activity. Lecarn could be heard bellowing orders as they accelerated. Resolute, Aiden jumped onto the railing and pointed at a cluster of ropes …

* * *

Lifting his hand from Ocean Star's railing, the chief cut short a flow of memories from the Great Expedition.

"Are you okay?" asked Criss, frowning.

"Yeah, I'm fine. Let's just … umm … let's go find the captain."

They walked across the deck. Ocean Star's marginal state, its sole purpose being to transport people and goods down the Wimau River, depressed Aiden. Ducking past a familiar set of wooden doors, the chief led the way through a narrow passageway to a ladder he used many times during his voyage two decades prior. Now, the ship carried a wealthy clientele, and the cabins were retrofitted to match their tastes. *Quite different from what I was given.* They climbed up to the captain's topside deckhouse. Aiden peeked inside.

The old man was sitting in the middle of the cabin, his elbow on a table and cheek resting in the palm of a calloused hand. Unhurried, he looked up then down, accomplishing nothing more than verifying the identity of the visitor. A weather-beaten face indicated work kept him busy. Dressed in a heavy coat that matched his dark pants, the balding captain gave off a rather unsympathetic countenance, granted one Aiden grew accustomed to long ago. "What're you here for?" He had not lost his proclivity for candor, either.

"Battalion business, I'm afraid," answered the chief.

The sailor spat into a tin cup on his desk. "Everything's up to code on this ship."

"That's not why we're here."

"By Gods, Two-Eyes, just let it out."

Surprised the captain remembered his nickname, the chief dithered about what to say.

"A suspect in a murder we're investigating was a crew member on this ship," Criss said in a formal tone. "We're going to need some information from you regarding his—"

"Oh, is that so?" The old man's eyes were now fixed on the agent.

"That's right. Can you tell us if anyone in your crew is missing?"

"Why don't you come over here, sweetheart?" The captain waved his arm. "You can sit on my lap and ask any—"

"Alright," cut in Aiden. "Enough."

"I'm your Captain, boy! You will speak when addressed."

As if hypnotized, the chief stood at attention, clacked his boots together, and raised a hand to his head in salute. "Yes sir!"

And for the first time in a while, Criss laughed.

"Very funny," muttered Aiden, embarrassed his muscle memory got the better of him.

The captain adjusted his chair. "Just kidding with you, chief." More cooperative, he proceeded to answer Criss's question. "Been missing a crew member for about a month now. Name's Drube. From some dread village, ended up running with a band down in Portown. That's where I picked him up. Was on board for a couple months."

Criss was collecting notes. "Where did he go?"

"Off the ship."

"I mean, in which city?"

"There's only one city in this dread land."

"So you're saying Phaidros?"

The captain rolled his eyes. "Is there anything else you need to know?"

"Yes." Aiden stepped forward. "Did he do anything out of the ordinary while on this ship?"

"I don't pay attention to my crew's private life." The old man spat again.

"Okay. Where did he live?"

As he rose to his feet, the captain exhaled with an exaggeration commensurate to his displeasure. He pulled out a large leather book from a shelf built into the ship's wooden hull and brought it back to the table. The sailor flipped one sheet at a time, breathing sharply with each new turn. He stopped. "Portown. Known family, a certain Zakus, brother. Also Portown."

"Why didn't you report him missing?" asked Criss.

"You think I've time to chase after every Source loving deserter? And anyway, I don't much care what a man does if he's not on this ship."

"Unless what he does is against Dominion law."

"Even if it's against Dominion law. It's just not my problem." The captain flashed them a snaggle-toothed smile. "That's what they got you two for." He slammed the book shut and returned it to the shelf. "Is there anything else I can help you with?"

"If we want to go to Portown, could you potentially arrange … you know?"

"You're more than welcome to purchase your fare, there's a ticket shop near the docks." Another spit. "I believe we're not sold out at the moment."

Aiden opened his mouth, determined it was pointless to pursue the conversation, and left.

"You want to go to Portown?" Criss asked.

"Don't you want to solve this case?" replied the chief, his tone gorged with sarcasm.

"Yes, but—"

"The guy's from Portown. He'll have living quarters there, we already know his brother's name, perhaps some friends. All potential leads. Someone has to go … I mean, it's all we've got." Aiden sighed and pushed open the doors leading to Ocean Star's deck. He walked toward the gangway and turned around to face Criss only once on shore. "What's happening?"

"Sir?"

"We're investigating arguably the biggest murder in history, and you're acting as if it's a trivial case. Why?"

"I don't know."

"It's because we have too much on our plate. When the news about the two Adepts came out, as absurd as it was, I thought it would resolve itself, but clearly not."

"Someone will find them."

"You think?"

"They can't stay hidden forever."

"I know people who have," said Aiden. "Anyway, we'll find out soon enough, now that a Temple hit squad's on the loose." He sighed yet again. "Then, the village attacks and not a dread-forsaken clue."

"And the Killer of Murcavis."

Aiden shot his colleague a quizzical look.

"It's what they're calling him," she added.

"Gods. Less than a day and they already have a name." The chief shook his head in disgust.

In the early hours of the morning, news spread that a delegation of Overseers had stumbled upon the home of a serial killer in the Woods of Murcavis. Details were still unclear. The psychopath would capture unsuspecting victims and keep them confined to the cottage where he was found. He employed a powerful narcotic, one with which Aiden had a decent amount of experience. Early in his career, he often witnessed junkies using the liquid for the hyper-realistic and powerful hallucinations it induced. Afterward, they would pass out hours on end, unable to be awakened.

"… we might want to get involved before it's too late," said Criss.

"Hmm?"

The agent rolled her eyes, frustrated with Aiden's short attention span. "I said if we want to get involved before it's too late, we might want to pay the Temple a visit instead."

The chief sighed. They had found a pit in the back of the serial killer's home, what would best be described as a waste disposal with a smell so vile, several Overseers were still feeling sick from exposure. The Battalion's inside sources submitted descriptions of the scene, and they were equally disturbing. The whole gamut of perverse tools and materials, and hardly any survivors. "You know what? I don't want anything to do with it. As far as I'm concerned, that cholee is the Temple's problem, not ours."

"But—"

"There are no buts here," interjected Aiden. "They can burn him, hang him, cut him up like a geega, I don't give a flying pip. Let's focus on our own problems first. One thing at a time."

"What if he's the one who hired the bomber? Or he's behind the village attacks?"

"Don't you keep saying these things aren't always connected?"

Criss turned around and walked toward the ticket shop.

"Where are you going?" called out the chief.

"To buy Ocean Star tickets."

"Are … are you sure?"

The nastiness of her reply was palpable. "Don't you want to solve this case?"

CHAPTER TWENTY-FOUR

He grazed his hand on her shoulder, and she leaned in a little closer. *Okay, this is it.* They sat still until, fingers trembling, the boy caressed the side of the girl's neck. Then, he tilted his head toward hers. She hesitated, but did bring her legs closer. The young couple sat motionless for what seemed like an eternity. *Come on, do it already.* The girl twisted away, and Ruan exhaled in disbelief, increasingly frustrated. *Gods, they're so scared.* The personal attendant looked up at the sky. *At this rate, they'll only kiss if I go down there and force them to.* As if she had somehow heard him, the girl turned again. And to the surreptitious spectator's delight, she laid her lips upon the boy's.

"Yes!"

The startled pair looked up and found a strange man observing them from the elevated deck of a nearby boat.

He had a scar extending down the side of his face. "Took long enough!" exclaimed Ruan.

The two grabbed their belongings and scampered away from the docks. Leaning on Ocean Star's railing, Ruan cleared his throat and spat into the water below. *They have no idea what's yet to come. All things considered, the trip to Portown will do me well. Our countryside's much more … ascetic.* The Temple's ubiquitous influence ensured most villagers considered acts involving sexual debauchery to be egregious sins. *But a prude society also produces a more erotic one.* A phenomenon the accuracy of which the personal attendant had demonstrated many times over.

A horn sounded, and he spun around, intent on making his

way down toward the ship's main deck to see the departure. *First, a stop in Fermantis.* The swamp city, home to certain locales that might otherwise be frowned upon in the capital, was always an interesting destination. Stepping off the last of the rungs leading to the boat's main deck, Ruan watched as two more passengers boarded. He had noticed them lingering around the docks and pegged them both as Battalion agents. *Or a lord and lady, perhaps? Too difficult to tell.* Regardless, Ruan had a feeling those two would somehow get in his way.

A flurry of activity interrupted the personal attendant's thoughts, suggesting they were about to leave port. Despite the absence of the captain at the helm, dock workers untied the thick ropes keeping Ocean Star tethered to land, while a group of sailors pulled in the gangway. When the captain showed up, they drifted away.

"Wait!" Two men came sliding around the corner of a side street. They tumbled to the ground, shot up, and sprinted toward Ocean Star. "Hold that boat!"

One was significantly shorter than the other, and the way they ran at the same speed made Ruan chuckle. The odd pair arrived at the edge of the dock, but Ocean Star was already out of reach.

"We have tickets!" shouted the taller one. The shorter and stouter of the two waved papers.

Ruan was mesmerized by the man, in no large part due to the incredible mustache he sported. Having never been able to grow any bristle, the personal attendant often admired the facial grooming of others. *And that is quite something.*

"It don't matter," barked the captain. "You're too late."

The bystanders expected a confrontational reply from the tardy passengers. Instead, without a word, the two men walked away. Then, they spun around in synchrony and raced toward the ship. Ruan's heart skipped a beat. Like all others on the deck, he dashed to the railing and looked over. The gap between the dock and the boat was at least a couple body lengths, and it kept widening.

"Stop!" the captain ordered.

Delighted to be witnessing such a bizarre scene, Ruan laughed. Even the sailors were watching with anticipation, some quick enough to place wagers on the upcoming leap's success.

"St—"

Joss and Pluto went soaring into the air. The gap had grown to three body lengths in Ruan's estimation, and he wondered how they would make it. Both flapping their arms, as if the motion might help them maintain altitude, the jumpers progressed toward Ocean Star. For a moment, time seemed suspended.

Pluto somehow managed to clasp the bottom railing of the deck. And while Joss came nowhere near doing so, he latched onto his friend's ankle, an exploit saving him from a tumble into the cold water below. The onlookers were stunned.

"Incredible."

"Did you just see that?"

"Amazing."

Aiden was the first to rush over, helping the two men onto the boat. "What a jump. Are you okay?"

Several sailors reached out to pat Pluto on the back but found their arms intercepted by a grip of steel. The livid captain yanked them away and came face-to-face with the two performers. "What in the Gods are you doing?"

They're about to get thrown overboard. Ruan opted to keep his distance.

It took Pluto only a few minutes to blather his way out of it. "… and that's why you should never give a kitchen boy more than five minutes to grill a balbak rib and—"

"Yeah, yeah, whatever," cut in the captain, at that point only seeking to avoid having to hear anymore of the ridiculous explanation. "Just go to your cabins."

The performers were about to dart away when something caught their attention. Ruan followed their fixated gazes to a short woman watching the entire scene with bemusement. Her long dark hair swayed in the light breeze. The personal attendant found her to be ... *striking.*

"What are you waiting for?" the captain yelled. "I said go!"

Pluto and Joss obliged, disappearing into the ship. As the rest of the crowd dispersed, Ruan, casual, made his way to the alluring woman. "How's it going?"

The way she looked up and assessed the personal attendant made him sweat. Beneath her black eyes lurked excitement and trouble.

"Did you think they'd make it?" she asked.

"You mean the jump?"

The woman nodded.

"No," lied Ruan.

"Seriously? I would have expected another answer."

"And why's that?"

"You seem like someone who likes taking risks."

"My scar, you mean?" The personal attendant brought his fingers to the side of his face. "That wasn't from a risk I took."

"What scar?"

Ruan smiled. "It's fine, there's no need to apologize."

"You sure like to flatter yourself, don't you?" She shook her head. "I wasn't talking about your scar, by Gods!"

"I—I think it was a reasonable misunderstanding."

"Well, I don't."

They stood in silence for a moment.

"Where are you going?" asked the woman.

"Portown."

"Me too."

"Then you'll join me for dinner in Fermantis?"

"Dinner?" She laughed. "Why waste my time with that when I could be in the Undergrounds?"

"The Undergrounds?"

"Come find me there, if you're up to it." The woman winked and walked away.

Ruan was impressed. *You can count on that.* He wandered back to his cabin and lay in bed, staring out the porthole. *Might be a good idea to get some rest.* The leg to Fermantis was the shorter one. They would arrive by early afternoon, spend the night and morning in the swamp city, prior to embarking on a full day's journey to Portown. It was a long trip, curtailed by the Dominion's pride of the sea.

Once it became evident no other lands existed, the Noble Assembly had not wasted time in repurposing Ocean Star. After all, the Wimau River was the fastest means of transportation across the Dominion. A river race even took place every year, pitting the quickest Source-powered motorboats against each other in a southbound dash from the capital to Portown. The record was on the verge of seven hours, though Ruan was willing to sacrifice speed for the luxury of his cabin and the additional stop in a city with little Phaidrosian oversight. *So long as I can avoid those dreadful Saryn plates.* It was far too easy losing money playing the villagers' favorite game.

They were now picking up serious speed, and the Woods of Murcavis flew by in a blur of green and brown. Merchants Road came into a fleeting view and vanished again. Ruan dozed to the rhythm of the rocking boat, until his eyelids fluttered open. The scene out of his porthole remained unchanged, identical trees interwinding with a moderately crowded Merchants Road. Unable to resist any longer, Ruan fell asleep for several hours.

Late in the afternoon, Ocean Star decelerated as she entered the perimeter of the swamp. Fermantis emerged, its expansive docks and elaborate network of canalizations exposed. Ruan exhaled in relief, eager to get off the ship. After his lengthy nap, he had been up and down restless, pacing the decks and passageways, looking at the Wimau stretching into the horizon. As soon as the gangway was put in place, the personal attendant rushed onto firm land. He hated confinement, and the boat, despite its opulence, was nothing but a large container.

Ruan paused to see where the others were headed. Pluto and Joss walked right by him and scampered straight into town, while the two Battalion agents followed a smaller canal to the north at a more leisurely pace. The dark-haired woman did not disembark. Disappointed, the personal attendant loitered around the docks in hopes she might still show up, but his hunger grew too important to ignore, especially in view of the numerous eateries to choose from. *The fried balbak at The Free Adept is the best I've ever had. Or maybe I'll go to Harsh Marsh Inn for their clam chowder. Mmmh. The Red Room? Closed ... What about the balbak special at Farm-and-Teas? I can't miss that.* Ruan raced toward the archway leading to the city center. The guards, positioned in response to the village attacks, were busy chatting and waved him through.

Fermantis boasted a large network of roadways and canals that funneled into a main square known for its fountain depicting the Cave of Dust and Bones. Of all the figures in the Book of Provenance, the hermits had accrued by far the longest narrative. Their home among the stalactites and the stalagmites was where the great heroes trekked for advice, starting with the first Overseer legend Lutigas and ending with Baratna, the final descendant in the line of Temple creators. The Fermantese rendition of the hermits had them hunching over in hooded cloaks that blended into the stone of the fountain, making the sculpture difficult to discern. A work of art befitting this complex city.

Swamp urban planning epitomized the ideals of disorder, with its mishmash of congested homes extending haphazardly, over the walkways, below ground, into the air. There were lodgings propped up by stilts high above the canals. Many of the wooden dwellings were connected by makeshift bridges and internal routes known only to locals. On a previous visit, Ruan had become lost in a network of buildings for hours on end, a mistake he did not want repeated. It was getting dark, and the personal attendant watched the Source-powered street lanterns flicker to life. They gave off a warm light, and he loved to stare at their reflection in the water, especially after frequenting one of the city's vintage smoking cellars.

The wait at Farm-and-Teas was too long, so he settled on a communal bench at the Harsh Marsh Inn where a hot trough of clams fed anyone to their heart's desire. *Anyone with enough coins, that is.* Feeling bloated far too fast, Ruan paid his bill and stumbled toward the main square. He approached Hermits Fountain and dipped his fingers in the water, wondering what the night might bring. *The Undergrounds* … It had been a while since he last visited the prominent dance room, that memory being particularly hazy. *I want to find her.* Ruan ventured along a side street. *She could be fun.* Zigzagging around the swamp city, he found a wooden bridge marked by a dozen Source-powered lanterns dangling from its railings. Across the way, a line of people had formed in front of a nondescript establishment. The attendant took his place behind them. *Appears to be moving swiftly.* Once inside, he walked down a set of rickety steps barely kept together. *It's only a matter of time before this totally collapses.* The Undergrounds had been dug out by amateurs with no experience in shifting sands and moving tides. *A problem for another night.* Ruan pushed open a last set of doors.

The music, muffled until then, hit him like a brick. And so did the heat and smell of energy. The partygoers were shaking their bodies, jumping frantically, and waving their arms to the beat. On stage, musicians banged on huge drums and other Source-powered instruments, creating a metallic and exciting sound that kept re-invigorating the adrenalized crowd.

Ruan was about to join in when someone grabbed him by the shoulder.

"Hey you," she said.

CHAPTER TWENTY-FIVE

Worn out, Sabine sat and leaned against a large tree trunk. Gazing up, she spotted a bird hopping along the lone dead branch of an otherwise leafy tree. It darted in erratic spurts, then stopped and stared at the ground, head cocked. The round body flaunted a long tail, short thin legs, and a brown coat glistening in the sun. Its yellow underbelly rapidly inflated and deflated, a movement the young woman found appeasing.

The creature leaped off the branch and furiously tugged an earthworm from the dirt, then flew back to a concealed nest in the forest. *Soaring freely through the air, not a thought on its mind.* Sabine sighed, envious yet forgetting the bird was on a constant task to feed its chicks. Never had she experienced a compulsion to fly away, escaping her worries ... *and fears. Everyone's out to get me.* Sabine had trouble understanding why. *What have I done to deserve this?* She glanced at the brothers. *And why am I still with those two?* Their time together was bizarre, like a nightmare, but for an odd reason, staying with the Adepts felt like the right thing to do. Her thoughts were reciprocated, given they had yet to kick her out. In reality, each brother was dealing with the situation differently. Witty and chatty, Kyran appeared to lack any appreciation for the grave circumstances. Edvon remained quiet and focused on moving them ahead in the journey.

"Maybe you've been exposed to it in the past?"

Sabine turned to face Kyran, irritated. "I already told you what happened."

"Do you seriously think the Gods came down here to wake

you up?"

"Yes, They saved us."

"You are—" Kyran paused for added emphasis, "—out of your mind."

Edvon snorted. "It was that stupid mushroom you ate."

"What?"

"Must have reacted as an antidote to his drug, whatever it was."

"Hmm," mused the younger brother. "That does make sense."

"I don't believe it," said Sabine.

"Oh, enough of your Gods." Kyran exhaled sharply as Edvon nudged him on the shoulder. "I do remember him offering us a sip from his flask. But for the love of Cholee, I can't remember drinking."

Sabine's eyes widened. "Watch your mouth!"

"Oh please, you think the Gods can hear me all the way from their Red City?"

"Well, they heard my prayers."

Gritting his teeth, Kyran was resolved to prove her position's lack of logic. "Okay, so you're saying the Gods listened to your prayers and woke you up? Well, did you pray to them while asleep?"

"No, how could I do that?"

"Exactly. What you're saying is nonsense."

"I pray to them every day," replied Sabine, refusing to surrender. "And anyway, I don't care about your opinion."

"Good, because I think the only God worth praying to is Cholee."

The young woman let out a gasp. "How dare you!"

"Alright, I've heard enough," interjected Edvon. "Can we concentrate on getting into this city?"

Kyran and Sabine looked away from each other.

Their elevated position at the edge of the woods offered an unobstructed view of Fermantis, which sat on an expansive swampland stretching to the horizon. The city was accessible only via the Wimau River or Merchants Road, and it boasted an impressive number of man-made canals and waterways converging onto the docks. There, laborers loaded crates on riverboats destined for either Phaidros to the north, or Portown and the smaller villages to the south. The main square in the center was lively, with a picturesque fountain and locals walking along rows of stalls where merchants sold their wares.

It was still early morning, the sun peeking out from the skyline, and already Edvon yearned for another night's sleep. He observed a pack of balbaks scampering across the swamp. *We'll need to follow the river for a long time before we can feel safe.* And even then, only the most remote villages were free of Overseers. Edvon had no plan in mind, and it disheartened him. His agitation was exacerbated by the two others who kept interrupting his thoughts with obtuse questions.

"Why are we even going in there?" asked Sabine.

"There's no other way around," Edvon answered.

"Not even way around?"

"Do you want to walk that?"

"I guess not."

Edvon pressed on. "What would you eat?"

"I'm not sure," Sabine replied.

"Where would you find shelter?"

"Okay," intervened Kyran, "we get the point."

"Great," said an increasingly angry Edvon. "Now how do we get into this city, by Gods?" His brother's proposal saved him from being chastised for the profane language.

"Why don't we just hide in plain sight?" Kyran shrugged.

"Let's just walk in there as if nothing's wrong."

"Are you crazy?" asked Edvon. "The city's swarming with Overseers."

"How would they know what we look like?"

The older sibling paused. "I don't know, and I'd rather not find out. So let's just sneak in like, well, regular fugitives."

"That's exactly the kind of suspicious behavior they'll be looking for, and—"

With no forewarning, Sabine left the cover of the trees, stepped out onto Merchants Road, and headed toward Fermantis. The Adepts, with little time to react, followed the young woman.

Kyran called out as they were catching up to her. "What's wrong with you?"

She stopped and swung around. "This was your idea, so just be quiet, by Lutigas!"

They walked in total silence while each formulated indisputable opinions that they kept to themselves. When the ground turned too wet, Merchants Road rose on stilts, protecting travelers from the swamp. Sabine, Kyran, and Edvon followed the elevated pathway to one of the city's side gates. A guard was asleep in the otherwise empty archway, and Edvon gestured to stroll straight through.

"Wait!"

The guard had awakened and risen to his feet. "Trying to sneak in, weren't you?"

"No sir," Kyran replied, his voiced marred by excessive urgency.

"Are you residents of the city?"

"Umm … we're not, I guess."

"Why would you need to guess?" asked the guard.

"What … I—"

"Just joking, my friend. So if you're not residents, what

brings you to Fermantis?"

"We're visiting."

"From where?"

"Phaidros."

The guard noticed the desperate condition of their clothes, giving him pause. "What's going on here?" He pointed at the tears in Sabine's dress. "Were you in a village attack?"

"Oh, this?" replied Sabine as she pulled on the fabric. "They're our costumes, silly. It's part of the act."

"You're performers?"

"That's right."

"What kind of act?"

Sabine smiled and grabbed both Adepts by the arm. "We're dancers." She proceeded to move her feet up and down, twirling them around in various nonsensical steps. Kyran and Edvon joined in, and the three, linked at the elbows, danced horribly in front of the guard.

"Okay, okay!" he exclaimed, pleading for them to stop. "Where are you performing tonight?"

Kyran chose an ambiguous reply. "Only the best."

"You mean the Red Room?"

"Uh … yeah, exactly."

"I thought the Red Room closed for good last year?" The Fermantese smirked, pleased by his crafty trap.

"Oh, you didn't know?" pressed Kyran.

"What?"

"They re-opened last month."

"Seriously?"

"Yep, new location. And by the looks of it, they've been, like, successful."

"Hmm, good to know." The guard nodded. "Alright. Enjoy your time in Fermantis. Break a leg!"

Kyran fought off an urge to heave a sigh of relief and followed his friends through the gates. A few streets further, they erupted into a fit of laughter.

"Dancers?" Edvon asked.

"More like clowns. Can't believe he fell for—"

"Watch out!" exclaimed Sabine.

They pressed up against the wall as a group of Overseers marched by. Not one of them batted an eye in the fugitives' direction. Kyran smirked. "Well, look who was right. I think we might actually be safe in this town."

"Don't be so sure." The ever-stern brother was not to be upstaged. "We should head to the docks as soon as possible and get on the first boat to Portown."

"Can't we eat, first?"

"It's too risky. And with what money, anyway?"

Sabine tilted her head back and removed her earrings. "These can sell for a couple coins, I'm sure." The young woman held two pieces of jewelry in her palm.

"Do they mean anything to you?" asked Kyran.

"Not really.

"Are you sure?"

"Yes, and I'm also super hungry."

They searched for the nearest eatery in the disorienting city. Farm-and-Teas, the first such establishment the trio stumbled upon, had a line of patrons stretching to the adjacent canal. So they continued to explore and came to an intersection, finding themselves on a busy street. *Is that fried balbak?* Kyran salivated, unconcerned as another group of Overseers walked by and paid no attention to the runaways. *And clam chowder?* A shout put an end to his gustatory contemplation.

The brothers and Sabine turned around, and their hearts dropped.

Gorgios was across the way, his rabid pack of Overseers at his sides, and he was pointing directly at them.

"Kill!"

The companions ran off in three different directions.

CHAPTER TWENTY-SIX

Her eyes followed the back wall from the ceiling down to the floor. It pitched in such a way that it produced a triangular shape, most likely to conceal ship machinery. From the floor, she continued to trace a trajectory, across the ravishing desk, with its generous spread of paper and quills, to the carved wooden door, an original antique. *Or made to look like one, at least.* Proceeding diagonally, her gaze twirled around the paintings on the wall, then went back to the ceiling where she had started. Along with most guests aboard Ocean Star, Neeta was amazed by the luxury of the cabins, the personal water closets, soft carpets, and large beds. *Which I've already put to good use, it would appear.*

She could feel him moving as he adjusted his arm around her waist. The Adept reached down to grab his hand, and their fingers interlaced. She pulled him in a little closer, their naked legs rubbing against one another. Neeta felt his manhood against the small of her back. *Still rocklike.* He repositioned himself, most likely embarrassed. *Men are so stupid.* She wanted him tight against her, intensely passionate. *Otherwise, what's the point of cuddling?* She closed her eyes. *Cuddling?* Neeta shot up her head as if she had just awakened from a dream. *What am I doing?* Letting go of his hand, she spun around. "Why in the Gods are you in my bed?"

"I … wh—what?" Ruan stammered.

"How did you get in?"

"What are you talking about? We came back together last night, remember?"

"Get out!"

Ruan made the mistake of trying to discuss the matter. "I'm very confused, is there a reason—"

"I said leave, you cholee!"

Taken aback by her aggressive behavior, Ruan scampered off the bed. He fumbled for his clothes on the ground, and Neeta yelled once more. "Out!"

Still naked, Ruan took one last look at her and left the cabin. Neeta heard a woman's shout of indignation coming from the hallway. The Adept let out a lengthy and affected sigh, sat up, and ran a hand through her long black hair. *What in the Gods happened last night?* She remembered being in the Undergrounds for hours on end, but the return to Ocean Star appeared a bit blurry. Neeta knew he had come into the cabin with her consent, and she cursed herself for being so halfwitted. *This is my big chance. I can't blow it. If I want to succeed, I should have been out in Fermantis at the crack of dawn, checking every street and alleyway.* Marrek was offering a significant opportunity, and she needed to pounce.

The officer was proud of herself for predicting Elias's demise, though she also pitied him. He was sitting on his patio, gazing in awe at his plants when he heard the anticipated commotion. Elias took a deep breath and marched to meet them, ready to be led to his execution. Neeta knew Marrek had no intention of reprimanding Elias. *Not directly, anyway.* But his message had been clear.

* * *

"Whoever finds the brothers will also find his or her responsibilities increased," the preceptor said, ending the meeting. He called out for Neeta to stay behind. "I know the way Edvon thinks. He's already left Phaidros, I have no doubt."

"But ... didn't you tell us to search the city?"

"A precaution," Marrek replied, stroking his chin. "They will hide in a remote village, and the only way to get to those is—"

"Through Portown."

"Exactly. And if you get there fast enough—"

"I'll be in position, awaiting their arrival," interjected Neeta, intent on completing the preceptor's sentences.

Marrek handed her a paper. "Here, take this."

"What is it?"

"An Ocean Star ticket."

Neeta raised an eyebrow. "Sir?"

"This situation calls for extreme measures. I want you on the fastest boat, and we got lucky. It's leaving tomorrow morning." The preceptor reached behind his desk and pulled out a package. "When you arrive in Portown, please deliver this to the tavern boy at the Golden Auralus."

Neeta held the small box. "May I ask what it contains?"

"The package?" Marrek smiled. "Personal matters unrelated to this, I'm afraid." A frown on Neeta's face prompted him to subtly invoke his rank at the Academy. "Surely you can do me a little favor along the way, no?"

"Of—of course," stuttered the officer. "Consider it done."

* * *

The box was still sitting on the cabin floor near the desk, and Neeta attempted to ignore it. *Gods, I want to tear that wrapping open.* Curiosity had been a predominant trait of hers since early childhood. *I wonder what's inside. Did the preceptor have a love affair? Or maybe he gambled too much in Mira, and that's his payoff money.* Neeta let out another exaggerated sigh. *Too much speculation for someone who hasn't even smoked yet.*

She left the bed, pulling the sheet along and draping it around her. Neeta went into the washroom where she found her tube of lipstick near the sink and brought it to the desk. She pulled out a small leather sachet from a drawer. The officer unscrewed a hidden container affixed to the bottom of the lipstick tube and poured in finely crushed herbs from the sachet. After twisting the container back into place, she opened its cap. Neeta applied gentle pressure to the base, until it snapped out. Swiveling ninety degrees, the lipstick gave way to a small, retractable mouthpiece.

The Adept opened the porthole and felt the fresh air enter the cabin. The lipstick tube was getting warm in her hand, an indication the little Source-powered device was functioning well. Her lips sealed on the mouthpiece, Neeta inhaled once, waited several seconds, and blew vapor out of the circular window. She swung the top half of the lipstick tube back into place, and a click confirmed the apparatus had shut properly.

As it should for someone who had practiced it so many times, the undertaking lasted less than a minute. Neeta walked back to the bed and sat down, contemplating the objective at hand. *Why am I doing this? It's not for money. It's not for fame. I guess it's for my career, then … But why? What would a higher position at the Academy give me? Power? Responsibility? No, I'm doing it for the reputation, for the way I'll be remembered. Is that what reputation means? How someone's remembered? Who cares about how they remember you if you aren't alive to witness it.*

The inundating stream of thoughts brought on by the generous application of lipstick seemed to die down for a moment, so Neeta got back on her feet to get dressed. Most people in the Dominion shared her views on mortality. Years past, a faction had preached ascension to the Red City upon death, but like any other religious sect, the Temple viciously stamped it out. *It doesn't make sense.* Neeta shook her head. *Why would the Gods ever want us, of all people, in their Red City?*

Once dressed, the Adept left her cabin, adamant that she would locate Edvon and Kyran. A frustrating task, for Neeta had no idea whether the brothers were in Fermantis. *Like playing hide and seek with someone who's left the house.* Then again, they had to be somewhere. *And if they're here?* Midway through Ocean Star's deck, Neeta bumped into the captain. "Oh, perfect, it's you."

"Why's that?" he asked.

"When does the ship leave?"

"Any of my sailors can answer that kind of question."

"Okay, good to know." Neeta's smile oozed insincerity. "But when do we leave?"

Irritated, the captain glanced at his pocket watch. "Six hours."

"Thanks." Neeta walked away, pleased at having inconvenienced the unfriendly captain. She proceeded to search the town and soon came to the realization her mission was unreasonable. Bored and unsuccessful, the Adept made her way back to the docks. She wanted to rest on Ocean Star and start afresh prior to departure. The captain was walking the gangway again. Neeta watched him march past the city gates and vanish down an alleyway. From the corner of her eye, she caught movement and saw a figure dashing from behind a set of crates toward Ocean Star. The man made it up the ship's ramp unnoticed. Intrigued, Neeta hurried after him and arrived on deck just in time to see him sneak through a hatch, one that led to the cargo bay below. The Adept followed the man to Ocean Star's hull. She poked her head around the corner and saw him frantically inspecting his surroundings. He turned in Neeta's direction. *Edvon.* Heart palpitating, the Adept forced herself to calm down. When she looked into the room once more, the young man was standing right in front of her.

"Neeta?"

She stepped out of her hiding place. "Edvon, what are you doing here?"

"Trying to find a place where I won't be killed!" he exclaimed, waving his arms.

"Okay, take it easy. Marrek sent me to help you."

"Have you found my brother?"

"No." Neeta frowned. "I thought you were together."

Edvon brought his hands to his face. "He might be dead."

"What do you mean?"

"The Overseers found us, and we ran, and … they were shouting the Recital Supreme … and …"

"And?"

"I don't know … I—I need to go back out there and find him."

Neeta put a hand on the Adept's forearm. "Come to my cabin, it's safe and comfortable, and we can talk more there."

Edvon's hesitation was clear.

"To make a plan," she added.

He walked behind her to the upper decks. Neeta unlocked her cabin and beckoned Edvon to go in first. But rather than following him, she slammed the door shut, locking the Adept inside.

CHAPTER TWENTY-SEVEN

"Where are they?"

Silence.

"Tell me!" the giant bellowed. "Tell me where they're hiding!"

"I d—don't know ..." The young woman was whimpering.

The slap on her face made a sickening sound, and onlookers cringed. Joss and Pluto rushed to join the crowd of Fermantese gathered near Hermits Fountain. They were watching a group of Overseers conducting a public interrogation of an alleged traitor. The besieging Overseers donned short white tunics, sleeveless and held firm by leather belts from which various weaponry dangled. "What in the Gods is going on?" The pack was ruthless and malicious, at least according to Pluto. Joss shuttered as another outburst resonated throughout the square.

"Tell me now!" The Overseer who kept shouting was immense, at least a good foot taller than his nearest companion. Not that the others were undersized, by any means. "It will only get worse for you. You filthy little traitor."

Pluto's laugh caught the attention of a few locals and Overseers. Oblivious, he turned to Joss. "This must be some kind of street theatre." The mustached man nodded, equally keen to watch the performance. After all, they owed a duty to support their brethren, no matter the medium. With a firm grip around her slender wrist, Gorgios yanked Sabine back toward him. She cried out for help, shaking her arm to free herself. Joss shot his friend a sharp look. "Well, she's obviously not the best actor," said Pluto.

A disruption in the crowd revealed a new character, an arrogant town official in fancy attire. Pushing the last spectators out of his way, the man strutted into the center of the circle. "What's going on here?"

The small group of short white tunics approached the man, who seemed to be regretting his decision to get involved.

"Temple business," said Gorgios.

"But ... I—"

"Temple business," repeated the ominous Overseer.

The town official had heard enough. "There's nothing to see here, people. Go on your ways!"

While most in the crowd shouted back, complaining of the Overseers' treatment of the young woman, Pluto instead bobbed his head in admiration of the town official's performance. It had been the one needed to save the show. "Boy, this guy's good," he whispered to Joss.

"Come on people, go along!" Seeing that nobody obeyed his command, the town official squeezed back through the crowd and receded from view.

Pluto and Joss gave him an enthusiastic clap before turning their attention back to the main stage. With no further interruptions, Gorgios had again immobilized Sabine who screamed out for help and fell to the ground. Grabbing her hair, the mammoth Overseer pulled the young woman off the cobblestones, and she cried out once more, tears streaming down her bruised cheek. Pluto rolled his eyes, finding the scene to be forced. "Gods, she's so bad."

"What did you just say?" asked a woman next to them.

"Just awful acting," Pluto whispered back. "She's detracting from the entire—"

The sound of another smack permeated through the air. An infuriated Gorgios had again resorted to physical violence, but this time, someone in the crowd spoke out.

"Hey! You can't just hit her like that."

Gorgios ignored the objection, but Vivian, one of his brawnier colleagues, made it a point not to and marched straight toward the man who had dared to speak up. The Fermantese put out his arms, waving them in an ineffective and, as it would turn out, detrimental action. When Vivian reached her target, she snatched one of the man's outstretched arms, twisting it to the left and sending her victim flying into the cobblestones with a thud. "Don't ever mess with Temple business!" The vicious Overseer brought her foot on top of the injured Fermantese in a triumphant display of authority. "And that goes for the rest of you." She glared aggressively at random people in the crowd.

Pluto was awestruck. "Wow. Now that was a powerful scene." Looking up to the sky, his buddy sighed. "Exactly, Joss … Marvis could take a lesson or two from that woman."

Sabine screamed not once, but twice, prompting more in the crowd to protest.

"This young actress has to stop wanting to take over the show." Pluto sniffed and grimaced. "They hate her. She's tanking the performance."

The young woman attempted to wiggle her way out of Gorgios's grasp to no avail, making the audience grow restless.

"Enough!" someone shouted.

The Overseers froze.

"Yeah, enough!"

"Enough of this!"

Pluto needed to intervene. "No, one bad fruit shouldn't sour the basket." His announcement quieted everyone, yet nobody understood the meaning of what he had said. Pluto pointed at the Overseers. "Let them perform!"

Many Fermantese disagreed.

"Shut up, Temple boy!"

"Yeah, shut up!"

"Teach him a lesson!"

One of them ran at Pluto. Confused, the Adept took a step backward, catching his foot on the edge of a cobblestone and falling. By a stroke of luck, his timing was such that it resulted in his assailant tripping over him and ending in Joss's arm. The man collapsed on the ground.

With a second of their own injured, the crowd went into a state of frenzy, attacking the Overseers as well as the Phaidrosian performers. Joss was hit in the back of the head by a well-targeted strike, joining the man he had accidentally floored. Pluto lasted a bit longer, then he too was knocked out. The Overseers, however, fared much better.

Swinging wildly, Gorgios sent a handful of Fermantese sprawling across the pavement. He lifted a young man by the throat and slammed him onto his back. The boy coughed blood on the senator's forearm, and the Overseer wiped it with a sweep of the hand. With no time to waste, he charged at another Fermantese, catching him under the collarbone and smashing him down. *I know that sound ... broken ribs.* Gorgios surveyed the field. His Overseers were doing well, dispatching the belligerents with ease. The senator cocked back his arm and landed a terrifying punch in a passerby's sternum. Without pause he put out a leg, impeding two audience members attempting to escape.

"Please, just let us go," one of them pleaded.

Gorgios demolished them, but felt a sudden sting in his left flank. The Overseer saw protruding from himself a kitchen knife stuck there by a brazen Fermantese. *A toy.* The hulk plucked it from his flesh. Then, in one swift motion, he unsheathed the sword from his belt and cut off the man's head.

"Overseers, to me!"

Gorgios spun toward the cry for help and watched as one of his soldiers fell to a knee, stabbed by an armed Fermantese. Roaring, the senator leaped and took a first swing that caught several limbs. It was too late, his man had already succumbed. Gorgios's wrath was out of control. After finishing off any Fermantese in proximity, the Overseer stumbled to Hermits Fountain. He washed the blood from his face, watching in disgust as another companion lost a fight. Vowing to kill them all, Gorgios ran back into the melee.

Sabine crawled away from the commotion and around the edge of the fountain. She stood up at its far end, dipped in cupped hands to cool her stinging face and pulled back, aghast. *The water's red! Like something from the Dread Days.*

"Where do you think you're going?"

She came face-to-face with an Overseer. He was bald and had a long gash running along the side of his leg. Horrified, Sabine stepped backward but found herself cornered by the edge of the fountain which jutted out on both sides.

The Overseer limped toward her. "You'll pay for—" He never finished his sentence, on account of a thick saber poking out of his neck.

The captain's strike had been quick, accurate, and even merciful, depending on the vantage point. For an old sea master who rarely ventured off his ship, it was an exciting turn of events. After a short struggle retrieving his saber, the captain grabbed Sabine by the wrist. "Come with me."

They went around Hermits Fountain and down the nearest street. The young woman followed blindly, unsure whom to trust. *This man just killed an Overseer.* Then again, it had become clear in the last hour that any future at the Temple was no longer a viable option.

"This way." Rushing through the docks, the captain led her

to Ocean Star.

"A boat?" Sabine asked, panting.

"My boat."

"Wait!" The young woman pulled back her arm. "Who are you? And what about my friends?"

"What friends?"

"Two Adepts, who—"

"No time. Do you want to die?"

"But …"

"Shut your mouth and follow me!" Ushering Sabine up the gangway and on the ship, the captain led her to his cabin. "Stay here!" He turned the lock shut on his way out, then rushed to the deck. "Ten minutes to departure!"

The sailors thought they misheard.

"Ten minutes, Captain?"

"That's what I said."

"But sir, some passengers are still on shore."

"Sound the horn, they have ten minutes."

CHAPTER TWENTY-EIGHT

The frigid water felt refreshing against exposed skin. But within minutes, the temperature sent his circulatory system into overdrive, and he could sense tingling through his fingertips and face. While most in such a situation would be alarmed, Kyran found himself enjoying it. *That's how a geega must feel.* The young Adept took another wide stroke before cutting short the agreeable albeit slow pace he had adopted. Cautiously breaking the canal's calm surface, Kyran inhaled and dove once more.

Every pull of his arms preceded a strong kick from his legs. *Pull ... kick. Pull ... kick.* The Adept followed a mindless rhythm, his breaststroke technique flawless. He had narrowly avoided apprehension by diving into the canal, just as the pursuing Overseers had turned the corner. Now Kyran wondered what had happened to Edvon and Sabine. And one disruptive concern was reoccurring. *What if they're together?* He clenched his teeth as he recalled the way his brother looked at her. The younger Adept could have admitted defeat, for the girls always had their eyes on Edvon. Progressing through the widening waterway, Kyran cursed himself for expecting it would be any different with Sabine.

He ascended to take in air. *Does that cholee need to ruin everything for me?* The young man made a fist. *Why her? Just stay away. But what does she think? Does she even like me? You're the one with her now. She'll fall for you, it's part of your plan.* Kyran felt irritated, confused by his own thoughts and the wide array of unfounded conclusions he was drawing. And for a brief instant, the Adept altogether forgot he was swimming underwater in a

Fermantese canal.

The momentum of one too many intemperate strokes caused Kyran to hit the silty bottom and rub against a patch of clams. He slowed down and regained control. *Let the water guide you.* The young man thought of Marrek who had convinced him to start swimming as a therapy, hoping it might help solve his fits of anger.

* * *

"When we are submerged," the preceptor explained, "our minds enter a meditative disposition. The movement of water is serene. The peacefulness of depth relaxes us, yet we are still required to stay alert enough not to drown." The psychological state of mindfulness, as the smiling Marrek called it, helped enhance mental clarity and lower stress levels. "Just try it."

"No, I don't want to."

The preceptor extolled the virtues of the sport until Kyran caved in to the pestering.

Any reluctance lasted one session because the swimming worked. Once in the water, he was freed from his burdens, emptying his mind and focusing only on the serenity of the task at hand. Kyran looked forward to those secret nights spent in the Academy pool, more often than not empty due to lack of interest from the other students. Besides the occasional presence of a professor, leading to nothing more than a raised eyebrow, he had access to his own sanctuary.

The rectangular pool sat in the middle of a hall, with a second-floor balcony held up by magnificently carved stone pillars. Above, a ceiling of tainted glass allowed for light during the day. Come evening, Source-powered lanterns were ignited, though sometimes, and it had to be late at night, Kyran would turn them off. Then, he could swim under the starlight, bathing in its bright and mysterious aura.

* * *

Brought back to reality by a growing humming sound, Kyran floated to the surface. He eyed a boat heading straight his way. The Adept dove back in and waited for the small raft to pass overhead, letting air seep out of his lungs to stay below. It left behind a modest wake as the resonance of the engine faded away. *I need to get out.* Unable to resist the cold, Kyran scanned the sides for a way to dry land. A small dock with a ladder was up ahead, and he used it to pull himself from the water. Dripping wet, he aimed for a narrow alleyway.

"Hold it right there!"

Someone grabbed his arm, yanking the young man back several steps.

"What the cholee!" yelled Kyran, trying in vain to pull himself away.

"Will you cut it out?" The much stronger Aiden barely moved. "And watch your tongue in front of a female agent."

"Agent?"

"Battalion agent. And we've got questions, primarily relating to why you were swimming in the canal."

Kyran spat out the first lie that came to his mind. "Oh, I've been doing that forever."

"Come again?" Aiden kept a firm grip. "You always swim in the canal?"

"My friends and I, we've been swimming in them since we're kids," continued Kyran. "You must be from Phaidros?"

Criss was sharper. "You swim in your clothes?"

"Oh yes, ma'am. Helps us … uh … it keeps us warmer."

The Battalion agents looked at each other.

"Chief?"

"Go ahead."

"Candidly, I think this kid's full of cholee, and—"

"Hey!" Kyran exclaimed. "Why can she say that word?"

"She can say whatever she wants," replied Aiden. "And anyway, I agree with her."

"About what?"

The chief did not hesitate. "Where's your brother?"

"My brother?"

"Come on, kid. Enough of the cho—umm … I mean … excuses. We can help you. It's better than being cut to pieces by some freak Overseers."

Kyran was impressed the two agents had connected the dots so fast. *Though, I was swimming in a dread canal.* "I don't know what you're talking about."

"Then, we'll arrest you," stated Criss, "and we can have this talk at the Main Complex."

"Arrest me for what?"

"Disturbing the Council of Five's peace."

"What? How?"

The agent walked up to Kyran, snatched his hands, and handcuffed them at the wrist in one swift movement. "I'll tell you about it in your jail cell."

"Wait!" exclaimed the Adept.

"Too late for that, now."

"Th—this is Battalion brutality!"

"So you want to talk, then?" Aiden peered at Kyran. "You can start by telling us why—" Stopping mid-sentence, the chief tilted his head. "Do you hear that?"

"Yeah," responded Kyran, "sounds like—"

"Shut up. Criss, that's Ocean Star's departure horn."

"I thought we had a few hours left."

Kyran cut in. "Wait, Ocean Star's here?"

"Will you keep quiet!"

Criss was surprised by Aiden's piercing retort. He looked more agitated than she had ever seen before. "Chief?"

"There's little time, it'll be leaving any minute," he replied. "We need to hurry."

They took off along the canal, forcing Kyran to keep up with them by placing him in the middle, each Battalion agent holding one of his arms. Ocean Star came into sight after a solid five-minute run. Without a break, Criss pushed the captive up the gangway and on the deck where she was accosted by the captain.

"Who's this?"

"I'm—"

"He's in our custody," Aiden interjected.

The captain was unmoved. "None of that on my ship."

"Battalion matters require this, unfortunately."

"Unless I say not on my ship."

"Frankly, sir," replied the chief. "I don't give a dread what you say. I'm bringing this prisoner on board, or you can explain your insubordination to the Noble Assembly."

Criss raised an eyebrow, impressed by Aiden's unyielding answer.

"Insubordination?" The captain advanced and came face to face with the chief. "Be careful boy."

"No, you be very careful, Captain."

The tense moment was short-lived, interrupted by Ruan stomping up the gangway. The personal attendant observed the strange scene. "Why is the horn blowing?"

"Because we're leaving," replied the captain, cutting eye-contact with Aiden.

"What? How were we supposed to know? I mean … I just

happened to be walking back here."

"You heard the horn, no?" challenged the old seaman.

"Not from inside the town."

"Too bad. We were forced to push up the schedule."

"What're you talking about?" asked Aiden.

"There was a riot near Hermits Fountain. And that's why we're leaving, before the port gets shut down."

"A riot?" Criss repeated.

"Group of Overseers captured some woman, and they were attacked."

"What!" Kyran broke loose. "What did she look like?"

Criss pulled the Adept back, but the captain did not miss a beat. "You let your prisoners talk like that?"

Aiden had already closed his eyes in frustration. "Not generally."

Then, the door leading to the passengers' cabins swung open, and Neeta came storming onto the deck. "Why is the horn blowing?"

"We're leaving!" the captain shouted.

"What? You told me six hours?"

"There was a riot."

"A ri—" Neeta stopped mid-word when she noticed Kyran. "A riot?" she finished, flustered. "And you're bringing dangerous prisoners onto the ship?"

"This man's in our custody," Aiden declared. "And he will cause no danger to you."

"If he does, I'll throw him overboard myself," commented the captain.

A sailor came dashing over. "Sir! Temple ship down the Wimau. The Lutigas."

Racing toward Fermantis was a large boat, white hull sparkling in the distance.

"You see!" cried out the captain. "Port's about to shut, so we're leaving. Now!"

The sailors were carrying out the orders when another loud command froze them in place.

"Halt!" Criss turned to Aiden. "We have a duty to investigate that riot, Chief."

"Yeah, the girl might be Sab—"

Kyran felt a stinging pain from a sharp slap across his face.

"Next time," warned Criss, "you'll actually regret talking."

The chief looked around, concerned someone might report them for mistreatment of prisoners. To his consternation, Neeta had a wide smile and seemed to enjoy the incident. The same could be said for the captain whose head was bobbing with delight. And Ruan, fascinated and intrigued by Criss's strike, lingered around in hopes of witnessing another one.

"Chief?"

"We stay on the ship," Aiden ordered. "We have a duty to solve this case, as well."

"No!" Kyran bolted for the gangway but was held back by the Battalion agents. The captain hollered his commands, Ocean Star drifted away, and the Adept's mind went blank. *No point in using the Source now. I'll never see them again.* Strangely, the young man had trouble deciding whom he would miss more, and as Aiden pulled him along, he cursed himself for having entertained such a dilemma. *They're already dead, so best not to think of it.* They arrived at an empty cabin, and the chief pushed Kyran inside. "Wait." The Adept turned around. "How did you know who I am?"

"Intuition."

CHAPTER TWENTY-NINE

Her next move would be crucial, potentially outcome determinative. So she leaned forward to better concentrate. Shifting anything back was not an option, the admiral had strategized too well. Rex Ruga raised an eyebrow and tilted her head sideways hoping to get a different and better perspective. Though several of her pieces were cut off from their end of the board, the commandant identified a viable lateral move.

Like in every other Mira game, the competitors had opened cautiously, exploring risk-free possibilities. Once pieces were taken, Rex Ruga and her Overseer colleague engaged in a rapid and lethal back-and-forth, one that wiped clean most on the board. Though the situation favored her opponent, the commandant was not willing to accept defeat. The stakes were too high. She slid a white piece seven squares to the right, forcing the other player to defend or risk losing one his own. The admiral elected the former strategy, leaving Rex Ruga on the attack. *When I'm at my best.*

She chased him around a few more turns, but he dodged masterfully as their last match in the series of fifteen came close to an end. With no better activities offered aboard the Lutigas, they had played the popular game throughout the day. It felt to Rex Ruga as though she had been sitting at a cafe in central Phaidros where old men could be seen leaning over Mira tables for hours and hours.

Such an uncomplicated game. Played on a twelve by eight board, each side had thirteen regular pieces and a special one whose name depended on the participant. While common

Dominioners used the word pawn, Overseers and Adepts projected their allegiance onto the game, naming the pieces pilgrim and scholar.

Each piece could move either horizontally or vertically, unless it ran into another one. The goal was to immobilize the adversary's pilgrim by surrounding it with enemy pieces. *And you can capture an opponent's piece by placing two of your own pieces around it, right?* Given the focus required in Mira games, the commandant often repeated the simplest questions in her head. Puzzle syndrome, she liked to call it. *Then I'll take yours right … here.*

"Good move," muttered the admiral, stroking his beard.

After a pause, he slid a black piece to the edge of the crimson board, trapping one of the commandant's. The admiral was aiming to kill the piece by herding it into the corner square. He succeeded, and Rex Ruga snatched the intricate statuette from the board, throwing it to the ground.

"I hope you didn't scratch it," the admiral commented.

"And if I did?"

"You'll pay to fix it."

"No, I won't."

"Well, not you personally. The Temple will when I submit the expense report."

"I don't care." Rex Ruga looked back at the board and at her hopeless predicament.

"Shall we discuss my winnings from this series?" asked the admiral.

"It's not over yet."

She moved in between two of the admiral's pieces, knowing a capture could only occur during his turn, and positioned herself for another strike. He had a two-piece advantage now and seemed ready to immobilize her pilgrim.

The ship slowed down. "Looks like we've arrived in Fermantis, Commandant."

Rex Ruga slid another piece forward. "Do you forfeit, then?"

"Don't be silly." The admiral responded by exchanging kills.

The commandant counted what was left. *Six to four.* If she lost another piece, winning the game would be impossible. A draw was equally unlikely, so Rex Ruga jumped up, scooped the pieces into the palms of her hands, and threw them across the admiral's large and luxurious cabin. "Write your requests," she spat out.

The admiral kept a straight face. "I won the series by a score of eight to seven. I believe we made a wager?"

Rex Ruga clenched her teeth. "I'll arrange for it." She slammed the door and navigated her way through a series of opulent passageways. The Temple's flagship was so large that by the time the commandant reached the deck, it had already docked. A small contingent of Overseers was waiting for her on land, and when Rex Ruga walked down to meet them, one called out.

"My Commandant, troubling news."

She hurried over.

"Erol, First Lieutenant in Fermantis." He held out a hand. "It is a great honor to finally—"

Rex Ruga yanked the Overseer toward her. "What is the troubling news?"

"It seems there was a bit of a mis—uh … misunderstanding in the main square."

"Misunderstanding?"

"Between Gorgios and some locals."

"And?"

"Umm, well …" said Erol, "the locals lost the argument."

The commandant exhaled. "Obviously. I'm asking how

many he killed."

"At least a dozen, if not more."

She shook her head in disbelief. "What about the two Adepts?"

Erol started to fidget. "Umm, no ma'am. They escaped, as did the defector girl."

Rex Ruga almost smiled but caught herself, adopting the angry expression expected of her. "Fools. Bring me there!"

They picked up the pace to get to the main square. *By Gods, that's a lot more than a dozen.* The scene was gruesome, the stench of death stifling. Blood filled the cracks between cobblestones, whilst bodies lay strewn about, most split open and missing limbs. Counting a handful of Overseers among the dead, Rex Ruga noticed Gorgios near Hermits Fountain, speaking to his thinned out squadron. She walked up to him. "Let's talk."

With a slight trace of surprise, Gorgios turned to face her. "Why are you here?"

"You know exactly why," Rex Ruga shot back. "Now, tell me what happened."

"An armed mob attacked us."

The commandant raised an eyebrow.

"It was only in self-defense," added Gorgios.

"Just like that? Out of nowhere?"

Her master of arms nodded. "Pretty much."

"You're a moron. Why are there still bodies here?"

Erol ventured a reply. "Th—that was … I … uh—"

"Clean this up! Before more people see it. And have the admiral shut down the port." The Fermantese Overseer sprinted away to get help. Turning back to Gorgios and his unit, Rex Ruga felt a surge of excitement. *Diplomatic games bore those who relish being out in the action.* She had trouble seeing herself living like Najara for the next fifty years. For now, the commandant only cared about locating and executing the Adepts. Even the serial killer Gorgios had stumbled upon would have to wait. *But he'll certainly be joining the others on that pyre.* "We need to find them today," Rex Ruga announced to the Overseers crowded around Hermits Fountain. "Understood?"

Gorgios huffed. "We?"

"You seem to forget what made me who I am."

"Right now, you're a commandant, whose role is to be back at the Temple."

"The Temple is in fine hands, rest assured." It was then that Rex Ruga saw two strange men standing among them. Much shorter than everyone else, at least two heads below the thugs in Gorgios's squad, one had a captivating mustache, unlike anything she had ever seen. His facial hair was perfectly groomed and twirled symmetrically on both ends. The second man was lanky. He was smiling at her, hair cut down to the scalp and eyes of an undefined color. *Are they gray? Black?* Strangely, the man gave Rex Ruga a slight tilt of the head, as if he knew her. "Who are these two?"

"They're friendlies. They spoke up for us, then laid the first defensive strike, neutralizing a belligerent villager."

"Spoke up?" inquired Rex Ruga. "Why was there a need for that?"

Gorgios absorbed a lethal glance from the commandant. "Because we were interrogating the traitor."

"Traitor? What are you talking about? I thought you didn't catch them?"

Pluto laughed out loud.

"What's so funny?" asked Rex Ruga.

"Oh, sorry … nothing."

The commandant stroked her hair, the frustration increasing. "Look, I don't know what's going on here, but it's starting to anger me!" The Overseers remained quiet, sulking school children scolded by their teacher. "Did you actually locate any of them?"

"Only the girl," answered Gorgios.

"Do we have any idea where they're heading?"

She was answered with silence.

"Commandant?" The Fermantese Overseer by the name of Erol had picked a poor time to reinsert himself into the picture.

"What?" snapped Rex Ruga.

"We rounded up many survivors, and—"

"Just make sure they never speak of this." She made brief eye contact with Gorgios. "And there's only one way to make sure of that."

Erol hesitated.

"Take these two as well," Rex Ruga ordered, gesturing toward Pluto and Joss.

"No," said Gorgios.

"Pardon me?"

"They stay here."

"These men are witnesses to your savagery, Gorgios. We can't have word of this incident spreading around the Dominion."

"They're not witnesses, they're my men."

"Your men?" repeated Rex Ruga and Pluto simultaneously.

"They fought alongside us and are therefore under my protection as Master of Arms."

The commandant threw her hands up in the air. "Fine." She eyed the two performers. "What are you, anyway?"

"We, umm …" started Pluto, "we do different jobs."

"Explain yourself."

"Well, the job we're doing now, it's … uh … to track something down."

"You're trackers?"

"Yes."

"Ah." The commandant grinned. "That's a good job you have."

Pluto played along. "Thank you."

"Men in your profession depend on secrecy, do they not?"

"That's exactly right."

"We may be in need of some trackers ourselves," continued Rex Ruga. "If it's not too much, may I inquire as to your clientele?"

"Our clientele?"

"Who do you cater your professional expertise to? Average Phaidrosians? Nobles?"

"Commandant," interjected Gorgios, but she waved him off.

"Only the highest ranked," Pluto replied, sensing a golden opportunity. "We're not cheap, you know."

"Excellent," said Rex Ruga. She was about to make a proposal when she noticed Erol out of the corner of her eye. He was still standing there, all smiles and listening to the exchange. "What in the Dread Days are you still doing here?"

"I … well, there was … umm—"

"Go!" shouted the commandant, and Erol ran off once more. She turned back to Pluto and Joss. "What are you being paid right now?"

"I couldn't possibly—"

"Double it."

Everyone remained silent, save Gorgios. "You realize the Temple has the very best trackers. Like myself."

Rex Ruga was undeterred. "I stand by my offer. Whatever you're making right now, I'll double it."

"We're being paid fourteen hundred gold coins," said Pluto in one breath. Joss made a hasty hand motion. "Each."

"I'll round up my offer. Six thousand gold coins, then," declared Rex Ruga. "To be paid when you bring us to the renegade Adepts we're searching for."

"Agreed." Neither of the performers had any tracking experience, a lie that became irrelevant when a panting Overseer came running down the street.

"Commandant, they're on the boat to Portown."

"How do you know?" Rex Ruga shot back.

"People on the docks saw two Battalion agents ushering an Adept onboard Ocean Star."

"Battalion? Ocean Star?" She turned to Gorgios. "Do you have any idea what's going on?"

He shook his head.

"Well, there's only one way to find out."

CHAPTER THIRTY

The pieces of metal twirled around to form a handle, leaving several gaps that made the utensil awkward to hold. Its pointed gold tines gleamed in the candlelight, exhibiting a curious contrast with the fork's otherwise dull copper hue. On the unpolished wood table rested the remaining cutlery with a similar dichotomy. A scrawny galley boy delivered yet another dish. *Surely the last one.* Sabine watched him struggle as he situated the latest addition to the spread. Breathing nervously, he slid the tray of clams to the left, placed the pickled vegetable bowl near the baked geega, and cleared away the empty dish of assorted nuts the captain had devoured long ago.

"Try some," the old man said when the boy left, snagging a juicy balbak rib with his fingers.

Sabine used her fork. *Auralus save me.* She ate the fresh greens and cooked legumes, and sampled the less-intimidating crustaceans. The main dishes looked overwhelming, as did the fat ridden chunk of meat before her.

"Come on," the captain urged. "Take a bite."

First the mushroom, and now, this. Sabine closed her eyes and brought the rib piece up to her lips. *Why me?* As her teeth dug into the flesh, the young woman gagged, and she dropped her fork onto the wood with a clang. "I can't."

"Good," the seaman replied, leaning back in his chair. "Far too long, I've been with women who'd tear that meat right off its bone." He sighed and made a not-so-startling statement. "Village port whores, really." Another groan as he rubbed his stomach.

"I've missed the company of girls like you, who are more," he grinned, "… sensitive."

In a cabin several decks lower, Neeta and Edvon were having a heated exchange.

"You can't just hold me prisoner like this!"

"I'm delivering you to the Academy whether you like it or not," said Neeta. "Get comfortable."

"What about eating? Sleeping?"

"I'll get us some food, and we'll figure out the rest."

Edvon clenched his jaw. "Isn't this ship sailing to Portown?"

"Yes."

"Isn't the Academy back in Phaidros?"

"Yes."

"So why are we here?" Edvon pressed on. "The best thing would be to—"

"Look, I don't care what you think," Neeta interjected. "All that matters is that you're both on this ship, and it's going to Phaidros."

"Both?"

Neeta bit her lip.

"What are you talking about?" asked Edvon. "Who else is on board?"

The officer ignored him.

"Tell me!"

What difference does it make if he knows? "Kyran's on board."

"What? Are you sure?"

"I'm positive."

"I don't believe you."

"I said I'm positive," Neeta fired back. "He's in Battalion custody."

Edvon's face regained color. "You need to let me out, so I can find him."

"I can't."

"Let me out!" He viciously shook the handle of the cabin door, trying to break the lock. "I said let me—"

A Source blast came flying at Edvon's head, and he ducked just enough to avert contact. Shocked, the Adept turned to confront the bright-eyed Neeta. "Did you just—" He blocked the next blast with a defensive one of his own.

The officer, resorting to something she was taught to eschew, realized she had blown her chance to win. The element of surprise was gone, and before Neeta could engage anew, Edvon's Source strike clobbered her. She gasped for air, clutching her abdomen and slumping onto the bed, unconscious.

Edvon rushed over to retrieve the cabin's key. It was absent from the small desk, and nowhere to be found on the bed. *Which leaves only one place.* Carefully, he slipped his hand into Neeta's front pocket, his fingers wriggling under the tight fabric and down her thigh. *Nothing.* He inspected the other pocket. *Still nothing.* Exhaling, Edvon reached underneath Neeta and felt the key in her back pocket. The Adept left the cabin to search for his brother.

One deck above, Criss relieved Aiden of his shift. Pacing around the cabin, she took note that their prisoner had yet to move. Slouched in the corner, Kyran's long hair concealed his face.

"Are you sleeping?" asked the agent.

No response.

"I can see you moving."

Still, the Adept ignored her.

Unlike most, Criss had witnessed first-hand the power of Source energy. *And I don't have any platinum to protect myself.* The Battalion had searched high and wide for the rare material, to no avail. *The Temple found it all. And apparently only enough to mold a dozen or so neck collars. Luckily, this Adept appears pretty harmless.* "I don't expect you to speak." The ship heeled as it followed the Wimau south. "But you will listen to me. There might be a way out of this for you."

Kyran lifted his chin.

"All I need is a little information. You live at the Academy, right? Has there been anything strange go—"

The Source blast knocked Criss off her chair. She slammed her head on the ground and went limp.

Twice! That's twice he's looked at my breasts. When the captain came back to tell Sabine the ship was making an emergency departure, she worried. After he gave her clean clothes and spoke of dinner, the young woman wondered if it had been an overreaction. She took another glimpse at the bed behind the table, though this time, her feeble attempt at subtlety did not go undetected. The captain pushed his chair and walked toward her. For a moment, Sabine believed she would have been better off with whatever fate awaited her at the Temple.

"Don't worry," the old sailor said, glancing at the bed himself. "I'm not forcing you onto it."

Sabine clasped her armrest. *I'm on a ship, alone.* Her heart sank, and she considered rushing toward the door. *Then what? There's nowhere to go.*

"We don't need a bed. We can start right here."

The captain pulled her up by one wrist. Yanking the back of Sabine's neck with his other hand, he shoved the young woman toward the corner of the table. In one swift motion, the seaman swiped the dinner service onto the floor. Plates and trays clattered, sauces spilled, and food tumbled around the cabin. *By Lutigas!* The captain pressed his guest onto the table, holding her face down. He clawed at the hem of the dress.

Just as Sabine let out a scream, a gust of wind rushed overtop of her head. The captain staggered back, releasing his victim and struggling to catch his breath. Sabine looked up. Kyran's arms were extended, and his eyes shone brightly. "Looks like I made it just in time."

The seaman recovered fast and swung forcefully at the Adept. They partook in a violent and hateful dance. The captain was gaining the upper hand when Kyran lost his footing on a broken plate. Despite being forced to a knee, the Adept not only blocked a kick to his face, he also held on to the captain's leg. Pulling it as hard as possible, Kyran lunged forward. The maneuver succeeded, and he smashed shoulders first into the captain who let out a groan. Snatching a porcelain tray, the sailor hurled it at Kyran's face. The young man used a defensive Source blast, stopping the object mid-flight and shattering it into a myriad of tiny fragments. Using the temporary distraction, the captain struck his opponent across the face, sending the Adept sprawling. Kyran hit his head and lay still.

"No!" Sabine looked around for an object to defend herself. The captain was quicker. In one swoop, he lifted Sabine off the ground and tossed her onto the bed. Pinning her arms with one hand, he pulled up her dress with the other. Sabine attempted to kick, but the captain used his own weight to immobilize her legs.

"You ain't an Overseer, are you?" He grinned. "Too bad, I always wanted to fu—"

A spurt of blood shot out the captain's mouth and landed near Sabine's head. The man seemed confused, his eyes darting

back and forth. He tried to speak but could not utter a word. "Fu …
Fu … Fu …" His gaze came into contact with Sabine's and for the
slimmest instant, she felt pity.

The captain fell over, leaving Kyran standing there, shaking
with an expression of disbelief. He contemplated the body at his
feet, as if to verify what had just occurred. Sabine peeked over the
side of the bed. Protruding from the base of the captain's skull was
the copper hilt of a dinner knife.

"Oh, no …" Kyran stumbled backward, catching himself
on the table. "What have I done?"

Sabine ignored the Adept and dashed toward the cabin's
entrance. She closed the door Kyran had left ajar and surveyed the
damage. Near the bed at the far end, the captain lay dead, blood
pooling around him. Leaning against the dining table was Kyran,
eyes locked on the floor and about to vomit. The ground was
covered in a jumble of food, shattered dishes, and cutlery.

The knock on the cabin's door was not opportune.

"Who is it?" Kyran whispered.

"How would I possibly know?"

"Captain?"

The voice from the other side was immediately
recognizable, leaving Kyran more anemic than before. "It's that
agent," he murmured. "You can't let him in, he'll kill me."

The young woman nodded. She slid both straps of the dress
down her shoulders to expose a little more bosom and opened the
door. "What?" Sabine asked, blocking the room with her exposed
frame.

Aiden hesitated, eyes darting up and down the young
woman. "Is … uh … is the captain available?"

"He's a bit indisposed at the moment."

"Um—"

"Why don't you try again in the morning?"

"Very well." As the chief turned away, he noticed something peculiar. "That's blood in your hair."

"In my hair?" Sabine repeated, adopting an expression of utter astonishment.

"What's going on?" Aiden pushed her aside and spotted Kyran. "What in the Gods are you doing here?" Glancing past the Adept, the chief noticed the captain lying face down, a knife sticking from his head.

"The captain's ... uh ... dead," said Kyran.

The chief lunged at the Adept, reaching him in one step and delivering a brutal uppercut. Kyran fell backwards, unable to halt a second punch right into his stomach.

"Stop!" screamed Sabine.

Twisting his torso, the chief cocked back his arm a third time. Before he could bring it down, Edvon crashed into him, and they fell to a floor littered with sharp glass and stray knives. Only one of the two would ever get back up.

PART IV

CHAPTER THIRTY-ONE

"Tap, tap, tap, tap, tap, tap …"

Footsteps echoed throughout the palace's immense corridor. Judging by their speed and frequency, they bore troubling news, as would have been the case with any sound so early in the morning. For no one dared to disturb the lord before he rose. *If he's even gone to bed yet.* The personal attendant responsible for the ruckus slowed down from his near sprint and rapped on a closed door.

"Come in!"

Joinus wasted no time in announcing the purpose of his visit. "My Lord, your son."

Lord Hanstun shot up. He was still in bed with what appeared to be a woman. Joinus squinted. *Or man with very long hair.* As a member of the Noble's personal service for close to three decades, the old attendant had seen just about everything.

"What has he done now?"

"He … ahem, a servant boy …"

"By the Gods! What are you saying, Joinus?"

The old man looked down at the carpet, unsure how to tactfully relay what had just occurred. No God himself, Joinus had been involved in countless political battles and power struggles, more often than not involving acts an adherent to the Book of Provenance would severely frown upon. Acts the personal attendant regretted with time. But nothing compared to what he was now witnessing—a younger generation pushing the boundaries of decency and doing so for no real purpose. "He slit open a servant boy's face."

Lord Hanstun brought a hand to his chin and grimaced. He turned around to nudge his sleeping companion. The figure got up and scurried away from the room, a sheet draped over their back, leaving Joinus still unable to determine the gender.

"Why?" asked Hanstun.

The personal attendant remained still. In a few years, he would retire to one of the luxury apartments in the center of the Noble District, as stipulated in his contract. A fair reward for one who had spent countless hours providing the highest level of service. And just in time, for Lecarn was growing older, a worrisome thought. "He had a little too much wine and boasted and, well … you know how he gets."

"What was he saying?"

"That he can get away with doing anything he wants."

"Obviously he can," Lord Hanstun muttered. "Why did he slash a servant's face?"

"Just to show the others he could, I guess."

Running fingers through his hair, the Noble took a deep breath. "How bad is it?"

"It will leave a scar. He used a kitchen knife, so—"

"Enough." Standing up and slipping into his satin robe, Hanstun walked past his personal attendant and into the hallway.

"My Lord," shouted Joinus, struggling to catch up, "wait!"

It was too late. The Noble kicked open the door to his son's chambers. Inside was a disturbing scene, even for a lord whose own tastes were often questionable. A boy cowered in the corner, black bangs covering a bloody face. He whimpered in pain, sealing the recently inflicted gash with both hands. It ran down from his temple to his jaw and made Hanstun nauseated. Diagonally across the room, Lecarn was lounging in one of several sofa beds, surrounded by girls and friends, laughing and taking large gulps from a goblet. An assembly of servants, unsure what to do, lurked in the background.

"What in the Dread Days is going on here?"

Lecarn looked up, waved at his father, and then turned back to the others.

"Get this boy to the medic." There was no movement or reaction, and Lord Hanstun gritted his teeth. "Now!" Within minutes, the maimed servant was helped out of the room, and the Noble marched toward the sofas. He yanked his son's long blond hair.

"What the cholee!" shouted Lecarn.

"Watch your mouth!"

"Oh, since when are you a Temple lover?"

Hanstun smacked him across the face.

"What the cho—"

Another smack. "Now, you listen to me. All your friends here, you tell them to go home."

"Home?" Lecarn chuckled. "They practically live here."

"Do you know what you've just done to that boy?"

"What boy?"

* * *

Wispy white clouds raced across the blue sky, rolling around aimlessly until they disappeared from sight. For the briefest of instants, one could see the Red City. Within seconds, a fresh cache of clouds materialized on the horizon, designed to curtail the exhibition. Lecarn brushed the hair out of his eyes and tried to forget the sickening memory that had come back to his mind unprompted. Focusing his attention to the main road, he concentrated on what lay ahead. *Almost there.*

Portown was visible in the distance, and Lecarn

accelerated, kicking up dust as his SPC charged along. Instead of driving straight toward the center, he veered off to the left and up a steep hill. Portown was so mundane, anyone who ventured into the city received curious stares, and the driver preferred to keep a low profile. At the top of the hill, Lecarn turned off the Source-powered motor, taking with him the only ignition key. Though he had, by his own volition no less, left a life of luxury for one spent on the road, the once-Noble still possessed enough wealth through his father to buy the best equipment. And this SPC had been custom-designed by the major source manipulator himself.

Lecarn jumped out, landing softly in grass still wet from the morning dew. Mirabel Crater extended to his left. He adjusted his tunic, and neck tilting backward, placed a loose brown cap over his head. Then, using an index finger, he poked into one of the dozen pouches hanging from his belt and pulled out a dried fruit. Lecarn flung the snack into his open mouth with pinpoint accuracy. Satisfied, he grabbed his leather gauntlets, proceeding to engage in the familiar struggle of stretching them around his wriggling fingers. Ocean Star would dock late in the afternoon, and he had plenty of errands to run before its arrival.

Just as he was about to walk down the hill, he spotted a ship in the near distance. *What?* Its colors were unmistakable. *Ocean Star. How's that possible?* Coming down the Wimau River at a steady speed, the vessel would reach Portown in no time. And the strangeness had only just begun. As Ocean Star turned to enter the docks, Lecarn whipped out his binoculars and watched as someone jumped out of a larger porthole, plummeting into the water below. Rubbing his eyes, the incredulous onlooker caught his breath at the sight of another individual. A woman leaned against the opening, hesitant to take the plunge. She too ultimately leaped, only to be followed by yet a third person.

The jumpers swam to the far bank of the river,

dragged themselves out of the water, and headed Lecarn's way. *Could it be the Adepts?* As the three drew nearer, he realized no one was paying him any attention. The first to reach the top, a slender young man with long brown hair and curious gray eyes, ran right by without so much as a glance in the once-Noble's direction. Lecarn made brief eye contact with the girl who had been so reluctant to jump, but she also went past without breaking stride. The last of the bunch, a strong man with an athletic build, wavered then followed behind his companions.

"W—wait!" shouted Lecarn. The three stopped in their tracks. "Are you the Adepts sent by Elias?

Elias? Edvon scrutinized the stranger. He was short and seemed well-traveled, given the state of his scruffy boots and the number of accessories dangling from his utility belt. The Adept peered underneath the man's light-green tunic and caught sight of chain mail. But it was the SPC parked nearby that attracted Edvon's attention. Though he was president of the Source-Powered Machinery Club, the Adept had never seen such a model. *It looks fast. We might not be the two Adepts he's looking for …* "Yeah, that's us."

"What're you doing?" muttered Kyran.

Ignoring his brother, the older Adept hoped a case of mistaken identity might afford them a better means of transportation.

"Wait, you are?" Lecarn raised an eyebrow. "You're Adepts?"

"Yeah."

The once-Noble put a hand around the hilt of his blade. "Prove it. And do so before you take another step."

"Fine."

Edvon lifted an arm in his brother's direction and flicked his middle finger off his thumb. The little squirt of Source energy flew straight into Kyran's forehead with a spark.

"Ouch!"

Chuckling, Lecarn walked over to shake Edvon's hand. "So you're both Adepts, then?"

A return shot fired by Kyran answered the question, and Lecarn laughed again before turning toward Sabine. "And you?"

She remained silent.

"Oh," offered Kyran. "That's our … uh …" Sabine was staring right at him. "Our assistant. She … umm, like, helps us out on these sorts of things."

"Things?" asked Lecarn.

Edvon stepped back in, convinced his brother was about to blow the entire plan. "Please ignore him, we've had a long journey. Should we just get going?"

Lecarn paused. *I've been around long enough to tell the difference between Source manipulation and sleight-of-hand tricks. They're definitely not lying about being Adepts.* He was wondering whether they were the right ones. "Tell me something, what does Elias look like?"

His mouth was about to open when Edvon realized he remembered not a single one of the officer's characteristics. "I'm … I'm actually not sure," he admitted, turning to Kyran for help.

"I thought I could picture him," said the younger Adept, scratching his head. "But when I try, I can't …"

"So you do know him," observed Lecarn.

"What do you mean?"

"Elias isn't the most distinct balbak in the pack, if you catch my drift."

The brothers were amused.

"Come to think of it, I wonder—"

The sound of a blaring horn startled the small group gathered atop the hill. Eyes darting around, Lecarn found it to be coming from none other than Ocean Star. He watched as the crew ran around, followed closely by passengers. The once-Noble glanced at Edvon who shrugged and looked away. Lecarn turned his attention back to the ship and spotted several sailors darting down the ramp and into town. *What the* … Whatever events might have occurred prior were not his concern. All he needed were two Adepts. *And now, I have them at my disposal.* Lecarn pointed at the SPC. "What are you waiting for? Hop in, let's go."

CHAPTER THIRTY-TWO

His face was covered with pustules, some red, others yellow. Neeta's chest was heaving. "Are you Zakus?"

"Yeah," the man answered.

She handed him Marrek's package. "Here, this is for you."

"What is it?" he asked.

"From the preceptor."

"Who's that?"

"Aren't you the tavern boy?" questioned Neeta with a frown.

"Yeah."

"And this is the Golden Auralus, right?"

"Yeah."

"And you don't know who the preceptor is?"

"Yeah." Zakus hesitated. "Uh … I mean, no … uh, I think."

Cursing under her breath, Neeta realized her conversation with the tavern boy would advance her to nothing. *What did Marrek possibly have to do with such a halfwit?* There were more important matters to deal with, and the preceptor's instructions had been clear. "Well, that's yours." Leaving Zakus confused, Neeta looked for the table where Criss was waiting. She spotted the agent near a corner, in an unlit part of the tavern. "Why did you sit all the way back here?"

Criss ignored the question, instead downing an entire glass of amber Portown ale.

"How many is that?"

"Gods strike you. You don't like it, go away."

"You know there're better ways to lament than turning your piss into liquor."

"Like what?"

"Um—" Neeta paused. *She is an agent, after all.*

"That's what I thought." Criss turned her head toward the main bar. "Another!" Zakus came with a refill. Taking a hefty gulp, the agent looked up at the ceiling and then, straight at Neeta. "They must have jumped out the cabin window, it's the only explanation that makes sense."

"Were they even involved?"

"Of course they were involved." Criss slammed down her glass. "You don't flee the scene of a crime unless you're guilty. Battalion training, day one."

She's probably right. Neeta knew the cabin had been locked from inside. *Unless the captain and the chief killed each other …* "How did no one see them, though? Or hear the splash?"

"Sound of the engine," Criss replied, her eyes closed.

Silence.

"What about being seen?" asked the Adept.

"Yeah, you already brought that up, didn't you? I don't know. Maybe they got lucky." She finished the last of her new ale. "Another!"

Neeta waved off the tavern boy. "That's enough. Let's go someplace else."

Pushing back her chair, Criss rose to meet the Adept eye-to-eye, and they stared each other down.

"I want another drink."

"Don't care. I know you're mad, and I would be too. This isn't helping." Neeta held out her hand. "Come on."

The grieving agent was led out the Golden Auralus. Together, the two women walked down Portown's main boulevard before turning down an isolated side street, one of many in the city.

Following along the lonely road for several minutes, they arrived at a cemetery. *Gods. Of all the streets to pick …*

The sight seemed to reanimate Criss. "Hilarious."

"I … I'm sorry, I didn't—"

"Don't apologize. I get what you're doing." The agent looked at the headstones scattered about the grounds. "Everyone dies."

"True, I suppose."

"Aiden lived a good life. Even though it ended too soon." Criss kicked a small rock. "You want to know something, Neeta? Crimes scare people. And when people get scared, they fabricate stories. Before you know it, the stories turn into conspiracy theories that only get more ridiculous as time goes on. But at the bottom of every crime is just some sad, bored person. Like the Killer of Murcavis, for instance. It's always someone you end up feeling kind of sorry for, the circumstances in which they were raised, or whatever." Catching her breath, the agent continued. "When those village attacks started, it felt like something different. A crime being committed by someone who isn't bored or sad at all. Rather, someone evil. Like, truly evil."

"What do you mean?"

"I don't think we, when we're born, have evil within us. We're by nature good-hearted, caring individuals. People do bad things because they're forced to, or because something in their lives altered their instinctive way of thinking. No one is naturally evil, in the true sense of the term."

"Definitely disagree."

"Okay, whatever. All I'm trying to say is that there is something evil going on, and Aiden got caught up in it."

Neeta had difficulty masking her surprise. "Are you saying Edvon and Kyran are implicated in the village attacks?"

"Whatever their names are, I'm not ruling it out."

"You're crazy, connecting dots that don't belong together."

Criss voluntarily overlooked the irony of the situation, in that she had been preaching the same concept to the chief for several weeks. "That Adept has something wrong with him," she said. "I could see it in his eyes."

"He's just a stupid kid."

"Well, it doesn't matter."

"Why?"

"I'll find him and make sure he spends the rest of his days rotting inside Crain Prison."

"You know I can't let you do that."

"And you're going to stop me?"

Shaking her head in disbelief, Neeta took the risk. "Do you wear lipstick?"

"What?"

"It just looks like you could use some."

"I don't get it."

"Here, let me show you." The Adept went about her usual drill, pulling the leather sachet from a pocket and using it to fill her transformed tube of lipstick with ground herbs.

The ingenious little piece of machinery left Criss rather impressed. "You know I could arrest you for that."

Neeta smiled. "Shame, I just had it sent in for Source refinement." She held out the tube. "You first."

The agent hesitated, looking around the cemetery to make sure they were alone. She snatched the apparatus from Neeta's hand. Criss had only smoked once or twice in her life, but the day's circumstances justified the transgression. After inhaling, she passed the tube back to Neeta who took a few puffs of her own. The two women looked at each other and burst out laughing. That they were standing in the middle of a cemetery made no difference at all.

"The first time I met her," Neeta said, musing on the lipstick.

"Yeah?"

"I knew I'd be with her forever."

Criss giggled.

"Even though I also knew," continued the Adept, "she had a million lovers, just like me."

"I guess I'm one of a million, now?"

"More like one in a million." Neeta sat down on a headstone. *Wait, what did I just say?* She was feeling it, which only meant conversations would get stranger and stranger. The Adept marveled at the herbs' effect. *You're eager to speak up, to become more involved. Before you recognize it, you feel you've been talking for twenty minutes, and the other people are just sitting there listening, or not listening. You don't know what you said, whether it was too loud or too soft, whether it even made sense. And then, suddenly, you want out, fast, and—*

"Hey, let me ask you something," said Criss.

"Yeah?"

"Did we both get locked into our cabins? Like, actually?"

The Adept took a second to consider the simple question. "Yeah … yeah, I think we did."

The women laughed again.

"What the dread?" Criss exclaimed. "Why can't I successfully lock someone in a cabin for once?"

"Beats me, feels like people have been locking me in cabins my entire life."

"Do this, do that." The agent shook her head. "It's not fair."

"Life's not fair. You think there's ever been a female preceptor?"

"Never mind a female chief," muttered Criss. "Gods only know who they'll bring in to replace Aiden. At least with him, I could tell he cared. And ... and I never showed him any gratitude."

The two women sat in the cemetery for quite some time before recovering a portion of their senses and walking back to the center of Portown. The Golden Auralus was busy. Not unexpected since the tavern offered one of the few forums of entertainment in the city. Smaller eateries near the waterfront looked appealing, so Neeta and Criss strolled in their direction. As the two women crossed the road, they were stopped by a recent acquaintance.

"Hey!" shouted Ruan. The personal attendant was at the sticks of a standard rental SPC.

Both Neeta and Criss walked over.

"Just wanted to offer my condolences," he said.

The agent acknowledged his sympathy.

"If there's anything I can do to help," Ruan added, "don't hesitate to ask."

Hollow words. Criss seized the opportunity. "Where are you headed?"

Biting the inside of his lip, the personal attendant cursed himself for stopping. "A small village."

"Which one?"

"You won't know the name."

"Try me."

"Tuka."

"What direction is that?" Criss asked.

Ruan pointed east.

"Can we hitch a ride with you?"

"Hold on a second," interjected Neeta, and she pulled the agent away from the SPC. "What are you doing?"

"I'm hunting those brothers down and bringing them to justice."

"Yeah, you already mentioned something about that."

"Good, now you've heard it twice, then."

Neeta sighed. "Not if I find them first."

"Why do you care?"

"I'm supposed to bring them back with me to the Academy."

"Looks like we're in a conflict."

"How do you even know they're going to this Tuka, or whatever it's called?"

"I don't," said Criss. "What I do know is that the docks are on the eastern edge of Portown. They definitely didn't come into the city, which means they took one of the roads going east."

"So you're just going to drive with this random guy and hope you run into them?"

"Exactly."

"Did I already mention you're crazy?"

Ruan's patience was wearing thin. "Are you two coming or what?"

Criss ignored his question and turned back to Neeta. "Our best shot at finding them is now, when they're still on the road, out in the open. Once they hunker down in some village, we'll never see them again."

Recognizing the validity of the agent's thought, Neeta nodded. "What about our conflict?"

"We'll just have to cross that bridge when we get to it."

CHAPTER THIRTY-THREE

The sturdy SPC was painted a rich green hue. All-terrain tires with deeply grooved tread blocks delivered the traction to travel through any region of the Dominion. A spare, fastened to the back of the vehicle, was covered by a gray tarp matching the color of the open air seats. On the front bumper, a barbed-wire grille allowed wind to enter, cooling an impressive Source-powered engine capable of carrying occupants at remarkable speeds. Behind the driver's seat, three rows of padded benches were bolted onto the chassis, each more elevated than the one ahead. And above it stretched a canvas tarpaulin that sheltered the travelers from sun and rain alike.

His hands on both steering sticks, Lecarn maneuvered his one-of-a-kind SPC across the countryside. In the seat next to him was Edvon, behind them Sabine and Kyran shared one bench. As they rolled on uneven ground, everyone jounced around. It became an ever-increasing occurrence. Long gone were the lush and flat fields of wild grass surrounding the Portown metropolitan area. Instead, a light-colored clay, one which rose into dusty clouds as Lecarn raced over it, was extending to the horizon. Bushes were strewn about the wilderness, replacing the majestic trees that grew to towering heights because of their proximity to the Wimau's nutritious waters. Yet the arid environment seemed well-traversed, with a number of tracks in the dirt creating routes leading to various destinations.

A short while back, Sabine had turned around and watched the lonely port town disappear. *We just managed to sneak off that ship. Now, we're returning to the unknown* … Riding in a Source-powered machine did little to comfort the young woman, though she preferred her new surroundings. *Anything other than that dreadful cabin.* Sliding over on the bench, Sabine leaned toward Kyran. "Where do you think we're going?" She hoped the sound of the motor would keep her question from reaching Lecarn's ears.

"I—I don't have a clue," replied the Adept, distracted by the sensation of Sabine's leg brushing against his and the warmth of her breath.

"This is such a big carrier," she continued, "he's probably not alone."

"Uh-huh," mumbled Kyran. He had barely registered the observation, all he wanted was to put an arm around Sabine's waist to pull her closer in. His thoughts might as well have been prayers because they came to reality. At that instant, Lecarn hit another bump in the road, and the young woman was thrust into Kyran's chest. The Adept helped back up an embarrassed girl, and she studied him for an instant, as if figuring out what to say. For Kyran, time had stopped, and he was content to sit there and stare back, enthralled by the beauty of her violet eyes.

"Thanks," Sabine offered.

"Oh, umm, don't mention it."

Lecarn shouted from up ahead. "Hold on! It's about to get a little rocky."

"Timely warning," muttered Kyran, and Sabine giggled.

A small mountain came into view. It appeared to have a flat top, with steep cliffs surrounding it. A strange formation in an increasingly desolate landscape, the elevated tract of earth captivated the three companions.

"It's called a tepui," Lecarn called out, sensing their piqued interest.

"What does that mean?" asked Kyran.

Edvon was ready. "It means—"

"House of the Gods," interjected Sabine.

"Exactly," said Lecarn, glancing over his shoulder.

"How did you know?" Kyran wondered.

"It's in the Book of Provenance. Sometimes, we even refer to the Temple as a tepui. But ... how? What is this place?"

"Oh, there's not much to understand," said Lecarn. "Means nothing whatsoever, just a way of naming things, I suppose. There are thousands of tepuis around here, and trust me, there's nothing special about any of them." He spun around in his seat. "Are you an Overseer or something?"

Sabine held her breath. *Am I?* She felt Kyran put his hand on her knee. "No, I'm not."

Lecarn nodded. "Okay, then. Not like I care either way." Pulling back on one of the steering sticks, he carried on with his explanation of the tepuis. "They're pretty cool from a geological perspective. Rain and wind have eroded the weaker rocks, leaving behind the stronger ones in a column. That's why they don't have gentle slopes like other hills or mountains, you see?"

"That's, like, really cool." Kyran pretended to be intrigued. He was focused on the fact that Sabine had yet to swat away his hand. The Adept pulled it back, worried he might make her uncomfortable. Little did he know his gentle touch had given the young woman exactly what she needed in the awkward moment.

"It will be cooler once you climb it," Lecarn continued. "One like this? You don't even need any ropes."

"What?" Edvon echoed his companions' sentiments.

"I'm just messing with you!" Their driver laughed. "Don't worry, we're camped just at its base." From a young age, Lecarn had been fond of teasing people. Perhaps it had been a way of coping with the death of his mother, or maybe it was just part of his natural temperament. Regardless, his harmless pranks had more often than not gotten him into trouble. Especially as he grew older, when the consequences of his actions increased in severity, until they culminated in a monumental breaking point. The once-Noble forced himself to expel the painful memory from his thoughts for the second time that day. The SPC was nearing the base of the tepui, and Lecarn slowed down before coming to a stop.

Edvon counted five figures around a campfire, three of whom were sitting on a makeshift bench. A large map of what appeared to be the Dominion lay flat on a foldable table, punctured by several pins marking specific locations. In the background, several heavy-duty tents, identical in size and color, were clustered.

A woman with dark-brown hair tied in a tight ponytail dispensed of any pleasantries and got straight to the point. "Why did you bring three?"

Lecarn grinned, as if he had been expecting such a question from her. "Why not?"

"We don't have room for another. That's why."

"Will you calm down, Zoel? I'm sure we can make it work."

She stood up, her leather pants clinging to well-sculpted legs. "Make it work in a tent other than mine." Zoel spun around and disappeared into one of the canvas shelters.

Another picked up where she had left off. "You're an Overseer, aren't you?" The man was tall, with a bony face and a distinct hook nose. His long dark coat, black turtleneck sweater, and sleek onyx hair made Sabine hold her breath.

"No," Lecarn answered. "She isn't."

"Anymore," added the man.

Sabine was stupefied. "What … what makes you think I am?"

"Oh, I've had quite some experience with that vile

institution."

"I can think of better terms than vile," shouted Zoel from inside her tent, causing the nefarious looking man to smirk.

"All right, enough," interjected Lecarn. "These people are part of our team now. Might I remind you of your origins, Xavier?"

The man named Xavier opened his mouth to protest, but coat twirling, he ducked into another tent. An awkward silence ensued.

"Well, you got to know two of the more charming members of our group. In any event, my name's Fionne, and that's Wick, and that's Gavin."

Sabine took a moment to examine the hosts. Fionne, an older woman, had trimmed white hair curling around her ears and neck. *She seems pleasant, at least.* To her left was Wick, and he too appeared eager to welcome the new arrivals. He was young, with dirty blond hair covering part of his eyes. This often forced him to run a hand through it or jerk his head. Wick's brown eyes darted back and forth as he observed the newcomers. *Who are these people?* Sabine looked at Gavin, the last camper of the bunch, who was leaning against a simple yet sturdy wooden staff. He had a leather hood over his head, a patchy gray beard, and a brown sack slung over his shoulder. Sabine frowned as she caught Gavin staring at Kyran. The Adept had also noticed and was ignoring the old man. *What's going on here?* She watched an uncomfortable Kyran give Gavin a sidelong glance. *This is so weird!*

Zoel had re-appeared from her tent. "I can't believe this is the best you could find."

"Will you stop it?" Fionne snapped.

Wick was in agreement. "We have Xavier for that."

Zoel laughed. "I'm not being a downer, just a realist. These three can't get the job done."

"Well, he seems pretty strong," said Wick, pointing at Edvon. "And anyway, Gavin doesn't look the most redoubtable, yet we know that's far from the truth."

The comment gave Zoel some pause. "True. Old man, you might not talk much, but there are few I trust more to cover me when things go sideways."

"That's why," Lecarn declared, "you never judge a book by the cover, especially when it comes to—"

And then, it clicked in Edvon's head. The reference to a job. The remote campsite, all-terrain carrier, strangely assembled crew. *These people, they're ...*

"—bounty hunters."

CHAPTER THIRTY-FOUR

Crushed bricks and splintered wood, scattered vegetation torn to shreds, smoldering SPCs, walls of homes reduced to mere rubble. Fragments of a once-thriving village devastated beyond comprehension. "What happened here?" the commandant asked to no one in particular.

Gorgios remained motionless, staring at the eerie reminders of life lost. Even the Overseers under his authority kept quiet, and observing the unimpressionable hit squad at a loss for words was as peculiar to Rex Ruga as the sight that had turned them into mutes.

Pluto elected to submit his point of view. "Looks like there was a raid."

Shooting her guide a nasty look, the commandant strode toward the carnage. *Perhaps they are trackers after all.* She had been wondering whether Joss and Pluto were ushering them around like a pack of balbaks, because there was no coherent explanation behind their decision-making process. *Left here, straight ahead through this village, bang a right there.* With not so much as a trace of the Adepts since their departure from Portown. Blindly following others was not one of Rex Ruga's assets, a straightforward fact that merely intensified her growing frustrations with the failing mission.

Now, the would-be trackers had spotted something. *And Gods is it morbid. Probably some Noble experimenting with his new toy.* A sign lying in the dirt caught the commandant's attention. It was charred like everything else, yet she could make out lettering in faded colors. *Inn.* The Overseer thought back to the Golden Auralus in Portown and to the conversations she had overheard about incidents occurring aboard Ocean Star, specifically the murders of both the ship's captain and the chief of the Battalion himself. *And apparently the two Adepts were involved.* There was something bigger going on, though Rex Ruga had trouble figuring out exactly what that might be. *Do I need to pay the Main Complex a little visit? The agents were obviously on the right path. How's it linked to these village attacks?*

"There's something wrong here," said Gorgios.

"Is that so?" she retorted. "You mean other than the apocalyptic destruction?"

The large Overseer huffed. "Yes."

"What is it, then?"

"There are no bodies."

The commandant frowned upon realizing the soundness of her Master of Arms' observation. "You're right."

"Maybe they all burned?" suggested Pluto.

"No." Gorgios shook his head. "We would see the bones. And smell the charred flesh."

"Ah, of course." Pluto shot Joss a dubious look, one that made explicit his desire not to know how the behemoth was so well-versed in such matters. "Maybe the village was already abandoned? After all, who would choose to live out here?" The comment elicited snickers. "Come to think of it, they probably killed each other, out of boredom." Now in full entertainment mode, the performer had most Overseers chuckling. He cracked several more jokes, a few prompting even Gorgios to smirk.

Rex Ruga ignored the others as they laughed and chatted in the heart of the fiery ruins. *What took place?* The question was alarming given the freshness of the attack.

"And that's the last time she ever talked to me!" exclaimed

Pluto, the others howling with amusement. "Mind you, whenever she—"

"Quiet!" Rex Ruga screamed. "Everyone!"

The Overseers stood at attention.

"You two." She pointed at Pluto and Joss. "Where are we going?"

"Come again?" asked the articulate performer.

"I'm paying you six thousand coins. Tell me where to go."

"For what?"

"For the Adepts, by Gods!"

"Oh, right."

"Track them!"

Pluto nodded. "Give us a minute." The two performers walked into the destroyed village until they were out of Rex Ruga's sight. "Any ideas?" Stroking his mustache, Joss shrugged, then held up two fingers. "Yes, we can do that," said Pluto, "but this stunt is ending soon. The woman's absolutely crazy. Gods, we should have never accepted this job."

Right on cue, Rex Ruga hollered out for them. "What's taking so long?"

"Let's just hope we somehow find these dread Adepts," whispered a wide-eyed Pluto. He waved at the commandant. "Yes, coming!" The two performers walked back and rejoined the group. "Our initial inclination was correct, as usual. The Adepts were definitely in this village."

"I sure hope so," Rex Ruga replied. "Otherwise, why did you bring us here?"

"Umm … right, exactly."

"So what now?" asked Gorgios.

"Watch and learn, friends." Pluto sifted through the cinders and tossed a handful into the open. The black ashes scattered in the wind. "Yes, it all makes sense," he said. Joss took five wide and exaggerated paces to the right, coming to a hard stop in front of a dilapidated wall. Eyes closed, he flattened the palm of his hand against it and stood perfectly still. Next to him, Pluto thrummed words no one understood, pivoted, and bent to the knee. "There!" Joss advanced straight to where his associate was pointing, crouched, and put his ear to the ground. He looked to the east. "They traveled that way," concluded Pluto.

Rex Ruga was dumbfounded. "What in the Gods was that? How could you possibly—"

"Did you not hire us to find the Adepts? We're doing our job here."

"Fine. We go east."

The group returned to the caravan of SPCs parked nearby. Before the commandant could climb in a vehicle, Gorgios pulled her aside. "Ruga, listen to me. You should go back to the Temple and let me deal with this."

"Are you out of your mind?"

"You're wasting your time out here, and Najara needs you."

"Gorgios, I already told you, Najara needs no one."

"All I'm saying is that it doesn't seem very wise for the Temple's leader to be barreling through villages when there are more important matters."

"Like what? There's nothing more urgent than finding these Adepts, as far as I'm concerned."

"And we'll find them. Let me take care of it."

Rex Ruga was livid. "Do you think I got where I am from being a diplomat?"

"I don't—"

"I rose through the ranks as a soldier."

"There haven't been any wars since the Dread Days, Ruga." Perhaps the only Overseer who dared to call the commandant by her real name, Gorgios looked at his love interest, but the answer was not what he sought.

"There are wars being waged every day, you don't see them." And with that, she lifted herself into the vehicle. "Onward!"

The Temple caravan rumbled through a barren countryside, save a growing number of tepuis dotting the landscape. That they were driving SPCs, Rex Ruga cared little. *Hypocrisy only matters for people who depend on others.*

Another village came into view. This one was intact, though when drawing nearer, they realized it stood as a haunting shell of a previous self. Formerly housing a few hundred families, the community now amounted to less than a handful. Residents had abandoned their homes and fled to the safety of Phaidros, leaving unopened packages on their doorsteps, blinds half shut, and the once-bustling square deserted.

"At least we won't have trouble parking," quipped Pluto as the caravan made its way down the main street.

The commandant jumped out and barked her orders to the Overseers who had already gathered around. "Search the village for the Adepts. And don't leave a single stone unturned."

They formed smaller units.

"Gorgios, I'm going to the tavern. Meet me there if you so wish." Rex Ruga then gestured to Pluto and Joss. "Make yourselves useful."

When the angry commandant disappeared from sight, the two performers braced themselves for the oncoming slaughter. "I know you're full of rubbish," said the blunt Master of Arms.

"Huh?"

"You two think I'm an idiot? It was obvious after the first village that you have no clue how to track something."

"What are you talking about?"

"Cut it out, I don't have time for this. In case you didn't realize it, I'm an actual tracker, the best in the Dominion."

Pluto knew there was no tricking the giant. "Why are you protecting us, then?"

"You assisted my squad in Fermantis. And anyway, we're moving in the right direction."

"How do you know?"

"Did I not just tell you I'm a real tracker?"

"They went east?" Pluto asked.

"Yes," answered Gorgios, "I picked up several trails outside Portown and have been on top of them ever since."

"So isn't this a big waste of your time?"

"No, not if it means she goes back to the Temple." The senator paused. "You didn't hear me say that."

"Hear what?"

"Very good," said Gorgios. "I'm heading to the tavern."

After several hours, the search units reconvened by the SPCs.

"We've looked everywhere," reported an Overseer. "They're not here."

"All right, I've had en—enough." A slightly inebriated Rex Ruga turned toward Pluto and Joss. "I'm losing my patience, in case you hadn't noticed."

"It's not our fault that, umm ..." Pluto glanced at Gorgios, "... they're good at hiding."

"Well, I will not hunt through every corner of this dread Dominion," replied the commandant. "I'm giving you one last chance."

"One last chance?"

"That's right. They'd better be in the next village we visit."

"And if not?"

"You're taking their place on the pyre."

CHAPTER THIRTY-FIVE

"It's always the remote ones that get hit."

Neeta frowned. "There must be a reason."

"Oh, I'm sure there is," said Ruan. "And I plan on finding out precisely what that might be. Don't you ladies worry, I'll tell you all about it after the next attack."

"Gods, you're cocky. How can you be so confident?"

"I spent an inordinate amount of time studying the maps."

"Well, good thing the Nobles have the best maps available," muttered Criss, one of her rare contributions to the conversation.

Ruan scowled at the agent.

"And the most time on their hands," piled on Neeta, and both women laughed at the driver's expense.

"In case you might have forgotten, I'm not a lord."

Criss was quick to chime in. "You might as well be one. I've heard about the lifestyle of you personal attendants."

"Maps, huh?" Neeta interjected, in a hastened effort to change the subject. "Why don't you tell us a bit more about them?"

"Yeah, sure." Ruan was also eager to avoid quarreling with the intimidating agent. "I marked the villages that were struck. On the surface, there were no logical connections. But when I dug a little deeper, patterns emerged."

"Patterns?"

"That's right. They all meet a certain set of criteria. First off, villages that have been destroyed are never neighboring. Second, their populations top at five-hundred. Third, the—"

"Okay, okay, I get the gist," cut in the impatient Adept. "You gathered your little data points and picked the most obvious site for the next attack."

"Correct."

"And it was Tuka?"

"Gods, no." Ruan rolled his eyes. "You think I want to die? No, the village closest to Tuka, you know, Jasper."

Neeta was unimpressed. "Ah. So you're going to wait in Tuka to discover what happens to the victims next door?"

"Is there a problem with that?"

"Don't get me started," intervened Criss. "All I can hope for is that your deductive skills are on par with your empathy."

Ruan laughed. "Do I want to see an attack? I'm trying to identify the offender here. More likely, someone of interest passes through Tuka, or they've planted the weapon in the area. And in any case, I'm on assignment, might I point out."

"Oh, so it's not your responsibility?"

"My responsibility? Why are we talking like I've done something wrong?"

"Who's they, anyway?" Criss asked.

"What?"

"You said that they may have planted the weapon."

Ruan shot a sideways glance at Neeta. "It's pretty clear what's going on here."

"Watch it," warned the Adept. "I don't respond well to Temple propaganda."

Criss could not hold back her inflammatory comment. "Propaganda and accuracy aren't mutually exclusive."

Tuka came into view against the windy horizon, drawing a merciful end to what would have descended into an even more toxic debate. Like the other villages they had crossed, this one was partly abandoned, its residual population too scared to escape.

Ruan drove up to the largest building, a three-story wooden inn.

"Are you staying the night?" he asked Neeta and Criss as they hopped out of the rental SPC.

The agent paused. "Maybe. Give us a second to talk it over."

"Very well. I'll get my room in the meantime."

"So?" asked Criss.

Neeta was unhappy. "So, your little plan was a complete failure. And now, I'm stuck in some dread-forsaken village in the middle of nowhere."

"I meant are we leaving now or in the morning?"

"Do you know how much time we've wasted?" pursued the relentless Adept. "And it's not like you were exactly pleasant during the ride."

"Will you answer my question?"

"And if you believe we'll find them now, then—"

Criss walked away.

"Hey!" shouted Neeta.

"When you figure it out, let me know," the agent responded, "I'm going to the tavern."

Kicking up dirt in frustration, Neeta went looking for Ruan. She found him arguing with a caretaker by the name of Stakel.

"You said the place is empty."

"Irrelevant. You want the better room, you pay the higher rate."

"You're going to let it sit, unused?"

"Yes." Stakel's voice was piercing, and the heavy Tukan accent did not make it any less annoying. Her white hair was curled up into little buns at the top, and she wore small glasses in front of her dull eyes. "Do you want the upgrade or not?"

Ruan slammed his fists on the counter. "Here, you Dread Shepherd," he said, handing her an additional pouch of coins.

"This better be worth it."

Stakel held back the room key. "What did you just call me?"

"Umm ... a Dread Shepherd, perhaps?"

"I expect an apology."

Ruan shook his head. "Seriously?"

"You're not getting a room in my inn until you apologize."

"Okay, I'm sorry."

"That wasn't heartfelt."

"I apologize," said the personal attendant, gritting his teeth.

"For what?"

"For calling you a Dread Shepherd. What else?"

"Say it all at once."

"Okay, you're about to lose my business."

"You'll sleep outside because we both know this is the only inn here in Tuka."

A prolonged standstill followed until Ruan forced the sounds from his lips. "I apologize for calling you a Dread Shepherd."

Neeta burst out laughing when Ruan snatched the room key from Stakel.

"Yes, I'm sure that was entertaining. Glad I could provide you with some comic relief. So what's the deal, anyway? You leaving?" he asked.

"What do you care?"

"Well ... if you stay the night, you're more than welcome to share my room."

Neeta poked the grinning personal attendant in the ribs. "You got lucky that one time on Ocean Star," she cautioned. "Don't you go thinking that was normal or something."

The wind had waned to a faint breeze. The Adept gasped in ecstasy, until Ruan collapsed from exhaustion. He lay on his back, staring at the ceiling. "Lucky, huh?"

Turning onto a side and resting her head on Ruan's chest, Neeta smiled. "People can get lucky more than once," she said, pulling herself a little closer.

"You always have an answer to everything."

"And you don't?"

"All I'm worried about is that dread caretaker finding out I have an extra guest in my room."

Neeta giggled. "Oh, she'll definitely charge you double."

"What a nasty woman. Chances are she's right there, listening to us."

"I hope so. Looks like the poor thing could use some warmth in her life."

The two-time lovers remained silent. Ruan took the officer by surprise. "How's it like at the Academy?"

"What do you mean?"

"I don't know, I'm curious what it's like."

"You want to be an Adept or something?"

"Who doesn't?"

"Overseers, for one, and—"

"Oh please, spare me the lecture," objected Ruan. "The Book of Provenance was written by people jealous they couldn't manipulate the Source."

"You think so?"

"Of course, that's why there's more of them than there are of you."

Though Neeta accepted the truth of the personal attendant's reflection, she changed the subject to avoid having to speak of the Academy. "So, who do you suspect is behind the attacks? Like, actually?"

"I'd put my money on you Adepts, with all the best—" The personal attendant picked up a smack across the chest. "Ouch!"

"Don't you dare say that again," said Neeta.

"I'm joking."

"Whatever." She sat up and scratched her thigh. "I wonder what happened to Criss."

"Why does it matter to you? By the sounds of it, you didn't care much for each other."

"I don't know, I kind of feel bad for her."

"So you have feelings?"

"No, I don't."

"By all the Gods, you do!" Ruan was delighted. "You might not recognize it yet, but you definitely do."

"How could you possibly know?"

"You're too narrow-minded, Neeta. We can have feelings for lots of different people."

"Oh, is that so?"

"Absolutely. And that's what makes this tolerable. When you love many, you can turn a blind eye to individual flaws.

"You're insane." Neeta stood up. "The faults you're so eager to avoid only enrich the beauty of a relationship, not the other way around."

Marrek's wisdom had influenced a generation of Adepts, if only it had forced its way to more minds in the general populace. Not that the citizens of Phaidros were uneducated, by any means. Mandatory schooling up to the age of twenty had been in place for several decades and offered various educational tracks. Some went directly to vocational school where they could learn a trade, while others pursued higher courses. Test results determined placement, with only so many open slots available at the next level. Those who made it to the top earned the most prestigious jobs in the metropolis. Urban architect, surgeon, mathematical historian.

Battalion agent. Criss took another swig of ale. *Being angry makes me even more ... angry! Because people only get mad when they recognize they're wrong.* A lesson she had taught herself long ago. The agent shook her head and walked toward the other end of the tavern where villagers were playing a game of Saryn.

"Place your bet," said one.

Another put down three coins.

"Okay, marble."

The gambler reached for a little glass ball. He hovered his hand over a flat plate with a coiled track that spiraled on itself. "I'll place it here." The villager put the marble onto the carved track, on the third coil to the inside.

"Okay, countdown." His opponent pointed at another part of the track. "Three ... two ... one ... shoot!"

The shooter hit the marble in the allotted time with nothing more than a gentle push of the fingertip, sending it circling around the coil. The marble stopped short of the mark.

"Not within a thumb's length, so I'll be taking those." The pointer scooped the three coins from the table.

"I'm up," said Criss.

The villagers scanned her from top to bottom and up again.

"You want to be shooter or pointer?"

"Shooter."

The agent tossed five coins onto the table. A villager agreed to cover the bet, and once Criss had positioned her marble on the track, he started the countdown. "Didn't even need all three seconds," mumbled Criss. The marble froze right on the villager's mark, and she waved at him.

"That'll be ten coins."

The men pushed one another, demanding to be next.

"I want a try."

"Will you play again?"

"Once more?"

Criss chugged down the rest of her ale and snapped her head toward the villagers.

They hushed.

"I'll be playing through the night."

CHAPTER THIRTY-SIX

When he was just a boy, Edvon often skipped down to the baqua courts in West Phaidros after school. There were always competitive games to watch and an occasional appearance from a professional or semi-professional player. He remembered wanting to throw curves like they did or make the incredible diving catches often witnessed by the small crowds. Edvon recalled one particular amateur who would show up on a nightly basis with his group of friends. He had long blond hair and a chiseled body that made everyone around him look unfit. The man was loud and cocky, often talking trash. He also rarely lost.

* * *

"Throw it, boy!" the blond man yelled.

Little Edvon gasped as the pip went soaring up high. The loudmouth sprinted around the pool before pulling onto the third railing and launching himself above the water. He managed to spectacularly divert the ball toward a teammate who passed it along for the easy triple out.

Lecarn emerged from the pool. "Throw it, boy!" The crowd was loving it, egging him on. He gave high-fives while pausing for shadow time, then switched sides. His teammate, a young man with a hazel right eye and blue left eye, stepped up to the wall first. The ball fell in the water.

"Hit!" shouted the spectators.

Next came Lecarn, and he slid a clever throw underneath

the front railing, narrowly avoiding a blocker's kick. The baqua player brought a finger to his lip, swiveled toward the crowd, and waved his bright-red glove around while strutting backward to the scoring circle. They would score many more runs, each increasingly fascinating to the little Adept.

* * *

It was ironic that Edvon had always wanted to meet the blond player. *I think he might be standing right in front of me.* The memory came from such a distant past that, perhaps, he was mistaken. Nonetheless, the similarities were striking.

"Are you from Phaidros?"

Lecarn turned to face him. "Why do you ask?"

"I think I remember you playing baqua when I was a kid."

"So what?"

"I … I don't know," said Edvon. "Small Dominion, I guess."

"It's not that big of a place, trust me. I've sailed around it multiple times. We're bound to run into a few people more than once."

The Adept remained silent.

"But yes, I used to play baqua quite a bit. Gods, that was a while ago. And what a team we had. I take it you're pretty good yourself?"

"At baqua?"

The bounty hunter nodded.

"I'm okay," replied Edvon. "Not a professional or anything."

"Forget that. The pro-leagues are for rich brats like me."

"So you're a Noble?"

"Not anymore."

"What does that mean?"

Lecarn took his time in answering. "I gave it up for something better."

"Huh?"

"You wouldn't understand, kid." Sighing, the once-Noble cut short the conversation. "Let's go back, there's little time left in the day." Stepping on a charred timber, he led the way toward the parked SPC.

The soil was pitch-black, leaving stains on Edvon's shoes that would probably never rub off. The Adept could barely tell where the houses used to stand, as if nothing had ever been there in the first place. *Gods, this is bad.* The others were already waiting for them at the meeting point.

"So?" asked Lecarn.

"We estimate the village was destroyed a week ago," said Wick.

"More than a week ago," added Xavier.

"That long?" Lecarn rubbed his forehead. "There could be dozens of these we don't know about." He turned to Fionne. "Was this town on our list of potential targets?"

"Yes, third one down."

"At least our methodology's right, we just arrived here a bit too late."

"Seems that way," Fionne replied.

"Fine. Then, we move on as planned. Anything else?"

"Yes," said Xavier. "Might be worth mentioning the lack of bodies."

"Like the other villages?"

"Correct."

"Gods," mumbled Lecarn. "Okay, we need to get moving. Tuka and Jasper are waiting." The engine sparked as he accelerated onto the open road, and they went flying, leaving behind a wasteland from which even the toughest scavengers would struggle to extract any use.

Their destination still several hours away, the riders had ample time to fraternize, though one of them harbored little interest in talking. Kyran glanced at Sabine who was again ignoring him. The young man cursed under his breath, unsure how they had reached such an impasse. It developed after a harmless argument.

* * *

"You think that was easy!" Sabine exclaimed. She was standing with Kyran at the far edge of the destroyed village, away from the others. "That captain tried to rape me."

"I didn't say he didn't."

"And then, I had to act like some prostitute in front of a Battalion agent."

"No one told you to do that."

"I can't believe you."

"Why are you always the victim?" shot back Kyran. "You too were in the dungeons, if I remember correctly."

Sabine stared at the Adept for several seconds before walking away. He called after her, but she ignored him and disappeared from sight.

* * *

Kyran cringed as he relived the incident, and he kicked the back of the bench in front of him.

"What the cholee, you little runt!" snapped Xavier.

The young Adept was in a particularly foul mood. "Shut up, you Dread Shepherd."

Xavier turned around. "Excuse me?"

Out of nowhere, Gavin erupted into laughter. Given how little he spoke, the old man's outburst caught them off guard, providing relief to the growing tension.

Lecarn seized the opportunity to change topics. "So, who do you think is responsible for the attacks?"

"Definitely the Temple," replied Edvon. "It's obvious."

"How?"

"They have the most to gain from it."

Fionne shook her head. "I'm not so sure."

"You can think what you want."

"Just consider the facts, Edvon. Politics are pretty simple in Phaidros. Sure, Nobles turn a blind eye to the Source because of its many benefits. But don't think that many don't end up supporting the Temple anyway. And Noble support is all the confidante needs to run her agenda. Who cares what the masses are saying?"

"The masses can create change."

"Where do you think you live!" exclaimed Fionne. "The books you're reading at the Academy forgot to tell you that never happens. We live in a society governed and enjoyed by the few. It's incredible. Nobles wearing jewelry around their wrists worth more than people's lives." She paused. "Though, you know the one benefit? When material things are irrelevant, it makes life perfectly clear."

"Yes," Lecarn pointed to his head, "and all that matters is your brain." Everything had changed in his life after meeting Fionne. The old woman had affected him in many positive ways, both intellectually and intimately. And then came Zoel. It had happened so seamlessly between the three of them, they soon became a triad. Bounty hunters by trade, they lived on the road, taking odd jobs and building their team. Lecarn had never been happier.

He was also getting hungry, as were the others, so they

stopped for food in a small outpost near the base of a tepui. They ate a simple yet invigorating vegetable soup and freshly-baked bread. Edvon chewed slowly and deliberately. He picked one of the large green leaves floating at the top of the soup. Bringing it up to his mouth, he swallowed the vegetable whole.

"I'm surprised you haven't yet asked what you're here for." Lecarn was in between bites of his own. "It's not like I gave Elias much detail on the job."

"You suspect the Source is involved in these attacks, and therefore, you want some Adepts in your crew." Edvon slurped down another mouthful. "Seems pretty clear to me."

Lecarn grinned. "Something like that."

It was quite late when they reached Tuka, hours after it had already turned dark. Lecarn parked the SPC on the outskirts of town, and the group unloaded the gear. Each member moved fast and efficiently, knowing exactly what task to accomplish. Wick hammered in the pegs from where the row of tents could be erected. Fionne and Zoel installed the table and chairs. In a quickly built fire pit, Xavier and Gavin had already managed to kindle a flame. Using it to spark the ends of two torches, Lecarn hung them on both sides of the camp. The brothers and Sabine quietly watched the sequence of activities.

Once they had finished, Lecarn addressed the group. "We'll need to share sleeping space."

Wick kindly volunteered. "I'll go sleep in Xavier's tent, and two of you can have mine."

"Thank you," said Sabine. "Edvon and I will take that one."

The younger brother could feel his blood boiling.

"Great." Lecarn's next suggestion went over poorly. "Kyran, you can share with Gavin."

Glancing at the surely perverted old man, the Adept shook his head. "I don't think so. I'm going to stay at an inn."

"What inn?" snapped Edvon. "And with what coins?"

Kyran tried to bluff his way out. "I'd like some of my pay from this job up front." He kept a straight face and stared at Lecarn, praying to the Gods that a pay was even in the works.

"Fine." The bounty hunter tossed him a small leather sachet from his belt. "Do as you wish, there's an inn in the center of Tuka. We'll pick you up early tomorrow morning on our way to Jasper."

With a conciliatory gesture, the young Adept walked away. Edvon, committed to the promise he had made to Marrek, rushed after Kyran, catching up to him as he stepped onto Tuka's main street. They proceeded without talking all the way to the inn, somewhat aware that Sabine was following. Kyran pushed the door open and came face-to-face with one of the vilest looking women he had ever seen. She was not deformed or disfigured but discharged a noxious energy.

"Will you be quiet?" Stakel snapped. "Guests are sleeping."

Kyran was confused. "We haven't even said anything."

"Are you here for a room?"

"Three rooms."

"That'll be nine coins."

"Just take it out of here," the Adept said, tossing her Lecarn's pouch.

Stakel sniffled before snatching three keys from behind the counter. She led them up the stairs, walked down the hallway, and opened a first door. Sabine disappeared inside.

"You're in 10," croaked the caretaker, pointing at another room.

Edvon bid them good night.

"What about me?" asked Kyran.

"At the end of the hallway, 6."

In number 7, Ruan and Neeta were doing it geega-style.

CHAPTER THIRTY-SEVEN

It originated in a dimly lit chamber, where four mortals relied on a God's aura to find their way. They were visibly nervous mostly because none of them were supposed to be there. Meeting a resident of the Red City was rare. What they were about to do, however, transcended mere formality. *Their meeting would shape the course of history.*

According to the Book of Provenance, Cholee was the first to break the silence. His words were memorialized in infamy. "Take It."

And the four mortals did so without a second thought. *So began the events that led to our castigation.* The only passage more notorious than the one Sabine had just read for the hundredth time was the resulting punishment. *Not our shackling to the Dominion.* Rather, Cholee's punishment. *For having bestowed upon us the knowledge of It.* Sabine flipped forward several pages, until finding the line she was searching for. "And he was bound to eternal flight, forever in limbo."

They said Cholee could still be seen outside the walls of the Red City, flying upward to return home. *Ironic, since he winged his way past the responsibilities of a celestial being.* Sabine heard a soft knock. She closed the inn's copy of the Book of Provenance, returned it to the nightstand by her bed, and looked through the peep hole. Holding her breath at the sight of Kyran's slim figure, she cracked open the door.

"You're still up?" he whispered.

"Well, I am now."

Kyran turned around. "Sorry, I didn't mean …"

"No, it's okay." Though still angry with the Adept, Sabine also felt an urge to see him. "What do you want?"

"I … I just don't like how it ended between us earlier today," he explained. "I didn't mean to argue with you, and … and I—" Kyran twiddled his thumbs. "I'm sorry."

The young woman remained quiet.

"I guess that's all I wanted to say." He was about to leave.

"Can I tell you what really happened?"

"What do you mean?"

"Why I was in the Temple's dungeons."

"Of course you can."

"Okay … but if I let you in, do you promise you won't—" Sabine hesitated, "—try anything?"

Kyran nodded. "I promise." He shut the door and sat on the bed next to her.

"When I was just a child," she said, "my parents sent me to Phaidros to join the Temple. I never got to know them well. They were farmers, toiling in the soil from dawn to dusk, and they didn't have time for a little girl in their house." She looked up toward the ceiling, contemplating whether to continue. "Or the money for an extra mouth to feed. Anyway, when I first arrived at the Temple, everything seemed so strange. But the more I embraced my study of the Book of Provenance, the more I enjoyed it. I made friends, and I trained to become a teacher, spending time at local schools in Phaidros to share the knowledge I had acquired in my classes."

Sabine paused, twirling a mesh of hair between her lithe fingers. "Only weeks ago, I passed my closing exams, earned the white robe, and became a cadet, and—" She shook her head. "Why am I telling you this? You don't care, it's boring and—"

"I do care," Kyran cut in.

"Okay, fine. Like I was saying, I became an Overseer,

achieving a lifelong dream of mine. For years, I had looked up to my teachers, to their knowledge and wisdom, and now, I was among them. I couldn't believe it, I was so happy. And then came the proudest moment of my life. At my graduating ceremony, the commandant herself made an appearance to congratulate me."

Kyran gave her a skeptical look.

"You dumb boys don't understand anything," replied Sabine. "The commandant is like a God to the women of the Temple. Phaidros is a city dominated by men. Your preceptor is a man, the Academy's highest officers are men, the most important Nobles are men, the richest merchants are men." She stopped to catch her breath. "For a woman to lead one of the most powerful institutions, you ... you just can't understand what that means."

"I understand," Kyran offered sympathetically.

"No, you don't. When Rex Ruga smiled and told me that my future was bright, it meant everything to me." Her eyes welled up with tears.

"What happened?" Kyran asked.

"I didn't realize that ... that she was smiling at me for a different reason. Later that week, she ran into me in a hallway. Before I could say anything, she pushed me against the wall, saying she'd been lusting for me ever since the graduation. I tried breaking away, but she was too strong. She reached down and ... put her hand under my dress, caressing my leg. I panicked, I didn't know what to do ... what to think. So I slapped her as hard as I could across the face." Again, Sabine took a long breath. "But ... but that didn't do anything, it only aroused her more, I suppose. She pinned me to the wall. I felt so helpless. Her face looked wild, like a madwoman. I wanted to scream, and nothing came out. I thought for sure I would die in that hallway, after she had finished with me."

Kyran remained motionless and quiet.

"Before anything else could happen," continued the young woman, "a group came from around the corner. They stopped in their tracks when they saw the commandant and me. She changed the narrative and yelled for help."

"What?"

"She lied through her teeth, Kyran, telling them I accosted her in the hallway."

"And they thought she was telling the truth?"

"Well, she showed them her red cheek from where I had slapped her. That's all they needed to accept her story. No one knew what actually happened, even after I explained it to them. I mean, who believes a young Overseer like me against the word of the commandant herself?"

They sat in silence.

"I can't believe it," Kyran muttered. The Adept cracked a smile upon realizing his poor choice of words. "No pun intended," he added.

Rather than angering Sabine, the light-hearted comment made her giggle. "You're so stupid."

"I'm sorry, I couldn't help it."

"How many apologies am I getting from you tonight?"

Kyran shook his head. "I don't know."

They could hear light raindrops tapping the glass window.

"Well, I don't know what will happen," said Sabine. "Everything was ripped away from me, so suddenly and … I … I just don't know."

At that moment, the old Source-powered lamp flickered.

"Again?" The young woman sighed. "It's been doing that all night."

"It must be low on energy."

"Yes, that's why I've always preferred candlelight."

"Candles also run out," countered Kyran.

"That's true." Sabine walked to the lamp, bringing it down to a lower setting.

Kyran's heart stopped when she turned to face him. As much as the Adept wanted to yank Sabine toward him and kiss her perfect lips, he remained true to his word.

"Why?" wondered the young woman as she resettled herself onto the bed.

"Why what?"

"Did this happen to me?"

"Oh, come on, that's pretty obvious."

"Really?"

"Because you're beautiful."

"That's not what I meant."

"I know what you meant," said Kyran. "I wanted to compliment you anyway."

Sabine's pupils darted around as she considered the young man sitting beside her.

"Sometimes," he added, "I think we just get unlucky."

"This isn't about luck. It's about … I don't know … I just hate them."

Kyran relayed a sage lesson Marrek had taught him long ago. "You shouldn't let one bad person ruin the good experiences you had at the Temple."

"You're right." She sighed. "What now?"

"I've been asking myself the same question for several days."

"At least you have somewhere to return to."

"No, I'm not going anywhere without …"

"Without what?" asked Sabine.

Kyran could feel his heart racing. "Without you."

"Me? We've only just met."

"And thank the Gods for that."

They kept quiet following the Adept's cunning reply, until she put a hand on his leg.

"I promised I wouldn't try anything," Kyran whispered.

"Yes, I know," Sabine whispered back. "I don't want ... that ... I just don't ... don't ..."

"Just don't what?"

"I just don't want to be alone." The young woman laid her head on Kyran's shoulder.

The Adept gently brought her closer in. He tenderly caressed her long brown hair. They stayed like that for a while, then leaned back onto the bed and cuddled under the covers.

Sabine pulled Kyran's arm tightly, and she could feel the warmth of his strong chest as she curled into him. For the first time in days, she felt safe. Her head rested on the Adept, his slow, rhythmic breaths gradually lulling her to sleep.

And the young man could think of not a single place he would rather be.

CHAPTER THIRTY-EIGHT

Rex Ruga barged into Tuka's inn shortly before midnight. "You!" Grabbing Pluto by the neck, the commandant dragged the performer to the nearest wall. "I vow to all the Gods, if they're not in this village, I will strangle you with my bare hands."

"Ruga?"

The commandant ignored her Master of Arms. "You've had chance after chance after—"

"Ruga!" shouted Gorgios.

"What?"

"Look!"

Edvon froze by the fireplace. The Overseers also remained still, too incredulous to act.

Gorgios barked out a familiar command. "Get him!"

The Adept reacted quickly, leaping across the room and grabbing a chair. He held it out, jabbing several advancing Overseers and keeping them at bay.

"Don't be stupid," said Rex Ruga. "There's nowhere for you to hide."

Edvon had just struck one of his assailants in the chest when a fairly drunk Criss came stumbling through the front door, struggling to cradle an absurdly large pile of coins. She dropped them at the sight before her. "What in th—the dread … were you two slee—ping together?"

Confused, everyone turned to the hallway leading up to the rooms, where a half-naked Ruan stood with Neeta by his side.

"I … I don't—" The officer paused, baffled by both the

question as well as the presence of Edvon and the Overseers. "What are you ... what ..." Noticing Joss and Pluto ogling her only added to her complete and utter confusion. "I don't know what to say."

"By Gods," Edvon muttered. "Did you two sleep together?"

"She just asked that!" exclaimed Ruan. "What do you care, anyway?"

"Not you. You!"

Standing even further back in the hallway, Kyran and Sabine were holding hands.

"Yes, we did. And if—" Sabine noticed Rex Ruga. "Wait, how did she ... how ..."

Deeming the ensuing silence auspicious, Pluto took the floor. "Okay, looks like we've got a full house here. So Joss and I will kindly see our way out, and—"

"You stay where you are," barked the commandant, without breaking eye contact with Sabine. "You two just made an extra twenty-five hundred coins."

Pluto looked at Joss with raised eyebrows. "Very well, then." The two performers casually sat down by the fireplace. "Carry on."

Rex Ruga was ready for immediate action. "Get the girl, too."

Her Overseers moved toward the stairs.

"Ev—everyone stop!" ordered Criss. "You're all u—under arrest."

The commandant laughed. "And in which capacity?"

"I'm the a—acting Chief of the Battalion."

"Then why don't you go act someplace else," warned Rex Ruga, "or you'll hurt yourself."

"I wi—ll do no such thi—"

Gorgios violently shoved Criss out. The agent went

tumbling into dirt still wet from the recent shower.

"Hey!" yelled Neeta. "You can't do that."

"I can do whatever I want," the behemoth Overseer answered. "And you're next if you don't get out of our way."

"Never!"

The dramatic one-word reply made Pluto giggle.

"I'm giving you two a last chance to move," declared Gorgios, "or I swear to Auralus, you will regret it."

Ruan obliged. "Neeta, come here," he implored, holding out his hand. "This isn't worth it."

The officer turned to face the personal attendant. "Gods, did I misjudge you ... I thought you had some pride."

"This isn't about pride. It's about self-preservation."

"That means nothing if you don't have something worth preserving."

"So be it." Gorgios charged.

The first bang to come that night, albeit the quietest of the three, resulted in the giant being launched across the room. He went slamming into the wall. Standing in the doorway was Gavin, eyes shining brightly and staff extended out in front of him.

"What!" Edvon exclaimed. "You're an Adept?"

Gorgios slowly rose to his feet and unsheathed his broad sword. "A dead Adept." He spat red mucus onto the carpet.

"Let's just calm down," said Lecarn as he entered the inn with his crew.

"Y—you!" Ruan stepped forward. "I don't know who's on what side, or what the Gods is going on. But whoever's trying to kill him, I'll be glad to assist."

The performers clapped their hands, delighted by the plot twist.

Rex Ruga was at the limits of her already notoriously thin patience. "You can figure that out some other time. We're here for the Adepts, and we're not leaving without them."

"Shut up," cut in Xavier, shocking the commandant. "Lecarn, this isn't a coincidence."

"What do you mean?"

"I mean that we specifically picked out Jasper as a probable target for the next attacks. And—"

"Jasper?" interjected Ruan. "Village attacks? You too?"

Lecarn was in agreement. "This can only lead to one conclusion."

"Someone here is the cul—culprit!" exclaimed Criss through the entrance.

They all remained perfectly still.

"I know nothing about the attacks," Rex Ruga claimed, "but I do know what will happen now. Kill them all!"

A second bang resonated throughout the inn and the fireplace crumbled. At the top of the stairs, Stakel was holding a fuming Source-powered gun dating from the Dread Days. She hobbled down the steps, her hair dripping wet.

"First off, you'll each be paying out of your pockets to fix that," the caretaker announced in her screechy voice, pointing toward the fireplace she had just blasted. "And what in the cholee is this ruckus?" Stakel reached the lobby. "You interrupted my bath."

"Bath?" repeated Pluto. "Are you sure those are working for you?"

The caretaker swiveled toward the performers. "In my entire life, I've—"

She never finished her sentence, on account of the third and final bang. A ray of blinding light cut straight through Stakel's head. Neeta, standing closest to the caretaker, gasped in horror as half the woman's face slid off, and her body slumped to the floor.

"We're under attack!" came a shout from outside.

They ran out of the inn. Wick, mouth wide open, was standing there, staring at the sky. From above descended an object of massive proportions, discharging beams of light into Tuka's houses and blowing them into smithereens. Frightened villagers besieged the inn as the surreal scene unfolded.

In utter terror, Edvon turned around to locate his brother, but Kyran was nowhere in sight. The older Adept pushed his way past the villagers and dashed back into the inn. Flames from the destroyed fireplace had spread onto the floor, consuming old wood and filling the entire area with thick smoke. Coughing, Edvon spotted Rex Ruga pinning Kyran down, and he sent a swift Source blast in her direction. The commandant keeled over in pain. "Come on!" shouted Edvon as he pulled his sibling to safety. They were only a few steps outside when a beam of light hit the east side of the building. The sound of the explosion was deafening, soon followed by a rain of rubble and shards that landed blocks away. Stakel's inn had been demolished.

A magnetic force field engulfed the village as the hovering object landed. Individuals bearing arms bolted out, yelling and shooting beams of light at the Dominioners. "Get on the ground!"

"What's going on here? I have the ..." The loquacious villager was promptly blasted in the head.

"I said get on the ground!"

Everyone held their hands up and knelt down. The invaders rounded them up, dispassionately executing those who did not immediately comply with their commands. They patted down the captives, confiscating anything they found. When the attackers got to Gorgios, he pulled out his weapon. Instead of handing it over, the senator hollered like a madman and brought it down on the unsuspecting Gavin standing right next to him. The sharp steel sliced through the old Adept like a knife through butter.

"No!" screamed Lecarn.

Gorgios tossed his sword to the ground.

The invaders howled with laughter. "What a big boga."

"Boga worth a fortune. Separate him from the others."

"Ay meseh."

Two of them grabbed Gorgios by the sleeve, walked him to their vessel, and disappeared from sight.

"Put the others in Cargo Bay T."

A large hatch opened, revealing an enclosure with metal walls. The invaders pushed the Dominioners inside.

Zoel protested. "I'm not going in there."

"Just be quiet and follow," Lecarn whispered.

"No, I'm not—"

The bounty hunters shuddered as another of their own succumbed, a fatal blast in the back of her head. Leaving no room for ambiguity, the abductors faced little resistance as they corralled the rest in the bay. And within minutes, they retreated into the sky, leaving Tuka smoldering and destroyed.

EPILOGUE

The large hatch had yet to shut and a cold wind whipped through Cargo Bay T as it ascended. A patch of turbulence sent the Dominioners tumbling in all directions. Lecarn lost his footing and caught himself on a floor railing, half his body swaying outside the craft. One man heard his shouting over the howling gusts.

"Need help?" called out Ruan.

Lecarn looked at the man he had maimed and understood the true meaning of fate. "I'm sorry."

Ruan nodded and stomped on the once-Noble's fingers. Lecarn plummeted toward the ground. He could see Phaidros in the distance, the streets of his childhood. The city he had wholeheartedly abandoned. A surge of memories flooded his mind. His parents. Friends. Love interests. Everything he had done, everything he had lived for. The visions faded from sight, along with the capital, the closer he neared his end. Beneath him, the tepuis were growing in size. Above, the little dot was about to disappear.

And while the others flew away to new beginnings, Lecarn smiled one last time.